Home to You

Jenn Faulk

ISBN-10:1500672173
ISBN-13:9781500672171

DEDICATION

To Ana – you don't have to be perfect to still be amazing.
Love you so much, sweet girl!

CONTENTS

For everything there is a season, and a time for every matter under heaven...

Ecclesiastes 3:1

CHAPTER ONE

Faith Hayes was in love with Sam Huntington.

He was just about perfect, in her estimation. With kindness and patience, a ready smile, and a genuine interest in all that she had to say, he had won her heart entirely. And because he was just about perfect, in her estimation, he had become her ideal, the standard by which all men then and forevermore would be judged.

She was going to marry him. She knew it with complete certainty. They would be together.

One day, of course. Because she was only six years old when she fell in love with him.

Their mothers were friends, the best of friends, so Sam and Faith had more than just a few occasions to be around one another. None happened more frequently than Sundays at church, where her father was the pastor. He had followed Sam's grandfather as the pastor of Grace Community Church, so the families were connected in a way that most families in the congregation weren't. And for Sam and Faith, that meant seeing one another. A lot. They usually found themselves on the same pew every Sunday, and Faith would forego a trip to children's church if it meant sitting next to Sam, which it often did.

Sam was a whole ten years older than her, so he likely gave it not even a second thought when she would climb across his other brothers to sit next to him. She would always carry a notebook and a box of crayons, and as her father took to the pulpit, she would draw pictures, making notes every once in a while, usually on what was being preached. Sam would praise her efforts with a thumbs up and would, very nearly every Sunday, sneak her a piece of cinnamon gum as they sat together.

He was better with kids than any of his siblings, and he honestly thought that precocious, curious Faith Hayes? Was a trip.

Like that one Sunday, when her mind drifted from the sermon and she drew what was an excellent first grader's rendition of a wedding. The groom was tall, with brown hair and hazel eyes, and the bride was short, very short, with blond hair and blue eyes. They were smiling – big, huge smiles that showed all of their teeth – and holding stick figure hands.

Sam smiled to himself, wondering at where Faith's mind was when she wrote, with a flourish, at the top of the page...

Sam and Faith

This caused him a bit of a fit of coughing. His younger brother, Scott, looked over to him questioningly, saw what Faith had drawn, and began laughing until their mother shot them both a silencing look.

Faith looked up at Sam with just a trace of hurt in her eyes. He took her crayon from her and wrote, underneath their names...

Your silly.

She read it and crossed it out, writing beneath it...

You're silly.

She was barely in school, and she was already smarter than him.

This made Scott laugh even harder, until it seemed that all the eyes in the church were on Sam Huntington... including the eyes of Faith's father, who paused just slightly in his preaching to glance their direction.

Sam elbowed his brother, ignored Faith, and kept his eyes forward for the rest of the service. And at the conclusion, when he looked at the little girl warily, she simply waved and said, "See you next week, Sam!"

And over time? He forgot all about Faith Hayes.

Ten Years Later

He hadn't told anyone about the orders.

He'd gotten word that Friday. After eight years in the Marine Corps, he was finally being sent somewhere exciting. He honestly didn't have good enough sense to be apprehensive about it because he was young, brave, and invincible, of course. But what good sense he had kept him from calling home and telling them all about it immediately.

"Sam!"

The voice brought a grin to his face as he continued to walk through the hallway of his small church there in Japan, pretending that he hadn't heard. This was standard, after all, the same routine he and his younger cousin, Kenji, played out every week. He'd been stationed in Okinawa for three years now, and it had been an ironic assignment as it came right when his uncle, Matt, had been stationed in the States instead of Okinawa, where his wife had been born, where they'd raised their children, where they were at home.

They had literally changed places. Camp Pendleton, Camp Kinser. But Matt had been transferred back that past year, and Sam had felt just a little more at home there by the East China Sea with his Japanese family just a few kilometers away. Aunt Shoko cooked for him at least once a week, Uncle Matt sat beside him in their men's Sunday school class, and there was always a throw down waiting to be had with Kenji, every time they saw one another.

Even now, as he surveyed the hallways around them, looking out for civilians who could accidentally get caught up in the battle, he readied himself. Kenji would have better luck if he didn't shout and make his presence known, but Sam rightly suspected that he did so because he liked them to be on even ground.

No surprises and all.

And no surprises just then, as Kenji appeared out of nowhere and attempted to grab him from behind in some completely illegal wrestling move. He held on for only a triumphant second before Sam threw him over his shoulders effortlessly, grabbed him by the neck, and slammed him right onto the ground.

Kenji lay there for a stunned moment... then burst out laughing.

Sam smiled down at him. "You're pathetic."

"If I think about it long enough," Kenji said, "I'm going to have to ask questions about why you've been trained to do things like that, Sam."

"Couldn't tell you anyway," Sam murmured. And he couldn't. And he hadn't ever told anyone. And never would.

"One day," Kenji grinned, moving gingerly, "I'm going to come at you and take you down. All super ninja style. Just wait for it."

"Most ninjas probably don't alert their enemies to their presence," Sam noted.

"Yeah, I know," he groaned. "That's my obnoxious American side showing. My Japanese side is super stealthy, but it can't shut the American in me up."

Sam held out his hand, pulling Kenji off the ground effortlessly. The kid was practically weightless. He would likely, one day soon, fill out like Uncle Matt and actually be a decent competitor at this game they played. But for now, he was slight and stood a head shorter than Sam. He was quick, though. Smart. So easygoing and so much fun to be around. Sam regretted that the rest of the family hadn't gotten to know him as well since they were so far away.

"You're still in one piece, then?," Sam asked, assessing him.

"I think you broke my butt," Kenji laughed again. "What's the name of the butt bone?"

"The coccyx."

Sam and Kenji turned at the sound of the bored, disinterested voice, their eyes landing on Kimmie, Kenji's twin sister, and Mai, her best friend.

"That's right!," Kenji said. "Mine's broken. Sam just broke my coccyx. Think it can be fixed?"

Kimmie frowned at him. "If you go to the base hospital, they'll just give you a donut pillow to sit on and tell you to suck it up."

"Awesome," he grinned. This prompted a shy giggle from Mai, which preceded the blush that covered her face as she averted her eyes from his.

Sixteen year old girls. They were all giggles and blushes like this. Sam praised God that he was no longer a teenager and that he dealt with real women now, not girls as young and silly as this. Not that he was dealing with women very seriously. There had been a few relationships in his short adult life, but none had gone beyond a few months of devotion. He was serious about Christ, about his faith, and finding a woman who was like-minded and able, at the same time, to handle what his future held in always being uprooted with the Marines... well, that was difficult.

"Hey, Sam," Kimmie said, regarding him with an assessing glance. She was her mother made over entirely except, of course, for the rather militant smugness on her face. All her father, that was. She wasn't rude, just frank and to the point.

Sam could appreciate this.

"Hey, Kimmie. Mai."

"You coming to the house after church for lunch?," she asked.

"Probably so," he said.

"I'd figured," she said. "Convinced Mom to make something a little more familiar to you because of it. Tex Mex."

Sam grinned. "What do you know about Tex Mex, Kimmie?"

"I know," she said, "that it makes you fat and gassy."

"Me personally?"

"In general, Sam."

"That it does," he affirmed.

"And that it's one of those things that everyone back in Texas raves over," she concluded. "I remember the trips back there, you know."

He did, too. His two cross-cultural cousins, wide eyed and astounded to be around the Texas family with their loud talking over one another, their big open houses, and all the food. The piles and piles of food. Kenji had embraced it all, but Kimmie had always regarded her American family as something of an oddity.

Sam knew her willingness to offer up food from home was a big deal for her. And that she did so meant she liked him.

He liked her, too. Okinawa had been awesome this past year, as he'd felt like he was back home with the four Japanese Fishers making him one of their own.

"Thanks, Kimmie."

"Yeah," she sighed, already dismissing him as she looked over at Kenji. "You ready to teach?"

"I am," he grinned, running back to bag he'd left on the floor before attempting to attack Sam. "Got the notes ready right here. Historical background, breakdown of the Greek in the passages, and an exegetical synopsis of the text."

Sixteen. He was sixteen, and this is how he talked. Sam shook his head at this.

"Kenji," Kimmie said, "they're second graders."

"Please, like you didn't do the same research."

She frowned at this. "Well, I did. But I incorporated some age appropriate methods to teaching them. What was your plan?"

"Uh... interpretive dance?"

Mai giggled at this. And blushed some more.

"Good thing I was actually thinking," Kimmie said, pulling something from her own bag, even as other people began streaming into the hallway. "Puppets, Kenji. This is a centurion puppet and a Paul puppet made from —"

"A pair of my socks," he noted glumly.

"Far be it for me to sacrifice to the Lord that which —"

"Cost me nothing," Kenji said. "Nicely done, Kimmie. And hey, this centurion looks like Dad!" He held it up and compared it to Uncle Matt, who was even now making his way down the hallway.

"That dirty sock doesn't look like me," their father said as he closed the distance between them. "And you're all going to be late to Sunday school."

"Mom already gone upstairs?," Kenji asked, as his father put his arm around Kimmie's shoulders and kissed her on the head as she smiled up at him.

"Yeah," he said. "Why?"

"I was going to ask her if she had some Tylenol or something," he said, making a face. "Sam broke my butt."

Matt looked to his nephew. Sam shrugged.

"Awesome."

They all said their goodbyes, and Sam made his way farther down the hall with Matt. Instead of stopping in their classroom, though, Matt continued on to an empty room at the end of the hall.

"Gotta talk to you," he said, pulling a couple of chairs off the stack in the corner of the room, the joints on the metal screeching as he opened them up and thunked them down on the linoleum.

"Yes, sir," Sam said, falling into work mode. Uncle Matt wasn't his commanding officer. Uncle Matt wasn't even in the same department. But he was a lifetime Marine, only a few years from retirement, and Sam respected everything he had to say.

Matt sat back, chewing his lip with a frown, watching his nephew silently for a moment. "I heard you got some new orders."

Oh. This. "Yes, sir," he said. "Afghanistan."

Matt kept silent for a moment. "You glad for it?," he asked softly.

Sam shrugged. "Well, it was bound to happen eventually," he said. "And I have no family. Better me than someone like you, don't you think?"

"Maybe," Matt murmured. "Sam, it's not what you're imagining. You know that, right?"

Sam did... kinda. He knew the work he'd be doing. He knew that it wouldn't be much different than what he'd been trained to do. The weather would be an issue, the lack of support crew, and the heightened vigilance. But he'd joined the Corps for this kind of assignment.

"Yes, sir. I know."

"You don't," Matt said, a sad smile on his face. "The physicality, the routine of it all... that'll be like you expect. But you can't let what you see, what you experience, mess with your head." He leaned forward. "Because it can mess you up, Sam."

Sam merely nodded. "Yes, sir."

Matt nodded at this. "And you do have family, talking about yourself like you're some random vagabond. You have a mother who's going to flip out about this." He grinned. "And I should know. Because she freaked out when I was sent into combat. And I'm just her brother. Not her son. You told her yet?"

"Am I sitting here with all of my limbs intact, sir?"

"That you are."

"Then, no, that's great evidence that I've not yet told her." It wouldn't be easy to tell her this, he knew. It was enough that he was half a world away. Deployment to Afghanistan would be too much.

Well, she'd just have to deal with it.

Matt sighed. "You need to tell her soon."

Sam sighed at this as well. He did. And he already had a plan. He had leave coming up, and he was going to head back to the States. There were orders for him to do so anyway, to do some paperwork back in California, and he'd figured he could swing out to Texas beforehand to deliver the news in person. He already knew the family would be on a mini-vacation to some lake house owned by some friend of the family. His mother had droned on and on about it in one of her calls, and he'd only been half-listening. He'd gotten the address, though, knowing that he could show up and surprise them.

"I'm going back to Texas next week," he said. "By this time next week, she'll know."

"Good man," Matt said. "And you'll get a little rest before you head out? Have some excitement before you get deployed?"

Sam doubted this very much. "Not much excitement in going home. The real excitement's going to come when I get to Afghanistan."

Matt nodded again. "Let's hope not, Sam."

Her alarm went off right at 5am.

She allowed herself a few seconds to groan and flop over in her bed, throwing a pillow over her head. These few seconds were

11

teenage seconds, spent acting like a normal teenager who needed to sleep in late.

Faith rarely allowed herself any teenage indulgences. Dates, drama, days spent thinking that high school would be the greatest part of her life – Faith Hayes was *not* into these things. She had bigger plans than this, and apart from these few seconds of normalcy she gave herself before anyone would see her, she was focused and certain.

She sat up in bed, reaching over to turn off her alarm clock. Flipping on her light with one hand, she gathered up her long, blonde hair in the other hand, slipping it into a no-nonsense updo without even glancing in the mirror. She'd normally start the morning with a run, just a few miles, and a quick, sensible breakfast. But today was her "off" day, Saturday, a day for being with family and having a leisurely breakfast after everyone slept in.

Everyone but her, that is.

They didn't know she woke up early on Saturdays, and because she stayed in her room quietly getting things done, they would never know. As Faith jumped out of bed, straightening it back up just right, just perfectly, she smiled over at her desk, where all of her research was laid out.

Neatly. Evenly. Perfectly.

The paper wasn't due for another three months. But Faith hardly considered the distant goal a reason to slack off now. She was in the middle of four different projects for her AP courses, but she'd spent a good portion of her time on that anatomy and physiology paper, color coding her research, organizing it all just so, and going beyond what was required.

She'd learned so much in the process, especially through the interviews she'd conducted. One with your standard, highly-acclaimed, widely-respected obstetrician – that was what her teachers were expecting of her research. And what they wouldn't expect, what they wouldn't think about... well, it had turned her research upside down, had given her a new perspective, a new thesis, and a brand new world of opportunities and possibilities.

She'd interviewed a midwife.

Faith didn't even know, prior to this project, that holistic, natural, female-affirming birth centers even existed. She'd felt academic about the entire visit to the hospital, talking about the sterile processes, the aid of medicine, the way a pregnancy and delivery was almost viewed as a medical condition, an illness to medicate, a disease to cure. But at the birth center, she'd been overwhelmed by the affirmation, of the support, of the beautiful way birth was described, as though it was what it actually was -- natural. And as she sat there and listened to the midwife speak, she felt as though God was tapping her on the back, gently whispering, "This, Faith. This."

It had changed the entire focus of her project. And it had changed her life, honestly.

She was still on track to finish high school a year early. She still had plans to go on to college.

But she was going to be a midwife when it was all done.

She was going to deliver babies, not in a hospital, but in a birthing center, one focused on Christ and His design, on the gift that children were, on the blessing that was inherent in the way He designed women to deliver and nurture.

She caught sight of herself as she continued poring over her notes, surprised to see how bright her smile looked, even for 5am. The more she researched it all, the more she thought about God's design, and the more she started to believe, just partially, that maybe God had even this in mind for her one day.

Motherhood.

Could it be? Faith couldn't imagine it. She had no time for boys now, couldn't imagine having more time for them as life got increasingly busier, and concluded that it might not be so.

Because there was the science of it. No matter how wonderfully creative God had designed the female body to bring forth life, it still required... well, it still required a man.

Faith was too busy for all of that.

She was so busy, in fact, that she, even after waking up two hours earlier than the rest of the family, was still the last one to sit at the kitchen table.

"Glad to see you slept super late, Faith," her mother said, as she slid into the seat across from her father and beside her sister, Gracie, who regarded her with a sleepy smile. While Faith's hair was neatly pulled back and her clothes were almost too tidy to have been slept in, Gracie was a mess. Her hair hung in loose, frizzy curls all around her round, sweet face, and her clothes looked like she'd fought whole armies in her sleep. She had traces of mascara and eye shadow still on her face, and she smiled over at Faith knowingly.

"You didn't sleep in," she said. "You were studying."

Faith frowned at this. "Maybe a little."

Gracie laughed out loud. "Maybe a little, my foot. Working on that economics project —"

"Already done," Faith sighed, helping herself to the food her mother had slipped onto the table.

"Already ahead of everything," their father noted. "With more to come."

"Yes," Faith agreed, thinking of the allowances that had been made at her school because of her exceptional grades. She was going to the community college in their part of the city this summer and had every hope of completing all eighteen undergraduate hours before she even began her third and final year of high school. She'd sped through it. "Full summer," she affirmed. "But enough that I'll be nearly done by this time next year. And if I do the same next summer, with my AP credits, I'll graduate with two years of college completed."

"Before you ever set foot on campus," their mother sighed. "I don't like the idea of sending a seventeen year old to college, Stephen. Especially when she'll already be halfway done." She looked to her husband with a frown.

"Mom, I'd be bored if I took high school at a normal pace," she said, taking a bite.

"Bored because you have no life," Gracie muttered through the pancakes in her mouth. "You don't do anything but study!"

"And you, Gracie," Faith said, primly wiping her mouth, "do everything *but* study. How are you going to be prepared for the real world?"

Gracie shrugged. "I don't know," she said. "Maybe I'll be prepared because I'll actually know how to have a life beyond books and studying. How to have fun." She watched her sister pointedly. "I mean, you totally won't join me in the drama club or the cheerleading squad --"

Faith suppressed a groan.

"But," Gracie said, wiping her sticky mouth with her sleeve, "I really thought you'd go for the cross country team. I mean, you already run every morning anyway."

"You're on the cross country team?," their mother asked, looking at Gracie, with her short legs and aversion to sweating.

"Oh, yeah. Cute little running outfits, you know. I'm on the 'injured' list," and here, she made giant quotation marks with her hands, "which means I 'have to'," again with the quotation marks, "sit out and hang out with the guys' team while the rest of the girls are running. Best. Team. Ever."

All three other Hayes family members watched her silently for a moment.

"Well," their mother sighed, "that's... something, Gracie."

"Sure is," Gracie affirmed. Then to Faith, "And when you get to college, you should take the time to really enjoy it! Phi Mu legacy and all. You should totally rush! I'm going to, and --"

"Gracie," Faith said, "why would I need to waste all that time making new friends when I already have the world's best friend and real sister right here?"

Gracie grinned at this. "You're trying to distract me from my argument. Because you know I'm right."

"I know that life is more than building everything around time-wasting activities that won't mean anything to me in ten years," she said simply.

"Everything in moderation," their father noted. "Fun and study both. But you have a good head on your shoulders, Faith. Christ in your heart. You'll do well, even if you allow yourself to have a little fun in the process."

"Absolutely," she said, agreeing at least with the part about Christ being in her heart. She'd believed from an early age. Her father had always been her pastor, and she'd been just eight when she'd given her life to Christ and become a part of the family of faith at their church in Texas. It hadn't been long after that when her father was called to Florida, to a pastorate there, and the Hayes family had been at River Fellowship ever since. It was a wonderful, affirming, challenging place, and Faith felt secure in who she was in Christ because of the teaching and the community she found herself in. "And the odds are good that I'll end up somewhere close enough to here, so that I can stay at our church, continue to sit under Dad's teaching, involved in our community. I'm doing all this for Jesus, anyway. Excelling, living, striving to be His in all that I do."

Her mother sighed. "You sure you don't want to pledge Phi Mu? I mean, Grandma Trish already had your recommendation written out five minutes after you were born."

Before Faith could speak to this, Gracie opened her mouth. "You've still got me, Mom. Phi Mu all the way."

"If you can keep your grades up once you get there," their mother noted.

"Oh, I will," Gracie assured her, pouring more syrup on her plate. "Already working towards success, just like Faith. I'm excelling, living, striving... to pass algebra. And maybe score myself an invite to the senior prom."

"You're not going to the prom as a freshman," her parents said. Together.

"Hey, I love Jesus, too," she said. "And that more than makes up for the fact that I don't have a good head on my shoulders."

"You have a great head on your shoulders," Faith said, smiling. "And a great head of hair. It's grown out. A lot."

"I know," she sighed. "I'm a mess of curls. I think I'm going to have Mom cut it before our spring break trip."

Faith looked up at this. "Spring break trip... what spring break trip?"

"We mentioned it last month," their mother said. "Grandma Trish will be wrapping up her trip to visit Beau and Melissa, and we're going to need to travel to pick her up anyway. We thought we'd make a family vacation of it."

Faith likely had only been half-listening, planning a research project in her mind, thinking on homework, counting the hours that she had left to work –

"Mom," she groaned. "I was going to use that time to get ahead on my research paper for English."

"When's the paper due, Faith?," her father asked.

"Not until the very last days of school," Gracie chimed in. "Saw that on Faith's color coded calendar."

"Then, surely," their mother said, "you can take a week without working on schoolwork and just *enjoy* yourself."

Faith sighed dramatically, prompting her mother to give her father a look.

"What?," he laughed.

"She's just like you," she said. "Heaven knows I didn't give two hoots about school back when I was her age. I was more concerned about things like –"

"So are we going somewhere where I can work on my tan?," Gracie said around another sticky, syrupy bite.

"Exactly," her mother said.

"We're going to the lake house," their father said.

"Nana's lake house?," Faith groaned. "All the way back to Texas?"

"Yes, Faith," her mother sighed. "It's been *years* since we've been back."

And it had been. Faith's memories of their former home, the memories of a little girl, were relegated to snippets of a large church, of the musty old lake house, and of a teenage boy whose name she couldn't even remember at sixteen...

"Ugh. Texas."

"Well," their mother said, "we're leaving on Monday."

"Nothing like advanced warning," Faith muttered.

Her mother ignored this. "I suggest that you pack a swimsuit, a book that has nothing to do with school, and plans to spend lots of hours just relaxing by the lake."

Faith frowned. "I don't even have a swimsuit."

"You can borrow one of mine," Gracie smiled. "The red bikini would look awesome on you."

Faith was about to open her mouth and tell them how she didn't think a bikini was appropriate at all, when her mother cut back into the conversation.

"And the Huntingtons are meeting us there," she said as she smiled. "Well, some of them anyway. It'll be so great to see Jess again."

"Who?," Gracie asked.

"Friends of ours from our old church," their father said. "You don't remember them, but Nick and Jess, and their boys.... well, grown men now, huh, Chloe?"

"Yeah," their mother nodded. "Very nearly. Seth will be there. Savannah, too. The rest of them are all out on their own."

"The rest of them?," Gracie asked. "How many are there?"

"Six," her father said, glancing over at his wife, smiling. "Let's see if your mother can name the ones left."

"I hear about them all the time from Jess," she grinned. "This won't be hard. Sean, Scott, Stuart, Seth, and Savannah. Oh, and Sam."

And at the sound of the final name, Faith dropped her fork to her plate.

Instantly, his face came to mind. Kind eyes, a reassuring smile, and attention, given to her as they colored together, as he slipped her a piece of gum.

"Sam," she said. "I remember him!"

Her father glanced over at her. "If I remember correctly, Faith, he was the one you followed around."

Her mother smiled. "Oh, yeah," she said. "I remember that! You were going to marry him."

Gracie grinned over her pancakes. "Was he cute?"

Their mother thought about this for a second. "Not really. But your sister didn't seem to notice. As soon as he'd sit down in church, she'd climb over anyone keeping him from her and sit right next to him."

"Yeah," her dad grumbled. "Not that it meant anything back then, but I'll have to keep an eye on him now, huh?"

"Dad," Faith said very simply, "I hardly think that'll be an issue. He's probably really, really old."

"Yes," he nodded, affirming this. "Practically ancient, right?"

"You won't even see him anyway," her mother said. "He's overseas with the Marine Corps. Japan. That must be exciting, huh?"

And as her parents talked about the world, Faith finished her breakfast, thinking about Sam, remembering more and more the longer she ate, blushing as she remembered how she had felt gazing up at his kind face, taking the gum he offered her in the pew, and cherishing every single sweet moment.

CHAPTER TWO

Spring break. The lake house. Nana's old, musty, empty, rustic lake house.

The Hayes family was only there for a handful of minutes when the Huntingtons showed up. Nick, Jess, Seth, and Savannah, with apologies from the rest. Faith and Gracie had barely managed a re-introduction before Savannah was telling them that the drive was horrible, that Seth had nearly wrecked the truck in the Burger King parking lot in Tyler, that she was quite certain that his skills behind the wheel would kill them all one day, and, oh yeah, was it going to rain this week, because that would mean Frizz City for her hair, and who wanted to deal with that?

Gracie had grinned at all of this while Faith had watched with wonder, as Savannah then launched into a detailed description of how this spring break would likely suck in comparison to the one she spent last year with friends from college, down in South Padre, with a new bar every night, so many boys, and --

The lake house was no longer as boring, obviously, as Savannah's words filled up every empty, quiet space.

The Hayes sisters didn't have much in common with Savannah, but Gracie had whispered to Faith that perhaps they would be a good influence on her, a godly witness, and an encouragement. Besides, Gracie had said, Savannah was really fun, as was Seth, her brother, who was a lot like Faith, serious, committed to Christ, and itching to get back to his books.

And besides just being fun, Gracie added, they were in *college*. This had gotten her even more excited, like the Huntington siblings were rare oddities, exotic animals at a zoo, captured from a thrilling utopia called university somewhere far away and magical.

They'd spent the first full night staying up late with all of the Huntingtons, getting reacquainted, then the first full day on jet skis at the far end of the lake, not too far from the dock and the start of the long winding road to the house. Faith had warned Gracie to bring sunscreen, and Gracie, as was her way, had ignored her older sister.

She was regretting that several hours in, as the sun climbed and her skin turned pink around the edges of the modest swimsuit she was wearing.

"Faith!," she screeched. "I'm burning!"

"Should've worn sunscreen," she and Seth said at the same time. She grinned at him. "I tried to tell her, but –"

"She wouldn't listen," he said. "I've gotten that about her since we've been here."

"Faith, please, can you go get some sunscreen for me?," Gracie pleaded. "It's not like you're even that into riding these things out here anyway. You didn't even wear a swimsuit."

She sure hadn't. She'd packed too many books and too much work for school to have room in her suitcase to even bring one along. She had absolutely no interest in the lake or anything that didn't involve studying.

If she went back now, maybe she could grab a book. There was the chemistry textbook, and she could sneak out a notebook, too, make some notes for a project she had coming up...

"Sure," she said, her mood lifting considerably at the thought of using her time a bit more wisely. "I'll head back up to the house."

"I'll come with you," Savannah said. "It'll give me a chance to grab a snack out of the fridge. You guys want anything?"

And with Seth and Gracie's requests noted, the two girls made their way to the dock, peering down the road as they talked, just as a cab pulled into the gravel driveway.

"Who's that?," Faith asked, as the back door opened and a young man stepped out, a camouflage pack over one shoulder as he leaned in to pay the driver.

Savannah squinted... then put her hand to her mouth. "It looks like... oh..."

Just as the cab began backing out of the drive, the mysterious stranger turned his face towards the two girls. He locked gazes with Faith immediately, even as Savannah cried out and began running towards him.

Faith's heart pounded as Savannah rushed into the stranger's arms, arms that were well defined, as was the rest of him... all as his eyes never moved from Faith's.

Savannah's boyfriend, maybe? She hadn't mentioned one in all the talking she'd done. Maybe a friend from college, then?

Or a brother. One of the others... Stuart, Scott, Sean...

Then, it hit her, even as he kept watching her.

Sam.

Oh... Sam. Sam Huntington.

Her mother had said he wasn't really that cute. This was one of those times when Faith concluded that her mother knew absolutely *nothing*.

He was gorgeous.

Sam. Just like she remembered him... except so totally *not* like she remembered him. Taller, broader, and a whole lot more interesting than he'd been to her back when she was six. And he'd been plenty interesting then, but now?

Well.

She found herself blushing the longer he looked at her, the longer she kept staring right back at him.

"What are you doing here?!," Savannah shouted at him, laughing and jumping up and down in his arms.

"Leave," he said, finally breaking his gaze from Faith and looking at his sister. "I'm on leave for a few days. I have to go to Camp

Pendleton later on this week, but I thought I'd come back to Texas to surprise Mom." Then, his eyes went right back to Faith.

Did he recognize her? Probably not. He probably didn't even remember her. And even if he did, it had been a long while. She'd been eight when they moved. She well remembered their last Sunday at the church, one of Sam's last Sundays as well. He was heading to basic training, and she was heading to her father's new pastorate. Even now, she could see herself in her memories, a little girl sharing a cookie with him in the fellowship hall and crying because he was leaving, she was leaving, and everything was going to change.

As she watched him watch her, clear interest in his eyes but no obvious recognition there, she wondered if things were about to change again.

Savannah backed away to hold his face in her hands, saw the question there as he continued watching Faith, and said, "Sam, do you remember Pastor Hayes?"

"Yeah," he said. Then, to Faith, "Wow, Pastor Hayes, you look really different."

Funny. Faith smiled at this.

"You dimwit," Savannah said, laughing. "This is *Faith* Hayes. His daughter. Do you remember Faith?"

He let out a slow breath. As she bit her lip and continued watching him, almost self-consciously, he finally managed an appropriate response. "Well. Faith Hayes. Wow."

"Sam," Savannah chided, giggling at him. "Your little buddy grew up, didn't she?"

Sam looked at his sister for a moment... then went right back to staring at Faith.

"Hey, Sam," Faith said, shyly. "Wow. Look at you."

Savannah laughed out loud. "Isn't his haircut awful?"

"Standard issue, you know," he said. "Faith Hayes. Wow."

This only made her smile again, as he stood there watching her. It was a curious thing. There had been boys who would look at her like this, but she'd never given them more than a passing glance.

But Sam? He wasn't a boy.

"Oh, good grief, Sam," Savannah laughed. "Are you just going to stand there and stare at her all day?"

He gave Savannah a look, to which she answered, "You're being rude. Go hug the woman. Seriously."

Before Faith could tell him that he really didn't need to, that she wasn't expecting anything, not even recognition, he made his way over to her, adjusting the bag on his shoulder as he walked.

And after studying her for just a moment longer, he reached out for her, cautiously and with an uncertain smile.

She didn't back away. She welcomed his embrace, exhilarated by the scent of him and his fullness in her arms. She could remember so many moments from when she was younger, of being so infatuated with him, and now, she felt them all again, like a rush of water from her head to her toes. She felt herself smiling as he backed away, his cheek brushing hers.

"It's really good to see you, Faith," Sam said, his eyes shining as he smiled at her.

And as he smiled at her, more memories clicked into place, causing her to sigh just a little at the enormity of what she had felt back then, what she was feeling even as he looked at her.

She smiled at him, echoing his sentiments. "You, too, Sam."

Faith Hayes, Faith Hayes, Faith Hayes...

He couldn't remember her.

Granted, his memory wasn't that great. And he had been a particularly non-observant teenager, especially during church. He could focus on the sermon, but that was about it most days. His recollections had left no room for a blonde goddess of a woman with a sweetly innocent, yet still seductive smile and --

He frowned, even as the clock in the front room ticked on loudly and the rest of the house slept.

He hadn't had much time to think about her, to wonder at how they knew one another, before Savannah had ushered him into the house that day. There was a whole lot of screaming and crying – all from their mother. Joyful screaming and crying, as he hadn't had the heart to tell her about Afghanistan yet. They'd spent the afternoon catching up with Pastor and Mrs. Hayes, whom he did remember...

... but not Faith. He'd watched her throughout the rest of the evening, catching her eye periodically even in the midst of the noise generated by the rest of their families. She and her sister had spent most of the afternoon retelling stories from the day with Savannah, and when Seth would cut in with his own interpretation of the events, Faith would laugh quietly as Savannah shrieked at him and Gracie corrected him. And Seth would smile at Faith over this, and Sam would feel a twinge of annoyance. With Seth for having her attention, with himself for not having gotten there sooner.

It was a bizarre reaction to a woman he couldn't remember.

Faith had cooked dinner alongside his mother, and he'd hung around the kitchen with them, trying to get more information out of her, trying to figure out who she'd been back at the church of his childhood, all while his mother glanced over at him with a curious, questioning expression. He'd given up finding out any information at all as his mother began loudly updating him on every member of the family, and blah, blah, blah...

Faith had glanced up at him knowingly as his eyes had begun glazing over. He caught the smirk on her lips and offered her one in return.

Faith Hayes.

He'd gone to sleep early, thanks to jet lag, wondering over his sorry, sorry memory.

Jet lag was the pits. To bed early, then up at 4am for no reason. Just about the time he would adjust, he'd be heading back, where he'd be forced to adjust again.

But he was suddenly immensely thankful for it when he found himself alone in the front room, just as Faith was tiptoeing down the stairs.

She was wearing an oversized shirt and a pair of shorts, her feet bare and a backpack hanging loosely from one shoulder. In her arms, she carried a stack of books, her fingers tracing the spines as she walked, then reaching up to the pencil stuck in the messy updo she had twisted her hair up into.

Beautiful. Even like this.

And totally unaware that anyone was awake and could see her right now.

"Good morning," he said softly, wanting to spare her the surprise, then biting back a smile when she gasped, dropped her books, and lost her pencil.

"Oh!," she whispered, as her hair fell down past her shoulders and she put her hands to her perfect, gorgeous mouth.

Beautiful.

"Sorry," he managed, standing to help her with the books.

"You scared me," she murmured. "Didn't realize anyone else was awake yet."

"I'm on Japanese time," he said, picking up each heavy textbook, wondering at the advanced subject matter. Anatomy, physiology, cellular microbiology –

"I can get those," she said, kneeling down with him, blushing when his eye caught hers.

"Let me help you, since I'm the one who made you throw them six feet into the air," he said softly, watching her.

She smiled at this, and his heart clenched reflexively. Faith Hayes, Faith Hayes, Faith Hayes... *why* couldn't he remember?!

"It wasn't six feet, was it?," she asked, a giggle in her voice.

"Close," he laughed as she demurely looked back down, gathering papers and folders.

He looked at the books he had stacked up. "Doing a little light reading this morning, huh?"

She smiled, even as she picked up her pencil and redid her hair, her eyes never leaving his as she did so. Sam watched, like a big idiot, mesmerized into adoring silence as she did so.

She didn't notice. "Have to finish some projects," she said. "Can't take much of a break with finals up ahead."

He stood. "Where can I put these for you?"

"On the couch is fine," she said, following him, tugging at her shorts, then sitting down. She watched him curiously, biting her lip, as he sat down across from her. She crossed her arms over her chest, almost self-consciously.

"I'm sorry," he said, thinking about it a second later. "I should probably let you get to your work, then."

"Oh, no," she said quickly. "You're fine. No need to run off, especially since you're so jet lagged and all."

He sighed. "I am. I've had worse, though."

"Seeing the world since you enlisted, huh?," she smiled. "I kept track of you for a long while, praying for you as you went."

This was surprising. They had known one another well, then. Well enough that she'd remembered him. Well enough that there was something knowing in her smile as she watched him.

"They have you ricocheting all over the world," she murmured, pulling her legs up onto the couch. "Or they did, but you've been in Okinawa now for... what, a few years?"

"A few," he said. "And you're all still in... um..."

"Florida," she grinned. "Didn't remember that, did you?"

He grimaced. "No."

She smiled even bigger at this. "You don't remember me either, do you?"

"Honestly?"

"Of course, Sam."

The sound of his name on her lips was incredible, actually. So incredible that it nearly distracted him from the question in her eyes, even as she continued smiling at him.

"No, I don't remember you. And you have no idea how much I wish I could."

She laughed softly at this, looking down at her hands shyly. "Well, it's been a while."

"Yeah," he nodded. "And I don't get home much, or maybe we would have seen one another again before now."

"Probably not," she said. "Florida, Texas... quite the distance there."

"Florida. Right," he said. "You said that."

She regarded him oddly for a moment while he kicked himself mentally. He was having trouble remembering his own name the longer she sat here with him.

"Jet lag, right?," she asked.

"Yeah." That, of course, and the fact that he was sitting in a dark, quiet room alone with the most attractive woman he'd ever seen in all of his young life, and –

"You know what's good for that, don't you?," she asked, standing to her feet.

He stood, too, regretting that he'd said anything at all about jet lag if it was going to cause her to leave the room. "What?"

"Breakfast," she said, turning towards the kitchen. "You hungry?"

Always. "I could eat," he said.

"We went to Africa several years ago to visit my Aunt Sophie," she said, pulling out a skillet and heading to the fridge for food, "and we were all so jetlagged for so long, coming and going. We'd have breakfast when none of us could sleep. Some of the best memories from that trip were from Uncle Willem and Aunt Sophie's kitchen, sitting around with bowls of cereal, laughing together."

"I love cereal." *What a dumb thing to say, Sam*, he berated himself.

But she merely smiled at him over her shoulder. "I could fix you a bowl of Cheerios," she said. "Unless you'd prefer bacon and eggs?"

"Whatever you want to fix," he said, settling in on a stool as she began frying up bacon in one skillet, scrambling eggs in another. "Can I do anything to help?"

"Just keep me company," she said softly.

Gladly. He'd keep her company all week, as long as she'd let him. In fact, he'd be okay with everyone else leaving, his own family included, so they could keep each other company without the distraction of other people.

Maybe he did remember her. Because there was something familiar, so natural, about being here with her like this. He watched her as she moved back and forth from the stove to the fridge, searching his thoughts for some remembrance of her...

"You said you have finals coming up soon," he said. "Am I keeping you from studying?"

"You're likely keeping me sane," she said, glancing over at him. "I haven't taken any time to relax in... oh, three years, at least."

Three years. So, she was almost done with college. Savannah's age. Just the right age for him, actually.

"What are you going to do once you're done?," he asked. "Career wise."

She turned to face him, biting her lip, moving to stand at the kitchen island where he sat. "I thought medical school, you know? Delivering babies. Women's reproductive health." A smile. "The female body is fascinating, you know?"

Uh huh. He hadn't given it much thought until now, as Faith stood before him, her feet crossed at the ankles, her fingers tracing patterns on the counter, her head tilted to one side as she watched him, as he struggled to keep his eyes on her face.

Fascinating. Oh, yeah.

"But now," she said, stretching and yawning as she turned back to the stove, oblivious to how this called Sam to attention even more, "I think I want to train to be a midwife. Same work, different philosophy."

"Mmmm," he murmured.

"You have no clue about any of it, do you?," she asked, grinning.

"Can't say that I do," he said. "Babies, pregnancy... not on my radar. But how is the philosophy different? What's so appealing about... well, dealing with all of that?"

"With life?," she said, turning back to him. "With being there, witnessing what God alone can do, seeing the story of someone's life here on earth begin, knowing that it began before time when God planned it? Using those moments to introduce people to Christ?"

He thought about this for a second. "Well, when you say it like that..."

"It's exciting," she said, smiling back at him. "An opportunity to share the grace of God, the goodness of God, the power of God with someone else, during a time when questions about life, eternity, and our place in it all are just there, waiting to be asked."

He watched her, amazed by the godliness in this statement, the heart behind her words. She felt his eyes on her and turned to face him. "Well, maybe that's not as exciting as the Marines."

"Maybe nothing," he said. "I've never even seen combat. It's all routine, all the time. Nothing changes much. But that's probably good for me, as I can't handle a whole lot. Probably couldn't remember anything if it wasn't so ingrained in me after all the routines."

"How so?," she asked, her forehead crinkling in confusion.

"Well, I can't even remember you," he said, feeling bold. "When clearly, you're someone I should never have been able to forget." A pause. "I certainly won't ever be able to forget you now."

And she blushed at his words and smiled even more, taking a breath to say something to this declaration he'd made, when Seth came down the stairs and kept her from it.

"Food," he said, yawning. "Food."

Sam bit back exasperation at this moment ruined. "Why are you up?," he asked his youngest brother.

"Food," Seth repeated, sitting next to him and smiling over at Faith. "Good morning. Early riser, huh?"

"Yeah," she murmured, her eyes drifting from Sam's. "But lucky for you since I started breakfast. Wanna join Sam and me?"

"You bet," Seth said, grinning.

Sam glared at him for a full minute before Seth finally glanced over at him. "What? Why are you looking at me like that?"

"Since when are you an early riser?," Sam asked him irritably, unhappy that he had to share the table with him, that he had to share the breakfast, and most of all, that he had to share Faith's attention.

"Since I've got to find time to study for finals, even on vacation," he said, smiling at Faith as she handed him a cup of coffee. "Thanks."

Sam's eyes followed her as she went back to the stove. "Aren't finals a long way off still?," he asked, turning his frown to his brother.

"Never too early –"

"—to study for finals," Faith finished with him. Seth laughed out loud as she smiled at this. "See? Faith gets it."

Sam didn't much like the inside jokes, the way that Seth and Faith were getting to know one another well enough that they could complete one another's sentences.

"You don't get it, though," Seth said to him. "Because you didn't go to college. Barely managed to finish high school, if I remember correctly."

"Yeah, thanks for that," Sam said, wondering what Faith thought of this. She probably had more in common with someone like Seth, could probably respect him more. Even he respected Seth for it. The high grades, the inevitable acceptance to vet school in a year, the internship he already had lined up for the fall, the fancy degrees he'd have so soon, the world's giant wink of approval because he'd learned to make a living using his head and not just his hands –

"Maybe the best education comes from being out in the world living, not just reading about it in books and hearing lectures about it," Faith observed quietly.

Sam looked up as she smiled at him appreciatively, slipping a full plate in front of him.

"Hey, why does he get the first helping?," Seth whined around his coffee.

"Because, like Faith just said, I'm smarter than you," he said. "Thanks, Faith."

"Yeah," Seth muttered, "you're only smarter than me if intelligence is measured by one's ability to kill someone with no weapons and –"

Sam kicked him as Faith turned around and watched them curiously.

"That's classified," Sam said, after a long moment of silence. "Which means that even Seth doesn't know for certain –"

"What you're trained to do," Seth finished. Then, he raised his finger to his neck and moved it across his jugular slowly, hanging out his tongue and then dramatically nodding his head as though he was... well, dead.

Sam glanced up at Faith, watching her with some concern.

"Well," she said, very simply. "There's science in even that. Knowing exactly how to go about killing someone with just your hands, I guess."

"I guess," Seth said as Faith slid a plate in front of him. "Thanks."

"No problem."

"So," Seth said, digging right in, his mouth already full, "how long has Sam been boring you with his stories?"

Faith smiled at this, looking down at her hands for a minute. "Hasn't been boring me," she said softly. "Just keeping me company."

Her eyes lifted to Sam's. And he was surprised... and thrilled, so thrilled, to see the tenderness there, directed solely at him, as though Seth wasn't even in the room.

"Best company I've ever had," he said simply, rejoicing to see the smile it brought to her lips.

When the rest of the group had woken up and made their way to the kitchen, Faith had slipped away to get cleaned up. She noticed that Sam's eyes trailed her as she left the room, and once she was in her room with the door shut, she released a deep breath.

Sam Huntington. Wow.

She pulled her hair down and made her way to her suitcase, looking for some clean clothes to wear, thinking about him with every footfall, every breath, every blink of her eye.

Maybe her memories were fuzzy, but she couldn't remember Sam looking like... well, like he looked. Or acting like he'd been acting.

He'd been watching her. Smiling at her. Saying the most wonderful things to her.

She wasn't a little girl anymore, obviously. She'd matured and grown out of little girl fantasies. And Sam was a grown man, so different than he'd been back when she had a childish crush on him.

But still. She had to keep herself from squealing and jumping up and down because Sam seemed to *like* her. *Like* like, you know.

What would he do today? Would it be pathetic if she stayed around the house, waiting for another opportunity to talk with him? She'd dragged her books back to the room once the kitchen got crowded, thinking that she'd have to study eventually... maybe. She was ahead in all of her classes, so what would it hurt if she spent her time here with him, and...

"Faith!," Gracie yelled as she came through the door, just as Faith was looking between her stack of books and her suitcase, wondering what to do. "You left your backpack in the living room," she said, glancing over at the books. "Please tell me you weren't up early this morning studying."

"Well," Faith said, "that was the plan."

"You're on vacation!," Gracie continued on. "The birds are singing, the water is warm, and the sun is shining! Not too much, though. Look at this." She wrangled her shoulder halfway out of her shirt. "Just pink! Not bright red!"

"Sunscreen," Faith nodded. "Told you."

"Yep!," Gracie grinned, beginning to pick through the mess of clothes she'd left lying everywhere. "I'm going to slather it on big time today. Seth said he'd take me and Savannah over to the far side of the lake and see if we can do better with the water skiing today. I was hardly able to stand up for two seconds yesterday. Which was still better than he could manage, but maybe that's because I have no idea what I'm doing with driving the boat, huh?"

"Could be," Faith murmured.

"He talked Sam into coming out, too," Gracie said, wiggling out of her pajamas and into her swimsuit.

"Sam's going?," Faith asked, going for a disinterested voice but sounding very eager even still.

"Yeah, though he didn't want to at first," she said. "Told Seth he'd rather hang out around the house. And I told him that he sounds just like you with all your studying and your aversion to the sun."

Faith frowned. "I don't have an aversion to the sun," she said. "And I don't appreciate that you told Sam something like that."

"But talking about you was what finally convinced him to go," Gracie said, looking at her arms in the mirror. "He said if I could talk you into it, he'd go, too. And I told him I've been talking you into all kinds of things since the day I could string two words together."

She had. She really had. And Faith had never been more thankful.

"Are you going to make a liar out of me?," Gracie asked, looking for her towel, even as she slipped her flip flops on. "Stay here and study?"

"No, I'll go. I love the lake."

Gracie frowned at her. "Since when?"

"Since now," Faith said, looking through her suitcase. "I should've brought a swimsuit."

"I told you that back at home," Gracie said. "Lucky for you, I brought some extras."

"I can't fit into any of your swimsuits," Faith argued.

"Yeah, it totally sucks that I got Mom's short genes," she said. "But can I really complain, since I was blessed with her personality? And I actually have a suit that'll fit you." She held up a red bikini.

Faith raised an eyebrow at this. "I thought you were kidding about that."

"Oh, no," she said. "I wasn't."

"And just where have you been wearing that, Stephanie Grace?," Faith said very pointedly, hearing the bossy, big sister in her voice.

"Outside by the pool, and that's it, you big prude," Gracie swore.

"I'm not a prude," Faith frowned.

"Yeah, well, whatever," Gracie said.

"A little modesty is warranted," Faith added. "Honoring Christ by remembering to --"

"Cover it all up," Gracie sighed loudly. "Yes, I know. And I never show off that much of my body. This is my tanning suit. Only worn in the backyard back home so that I can get a tan, finally. You know, on the off chance that I have a horrible accident of some sort, end up on an operating table, and need to have my insides cut open, I would like to have at least some semblance of a tan on my midsection lest I blind the whole medical staff with my pasty, white self."

Faith narrowed her eyes at her sister.

"Oh, fine," Gracie said. "It's because I'm vain, and I like the way I look in a bikini. Even if I'm the only one to see it. There, happy?"

"Give me that," Faith said, taking the bikini out of her sister's hands, getting undressed, and slipping it on. The bottoms were fine, but the top... "Gracie, not only did you get the short genes, but you got the small *everywhere* genes."

"Truth, sister. Can you cram all your business into that?"

Faith bit her lip as she tied up the back of the top. "Just barely. Wow. Look at that."

She turned around to show Gracie. "Hmm," her sister managed.

"What? Just say it."

"Well," Gracie said, "your cups are overflowing. Literally."

"And how!," Faith groaned.

"Well, you look better in it than I do... but..."

"It doesn't fit," Faith whined.

"Maybe you shouldn't be wearing it if it doesn't fit," Gracie noted.

Faith looked at herself in the mirror, wondering at the truth of this. "You're right. It's... too much, huh?"

"Here," Gracie said, going to her sister's side, "maybe if we just stretch the material as far as it can go..."

"That looks worse," Faith protested.

"Nothing about this looks bad," Gracie said, her hands holding the material in place for a moment. "Well, except for how we probably look, me with my hands on your –"

"Don't make this weird, Gracie."

"Oh, it's already weird," she said. "But I'd subject myself to weirder to get you out on the lake today and out of your books." She put her hands down and sighed. "I'm not sure anything can fix this problem."

"But what can I –"

The door opened, and in walked Savannah, who whistled low and said, "Whoa, Faith, are those real?"

Faith frowned. "Okay, that settles it. I'm not wearing this."

"Well, you look great," Savannah said, grabbing her own swimsuit. "But Seth will probably wreck the boat if you come out in that. I mean, he's a good guy, but he's a guy."

"Go get one of Dad's tshirts to wear over it," Gracie said.

"I can just grab one of mine –"

"You may not have enough left because I borrowed... a few."

Faith groaned. "Gracie! I had all of my outfits lined out for the week, all organized, and --"

"We'll do laundry tonight, and boy, am I glad you agreed to go to the lake, because you'd just look silly sitting around the house in my bikini."

Faith frowned even further. "Savannah, is there anyone out in the living room? I'm going to try and sneak through to my parents' room."

"It was clear when I left," Savannah answered.

So, Faith made her way out to the living room, checking both ways before scurrying down the hall towards the room her parents were staying in. Before she could get there, though, the door to one of the extra rooms opened up, and Faith ran right into Sam.

"Hey," he laughed, reaching out to steady her, then pulling his arms back and standing up straighter when he saw what she was wearing.

He stopped laughing, and his eyes went right to her face.

"Faith."

"Sam."

Mortifying, standing here like this with him... and oddly thrilling. Not because she was half dressed but because Sam had the decency to look embarrassed on her behalf and the even greater integrity to keep from letting his eyes roam –

"I need a tshirt," she offered lamely. "I was just heading to my parents' room to see if my dad had an extra –"

"Tshirt, got it," Sam said, ducking back into his room.

Before Faith could wonder at the oddity of this, he stepped back out with a gray shirt in his hands.

"Here." He handed it to her without looking anywhere south of her neck.

"Oh, I wasn't asking you, Sam," she said. "I was just —"

"It's no big deal," he said. "I've got more than I'll need. Besides, all of our parents have left for the day."

Faith nodded and slipped the shirt over her head. It fell perfectly, covered everything, and brought a very distinct Sam scent to her nose. She sighed appreciatively.

"Thanks," she said.

"It looks great on you," he said, smiling again.

And she fell just a little further as his eyes stayed on hers, warmth and tenderness in his gaze...

He thought he knew her for a minute there.

As he'd gotten ready for their day on the lake, something finally clicked.

There had been a little girl, a very young girl, back at Grace. She'd sit with him during the morning service, have him color pictures with her, and tell him the best stories, in her precocious way.

He'd felt a little disheartened connecting this girl to Faith because it meant that she was much too young for all that he'd already begun to envision for them. How this could be, how she could be just a child, when she was studying those college textbooks... well, he didn't know.

But he intended to ask her. Surely, she hadn't been that young. Surely, she wasn't that young. He was even laughing at the improbability of it, the complete absurdity of it, when he left the room, ran right into her, and –

Hello.

He didn't look more than once, and he didn't look for very long. But that accidental glance had wiped away any suspicions that Faith Hayes had ever been that young girl at church whose name he couldn't remember. How could she have been when she was standing in the lake house, looking like a centerfold in that tiny –

He'd successfully managed to push the image out of his mind (kinda) when she'd slipped on his shirt self-consciously and smiled up at him shyly with the USMC letters covering her. And he'd told himself then that it didn't matter that he had no idea who she had been... he would learn everything there was to learn about her now.

And he did. They spent the whole day talking to one another and practically ignoring everyone else from the moment they left until they returned back to the lake house just after sunset. He and Faith had eaten dinner with the whole group, but they hadn't paid any attention to anyone else.

Savannah had declared that their parents were tragically boring and had insisted that the five younger friends go out for ice cream. Sam had slid into the driver's seat of his dad's truck, gently pulling Faith up next to him, sitting close as though they were all alone... with Seth following, Savannah behind him, and Gracie jumping into her lap, all of them chattering like a bunch of annoying monkeys while Faith smiled at Sam. The loud laughter and talking over one another had changed when he leaned over her, his arm brushing against her leg and diverting her attention from the story Seth was telling her, as he turned on the radio.

And Savannah had groaned loudly at the old country station Sam found, causing both Hayes sisters to wonder at what the protest was. Until Sam began singing along, in a horrible off-pitch voice, crescendoing to a ear-splitting falsetto as he tapped the steering wheel, his horrific attempts at sounding feminine in comical opposition to the biceps and shoulders that flexed and bulged as he winked over at Faith…

She had never laughed so hard. And she had joined in on his song until everyone in the truck was pleading with them to stop. It was no wonder that the other three made a beeline away from them at the ice cream shop as Sam reached out for her hand tenderly, pulling her away so that they could sit together alone, talking in between bites. And before long, they made their way back to the lake house, more quietly now, where Gracie and Savannah left to go to sleep, where Faith sat with Sam and Seth for a while longer. As they played video games, they talked about church, about Christ, about spiritual things, and Sam found himself watching her even more as every word sounded so deep, so profound…

At midnight, Faith said goodnight to them, waving softly to Sam as he and Seth were finishing up the last game of the night.

He watched her leave, then turned to his brother. "So… you and Faith seem to get along pretty well," he said to Seth.

"Yeah," Seth nodded, his attention still on the game. "She's got it together for someone her age. Spiritually together, which is rare."

Sam hardly heard the mention of her age. "You're not interested in her, are you?"

Seth looked at him, frowning. "No. She's way too young for me."

Silly Seth. He had always been an old soul at heart.

"Very funny," Sam said, slapping his brother on the back and standing up.

"Sam, she's only –"

"Only here for a week," Sam said. "Not nearly enough time, but... it'll have to be. I think there could be more to this."

And Seth opened his mouth to clarify things for his brother, but Sam was already making his way to their room, his mind on Faith.

They'd just won the last of a series of card games that next evening as Team SamFaith, a name that Savannah had said was completely unoriginal. But neither of them were listening to her or any of the others as they left the room in shifts, each to their rooms for the night, others back down to the lake, after a long day spent in town shopping, this time with everyone.

Their parents had all been there, and Faith had wondered if she'd have less time with Sam. She'd spent most of every day with all of his attention, and it had been a thrill. And it was still a thrill, even as their families were there, too, to find that he always took the seat next to her, that he was always part of the conversations she found herself in, and that, when she slipped out of the dressing room wearing the sundress Gracie had insisted she try on... well, that he was standing there, waiting for her, simply murmuring "beautiful" as she'd stepped out in it.

He'd paid for it himself while she'd been putting her own clothes back on, and when she'd protested this kindness, he'd simply squeezed her hand, smiling at her quietly, as the family around them continued on chatting obliviously as they looked over the rest of the store.

That night, Sam and Faith continued watching one another, talking from where they sat beside each other on the floor, their backs to the couch, even as they cleaned up what was left of the card games.

"I take it you're quite the card shark in Okinawa," she said softly, smiling up at him, totaling up how many games they'd won together. He'd already told her so much about his life overseas, and she could almost picture it, could imagine him late at night, still in his fatigues, coming in from a long day of work, tired and worn out... looking just like this, with a smile in his eyes.

"Not really," he said, turning to face her, leaning his arm on the couch, his fingers so close to her arm that she could feel her skin buzz. "To tell you honestly, I spend most of my free time mooching off my family. Begging for homecooked meals, making a nuisance of myself."

"Really?," she asked, matching his grin, thinking of him overseas, the hero from her childhood dreams...

"Yeah," he said. "Before, when they were still stateside, I spent a lot of time by myself. Was stuck with a group of guys who were pretty wild. So while they were going out finding girls and bars, I was always by myself."

"Hmm," she murmured. "You're a good guy, Sam. You've always been a good guy."

He didn't say anything to this, watching her as she glanced up at him shyly.

"But still," she said. "Overseas living. Seeing the world like that. I'd give anything to experience those places in real life, you know? Not just in books. You can see it all. Take some time and see the world, you know?"

"Well, I'll be seeing more than I want to soon enough," he said. "Or at least another part of the world."

"Change of orders, huh?"

"Yeah," he nodded, watching her. "Haven't told the family yet."

She blinked at this. "It's... not good, then?"

"Could be better, likely. But I'll be okay."

She smiled at this, tilting her head and watching him closely. "Where to, Sam?," she asked softly. Then, shaking her head, "Well, you don't need to tell me, if you haven't even told your family..."

"I want to tell you," he said softly, surprised to find that he wanted to tell her everything.

She gave him that smile. That incredible smile. "Where, then?"

"Afghanistan," he said, very nearly forgetting the question as she watched him.

"Oh," she sighed, a slight tremble in her voice. "Is it dangerous?"

"Probably," he said. "But I'll be okay."

"I'll pray for you," she said. "Every day. Just like when you went to basic training."

He watched her for a long moment. "You did that?"

"Yeah," she nodded, smiling. "I promised you that. Don't you remember?" Her smile excused the memory loss. It had been a long time, after all.

"No," he sighed. "I wish I could remember more. What else have I forgotten from then?"

"Well," she said, pulling her knees up towards her chin, thinking, "you were always good for a piece of cinnamon flavored gum."

"I did chew a lot of that," he said, grinning. "Still do, when I can find it in Okinawa."

"And," she said, "you shared the Gospel by drawing stick figures and using a lot of verses from Romans."

He sat back, wondering at this. "I still do that, too. Did I share Christ with you?"

"You did," she affirmed. "Of course, it was on top of what my parents did already. And it was my dad who led me to Christ. But I still remember the drawing you made for me, how well you explained it. Made good sense to me. Made a difference."

What an amazing thought, that he'd played any part in leading her to be the godly woman she was now.

"I was going to marry you," she whispered, smiling at this.

What an even more amazing thought.

"Wow," he said. "So we were an item?"

"In my dreams and my prayers, yes," she said. "And I did pray for you, when you left for basic training, just like I said I would."

She would have been a teenager by then, he thought. Which is why he couldn't remember her. Why would he have taken note of a thirteen year old girl back when he was eighteen?

"Thank you," he said. "For all that praying. For thinking about me, remembering me while I was gone."

"Yeah," she nodded. "I wrote about you in my journal every night. Asked God to keep you safe. To bring you home to me. Drew little hearts around your name."

He smiled. "You still keep a journal?"

"Oh, yeah."

"Are you going to draw little hearts around my name tonight?," he asked.

"Well, Sam, you assume a lot if you think I'm going to write about you at all," she laughed.

He reached up and put his fingers to her cheek tenderly, the first time he'd been so bold with her, gentle even in this. "Surely you will. If you're going to be praying for me."

"Yeah," she breathed, putting her hand to his, tentatively, shyly, leaning closer to him. "I will, Sam."

And before he could lean in and finally kiss her, they heard the door to the kitchen open, along with Savannah and Gracie's loud voices, signaling that the moment was lost.

But there would be others, surely.

Every day that week, more of the same.

Faith had remembered him, of course, but she hadn't figured on these feelings in addition to the warm memories she had of the teenager who had so well tolerated her childlike affections. Her affections went well beyond that now as she watched him watching her during all the time their families spent together. She had never felt anything like this, this pounding of her heart, the loss of breath, and lightheadedness that overtook her every time Sam leaned over to tell her something, every time he smiled in her direction, and every time she made him laugh out loud as they watched the hours slip by at the lake house.

And Sam? Was baffled by his own feelings as Faith occupied all of his thoughts. She was younger than he was obviously. But certainly not too young, as she spoke so maturely and seemed to be so knowledgeable about so many things as they spent hours talking. He wondered at times if her affection was of some entirely innocent variety as it must have been all those years ago... then concluded it most certainly wasn't as she glanced up at him from lowered eyelids, then went underwater to swim his direction in the lake when Seth, Savannah, and Gracie were busy and not paying any attention. And his affection? Not at all innocent but deeper and stronger and hard to ignore as she'd surface right next to him, where he'd put her arms around his neck, float farther away from the group, and breathe her in as she brushed her cheek next to his and put her hands in his hair. And when they'd hear their names called, always before he could say what he felt, their eyes would meet, even as she'd break away with another smile.

Faith discovered in Sam the same teenage boy she had loved back when she was a little girl, except grown and matured and more alluring and intoxicating than she would have certainly noticed back then in her innocence.

And Sam discovered in Faith everything he'd never even known he wanted.

They'd gone down to the dock one afternoon and sat there, watching as Savannah and Gracie convinced Seth to play a game of tag in the lake. The further they got out, the closer Sam scooted to Faith, until he was sitting with his arm around her back.

"You told them about Afghanistan yet?," she asked softly, leaning into him.

He shook his head, glancing over at her, before he squinted out at the water. "Not yet. Kinda wanna spare my mother the grief while we're here." He shrugged. "Or maybe I just want to spare myself the grief of dealing with her grief."

"Well," she said, "it's not like they won't find out eventually. Like, when they get your first letter from Afghanistan."

He grinned. "Or a call. Set up to video chat, like they're right there with me. Hey, Mom! I'm not in Japan. Surprise!"

She smiled at this. "Not such a great surprise."

He looked back out at the water. "I don't suppose," he said softly, "that you got that part... about how I'll be able to get letters, calls, all that."

"Your mother will be thrilled," she murmured.

He shot a glance her way, saw her smile, and smiled back. "Wasn't my mother I was hoping to hear from. Would you keep in touch?"

"Yeah," she practically whispered. "For as long as you're over there."

"It'll be a while," he said, thinking on this. "But I'd come home, every chance I got. I'd usually just head back to Okinawa, but... I'd come home to you."

She sighed a little at this, watching him, smiling softly. Before he could move in to kiss her, finally, she exhaled. "Hey, I've got a question for you."

He sat up straighter. He was ready to lay it all out for her, if this was what she needed. "Okay. Ask anything."

She bit her lip thoughtfully. "What's your best memory from Grace?"

"Our church?," he asked.

"Yeah," she nodded.

"Why do you ask?," he said.

"Because I have a feeling," she smiled, "that you still don't remember anything."

True enough. He thought for a moment, eighteen years of memories sweeping through his mind. And his grin prompted a laugh from her.

"What, Sam? What are you thinking?"

"Oh, this is going to sound completely unspiritual, but my favorite memory is of the time Scott pulled the fire alarm during worship."

Faith smiled at this. "I remember Scott. And I remember that Sunday. Hard to forget when it was the one and only time it ever happened."

Yeah. Because his parents had threatened Scott with a visit to the police station afterwards, trying to scare him onto the straight and narrow.

"Can't even remember now," he said, "why we weren't in worship."

"Probably working children's church," she murmured. "You did that once a quarter."

He looked at her. "I did. Yeah, and I guess I got Scott to help out. I'm surprised that you remember that, Faith."

She shrugged. "I remember the evacuation, my mother looking for me all in a panic. And her finding me sitting with you." She smiled.

He didn't remember this. Little surprise.

"Any other memories?," she smiled.

"Your dad," he said, "asking me questions in the pastor's office about what Christ had done in my heart. I was five. He wasn't sure I was old enough to understand what I'd done. But he baptized me after I'd explained the assurance I had to him." He watched her for a moment. "I don't suppose you were around yet, huh?"

"Not quite yet," she affirmed.

"How about you?," he asked. "Your best memory from Grace?"

"So many," she sighed. "But definitely one of your mom's tea parties for the elementary aged girls. I felt so big and grown up."

Sam remembered the parties... but had his mother been doing them all along? Even back when he was a kid? He could have sworn she hadn't started that until he was a teenager, but...

Well, he couldn't trust his sorry memory.

"One more question," she murmured.

"Yeah?," he asked.

"What's your best memory since Grace?"

And he thought of all the years that had led up to this as he and Faith stared out over the water together. He put his hand over hers and said, very simply, "This one."

She knew when she woke up that next morning that he would be leaving. Just a few days back to California for some paperwork, but he wouldn't be back here. She would be gone in another day, he'd spend the rest of his leave with his family in Texas, and that would be that.

It was a sad thought and one that she didn't linger on that morning as she woke and showered while the house was still quiet, fixing her hair and slipping on the sundress that Sam had gotten for her, then made her way back to the room she was sharing with Savannah and Gracie, who were still asleep. She sat up in her bed and began putting on her makeup, trying to stay as quiet as possible.

Even in the quiet, Gracie didn't stay asleep for long. And just like she had when they were little girls, she woke up groggy and grinning and made her way over to Faith's bed, where she snuggled up next to her sister, stole all the covers from where they sat in her lap, and breathed, "Good morning, Faith."

"Morning, Gracie," she whispered. "Savannah's still asleep. Pretty sure the rest of the house is waking up, though."

"Mmm," Gracie murmured. "Why are you up so early? And why are you all dressed up?"

Faith looked down at her. "No reason," she said softly. "Just want to look nice."

"And send Sam off with a smile," Savannah murmured from her bed.

Gracie began to giggle while Faith blushed.

"That's not it," she whispered.

"No need to whisper," Savannah said simply as she threw her covers off. "Everyone's awake. And everyone knows what's going on with you and Sam."

"Do they?," Faith asked, concerned. There was the age thing, of course. Faith had wondered why no one had said anything. She had been careful to make sure that no one saw what was going on, going so far as to deflect Sam's attentions when others were watching. He'd watch her oddly at some of these moments, then smile, assuming probably that she was just shy, just private.

"Oh, yeah," Savannah said, glancing over at her.

"Well, nothing's going on –"

"I'm surprised your parents haven't said anything," Savannah interrupted, gathering up her clothes, sniffing to figure out what was clean and what she could take to wear after her shower.

"Why would they say anything?," Gracie asked, crinkling up her nose.

"Because Sam is twenty-six," Savannah said, finding a clean shirt finally.

Gracie gasped out loud. "Faith! Did you know that?"

"Of course, I did," Faith said. "He's always been ten years older than me. That hasn't changed in all these years. I'm sure he knows it, too."

Savannah raised her eyebrows at this. "Well, maybe. Though I'm pretty sure Sam stopped thinking with his head the minute he saw you –"

"We have a lot in common," Faith said, shyly, her face blushed again. "And there's nothing wrong with us talking, like we've been talking."

"Have you kissed him?," Gracie asked.

Faith shook her head. "No." Then she looked up at Savannah. "See? Nothing's wrong with that."

Savannah shrugged. "I don't know. It just seems like there's a big age gap there, and –"

"Our mother is fourteen years younger than our dad," Gracie yawned.

"Yeah, but your mother wasn't sixteen when they met. And I think your dad knew from the first day how old she was. I don't think Sam remembers." She looked at Faith. "But whatever, you know? The heart wants what it wants."

And it did. And her heart wanted him. So she finished putting on her makeup and made her way to the kitchen, where all four parents were already up and fixing breakfast.

And there he was with them, all dressed in his fatigues, smiling over at her as soon as their eyes met.

Him there, smiling like that, dressed like that... she felt her heart doing strange turns and twists, even as her mother tried to get her attention.

"Faith," she said, staring point blank at her daughter. "Are you listening to me?"

"Yeah," she breathed, tearing her eyes away from Sam. "You wanted my help?"

"No," Sam's mother said, smiling over at her, "she wanted to know if the other girls are awake yet."

"They are," she sighed, "but it'll still take them an hour to get ready likely."

"Let's only make for us and these two, then," her father concluded, glancing over at her, raising his eyebrows at the way she was dressed.

But she hardly noticed, as she'd already made her way over to sit next to Sam.

"You look amazing," Sam whispered, leaning over so that his lips just barely brushed her ear, even as she glanced up to make sure that no one was watching.

They weren't. So she turned to him and smiled again.

And after a breakfast of looks traded back and forth and Sam's leg up against hers underneath the table, thrilling every part of Faith, he leaned over again as their parents cleared the table and said, "I only have about an hour before I have to leave for the airport. Will you take a walk with me?"

She nodded wordlessly and let him take her hand in his as they slipped out of the house together.

As they walked, she watched him from the corner of her eye, strong and confident, capable and sure. She thought on Savannah's words and knew, in her heart, that Sam felt like she did and that it made age nothing but a number. She certainly wasn't like most girls are at sixteen, and he knew this, surely.

"You know," he said softly beside her as they walked, "the best part of this vacation has been you."

She smiled at him. "I could say the same about you, Sam."

"You could?"

"And I do," she concluded, as he stopped by the water, just beyond the view of the lake house, and slipped his arms around her.

She took a breath at this familiarity that she had felt all along, that was now made clear, by the way that Sam pulled her closer.

"You're so beautiful," he murmured.

"Hmm," she managed. Then, she offered, "I love your uniform."

Ugh, Faith, she berated herself. If that didn't sound like a goofy, silly sixteen year old —

He grinned at this. "I like wearing the same thing over and over again," he said. "Makes life easy."

"Sounds really awful to me," she said. "But you look nice, all the same. Very nice, actually." And she put her hands to his arms, biting her lip and watching as her fingers traced the cuffs of his shirt and the muscles underneath.

Oh, Sam was *not* sixteen like she was. Not even like he had been when she'd known him back when he was eighteen. She glanced up at him shyly, unsure of how to handle where they were right now, and was caught breathless by the look in his eyes.

Kindness, sweetness. Gentleness. Even as he had been so many years ago. Tender and careful, even in the way he moved closer to her, their faces only inches apart.

"Faith, may I kiss you?," he whispered.

He would be her first kiss, and this moment would be the first like it for her. And she was confident that there would never be anyone else but him, because he was the world to her, right here and right now and likely forever.

Robbed of speech because of all she felt, she simply nodded.

Beautiful.

He had said it and meant it, but it went beyond what he saw. She was sincere. She was thoughtful. She was so sweet, so precious, so special to him, even now. He wondered at how she could be all that she was already, after just a week, but he knew it was the way they understood one another, the way they spoke the same things, the way they loved Christ, the way he finally felt like someone in this world was made for him, the way he finally felt like there was someone to come home to.

She was beautiful, completely, wholly, purely.

And so he put his lips to hers softly, praising God for orchestrating this moment, losing himself in her, rejoicing to feel her sigh at his touch, triumphant that he was the one who could so move this beautiful woman even as she wound her arms around his waist.

And even after his lips left hers, he held her close, smiling to see her open her eyes and stare up at him with the same adoration he felt for her.

"I've been wanting to do that all week," he sighed.

"I'm glad you did," she sighed with him, pressing her cheek to his shoulder, holding him close. "I don't want to go back to Florida tomorrow morning."

And they stood silently for a moment, Sam sorely dreading that he would be returning to Japan in another week, and –

"Hey," he said softly, prompting her to look up at him, even as he brushed a strand of her hair away from her face. "You're on spring break, huh?"

"Yeah," she breathed softly.

"And you… just get a week?"

She nodded, thinking on how a week away from school had sounded unbearable and now, it seemed too short indeed, here in Sam's arms.

"Could you… would you consider blowing off classes for a week and coming back home with me? I mean, not just me. With my family, of course. All of us. I have a week left in the US, and I want to spend it with you." He leaned down to kiss her again.

She returned his kiss eagerly, then smiled up at him. "You're going to California, though," she murmured.

"Just for two days. Then, back to Texas," he said. "And I'll rush through it all, get on the first flight back, if you're waiting there for me."

She smiled at this, overjoyed that she was his choice…. then, her face fell. "Sam, I can't."

"Why not?," he asked, playfully. "It's no big deal, right? Just a few college classes. Everyone skips every now and then, huh?"

She regarded him oddly for a moment. "College classes?"

"Yeah," he said, more excited by the prospect of a week with Faith the more he thought about it. "I know Savannah has skipped an entire week before for much less than comforting a sad, lonely Marine on leave…" He gave her an exaggerated, sad look. "Come on, Faith. Do your patriotic duty and keep me company… please?"

"I'd love to keep you company," she laughed. "But… I'm not in college, Sam."

He gave her a confused look. "But all the studying you've been doing —"

"Yeah," she said, smiling, pulling him closer, "for high school."

"What?," he asked. "Are you... doing student teaching at a high school or something?" But, no, that wasn't right. She wasn't going to be a teacher. So, it must be...

Sam swallowed, trying to figure out any other explanation for what she was saying, never guessing that her meaning was the obvious —

"Samuel," she laughed, and his heart very literally pounded at the way she said his name, "I'm in high school."

This? Was a shock. Sam had neglected to do the math, reconciling the little girl of Grace with this woman here now. He had neglected to think through the numbers, thinking only of how she made him feel. And he had neglected to question any of the things he normally would have questioned, given how mature and wise and unbelievably amazing Faith was —

"Oh," he said, still holding her. "Are you... well, you're graduating soon, then... right?"

"No," she said, laughing. "I'm a sophomore."

Sam, just a tiny bit horrified, breathed a shallow breath. "Faith, how old are you?"

"Sixteen," she said.

And this? Made a difference. Oh, wow. It made a huge difference!

"I thought you were the same age as Savannah," he barely squeaked out. "Which is still really young, but at least it's..." He swallowed. "Legal."

She smiled oddly at this. "You really don't remember when we were kids? At the church?"

He didn't. He really didn't. And it had been a praise, apparently, because he'd only been able to think of her in this context, the lake house, where she was so mature, so grown up, so —

So *this*, he concluded, as she reached out for his face and kissed him again. She was sixteen, but he sure couldn't tell when she smiled beneath his lips like this.

"Faith," he breathed, backing away just slightly.

And it hit him, as she smiled up at him and ran her fingers over his lips, gazing up at him with adoration... Faith Hayes. Sitting next to him in church, coloring a picture. Finding him at every fellowship meal, telling him the stories she'd heard in Sunday school. Running ahead of the rest of the group on those occasions he'd do children's church, so that she could walk with him, her hand in his, her smile only for him.

Faith Hayes.

So. Young.

"Oh... Faith," he barely managed.

And she saw the recognition there but failed to see the horror that came with it. "Sam," she murmured, his face in her hands as she pressed her body against his. "You remember me. I knew you would."

He tried to think, tried to justify any of this, but it was impossible, as Faith put her head to his shoulder again and they continued to hold one another. As they walked back to the house in silence, he thought of the words to say to explain his mistake to her...

... but she gave him no opportunity to, as they came up to the house, and she let go of his hand, smiling back at him and putting her finger to her lips.

Their secret. That made it seem even worse.

The goodbyes had taken up the rest of his time, and Faith had stayed on the fringes of the crowd, smiling to herself. When he'd gone to awkwardly hug her goodbye, she'd stopped him, holding out her hand instead as both sets of their parents watched. And their hands touched as their lips already had, with a small piece of paper folded in hers, passed to him.

He opened it in the cab, saw that it was her phone number and her address, and even though his heart screamed otherwise, his head told him to throw it away. And he did.

Faith never heard from him again. And though she cried and mourned and felt the loss, she somehow knew that one day, she would see him again.

CHAPTER THREE

Eight years later

The prayers Faith had been voicing on the drive over to the clinic continued on, even as she sat before the matronly, no-nonsense woman who would, hopefully, become her new employer. Elaine Charles was typical for the profession -- soft, welcoming, warm, and just a little eccentric.

"Now... where did I put my glasses?," Elaine muttered to herself, patting down her large bosom as she finally sat at her desk, blowing her hair out of her eyes as she did so. "Is it hot in here, dear? Or is that just the change of life? As if you would know, right?" She smiled brightly, even as she continued searching pockets and the floor around her chair. "So young yourself. But you know all about it, I imagine. Your degrees, experience, all those ovaries and uteruses you've checked out even this early on in your career." She frowned just slightly. "Well, good gravy! I have completely lost my glasses!"

Faith nodded softly. "Um... they're on top of your head."

70

Elaine put her hand to her messy updo and laughed out loud. "That they are! Look at you, already making my life easier!"

It was a wonder that Elaine Charles hadn't misplaced a baby in all of the deliveries she'd done, honestly. She was scatterbrained, distractible, and forgetful. But her clinic was different from most, in its faith-based philosophies and overtly evangelical purposes. Elaine was an amazing midwife. Faith knew all about it.

Just thinking of the praises she'd heard, the things she'd read, the talk surrounding this clinic, so far from her home state, had Faith once again uttering silent prayers in her heart as Elaine ("you must call me Elaine, dear") smiled at her, glasses finally on and Faith's resume in hand, putting it on top of the mess already scattered over her desk, overflowing to the floor.

Faith's organized, ordered mind shrieked a little as patient files spilled from the desk and likely mixed with others that were stacked haphazardly on the ground. Silently shrieked, of course, because she wanted this job more than she'd ever wanted anything.

"So, so, so, tell me more about yourself!," Elaine trilled, her hands folded on the desk.

"Well," Faith said, thinking of all that she'd gone through to get to this moment, "I completed the BSN to DNP program at the University of Florida a couple of years ago, with a concentration in nurse midwifery. As soon as I was licensed, I began full time work at a clinic in Orlando. Mainly birthing center deliveries with some home births done as well." She'd been the youngest midwife on staff and the only DNP in the clinic, and it had served her well as she'd connected with the younger patients especially. There had been more than one spiritual conversation leading to Christ with those young mothers as Faith had walked with them through their pregnancies and their deliveries.

Elaine clasped her hands together and leaned back in her chair. "And how did you find the home births, dear?"

"Referrals from the clinic, of course, and I'm listed as a CPM with the Florida registry --"

"No," Elaine giggled. "I mean, how were those home births? How did they go for you?"

Faith thought back to the first one, in the home of a mother of five who had done most of the hard work of labor before Faith arrived, moved to check her progress, and saw a head already halfway out. She'd done deliveries at the birth center, of course, with its safety measures in place if things went wrong, if heart rates dropped, if the bleeding was too heavy... but this was something else entirely, being on her own, knowing that the birth was happening with or without her, yet still feeling great responsibility as she helped ease the infant into the world, her capable hands trembling as his siblings played in the next room, as the warmth of this family home welcomed him, and as he took his first breath and Faith felt as though she could breathe herself, her relief so great.

"They were terrifying," Faith said honestly. "None as much as the first, but... well, they're always still just a little terrifying. And exhilarating, all at the same time."

Elaine grinned. "I've done hundreds myself," she exclaimed. "And it's the same! Terrifying, the enormity of it, and almost holy. Knowing that each and every one of those babies is called out for a purpose and a plan, singled out for God's purposes and His glory." She gasped and put a hand to her large chest. "Just gives me goose bumps!"

Faith smiled. "Exactly." This was why she'd gone this way, of course. This was why she'd spent those years in school, those years in real-life practice, and those hours of sitting around with so many laboring women, praying and sharing Scripture.

There was more to this than delivering babies.

This was why she was at this clinic now, knowing that Elaine Charles was running a ministry, not just a medical practice.

"You know, of course, that we're evangelical," Elaine said simply. "That we adhere to a doctrine and statement of beliefs, requiring all of our midwives to be in agreement theologically."

Faith did. She'd already read through it all, researched it, and found herself in line with all that this ministry backed and believed. "Yes," she said. "It's exactly the kind of clinic I had hoped to work in when I began my career, honestly."

"You're a... pastor's daughter, right?," Elaine said, glancing at the resume that teetered on the edge of the desk. "With some hours of seminary yourself?"

"Yes," Faith said. "At the suggestion of my father. Just some winter terms, a couple of systematic theology classes, to supplement what he's taught me all of my life."

"You enjoy school, obviously," Elaine smiled at her.

Understatement of the year. The seminary classes had been a hobby, completed during the two vacation weeks that the birthing center made her take. She'd felt at home, slipping right into the routine of lectures, papers, exams, hours and hours of reading...

"I do," Faith said, smiling as well. "We never stop learning, do we?"

"We sure don't," Elaine said. "You're overqualified for the job, Faith. You know that, don't you?"

And Faith's heart clenched at this, fearing that the job could be slipping away before it was even hers --

"Which means I would be crazy to not hire you before you can think twice about it, huh?"

Faith bit back a smile at this, knowing what Elaine's words meant. "I would be honored and truly, truly blessed to work alongside you."

Elaine literally clapped her hands at this as she shot Faith another winning smile. "Well, we're understaffed at the moment. If you came on, you'd start out full speed ahead. Our client list is long, and we make ourselves accessible to them at all hours, every day."

Faith nodded. "Excellent. I can handle it."

"Then, you, my dear," Elaine said, extending her hand across the desk, "have the job!"

Faith spent the next hour filling out paperwork and making plans for her move to Texas, contacting clients who would be her patients very soon, making lists in her head of all that she had to do, even as she made her way out to the rental car, unlocking the door just as her phone rang.

Expecting that it was Craig, she took a deep breath. How to explain to your fiancé that you had indeed taken a job that would separate you from him by three whole states...

It was complicated. The whole relationship had been complicated, honestly.

There had been that spring break when she was sixteen, back at Nana's lake house... back with Sam Huntington. Faith had been heartbroken when she hadn't heard back from Sam, of course, and even after she'd resolved that she wasn't ever going to hear from him or see him again, she'd wondered about him.

It had been her age, surely. She'd replayed the conversation by the lake over and over again, searching for any other reason why he would have become so strangely silent. He didn't seem the type to play around with women, and she knew his heart for Christ, knew that he was sincere, and knew that he would never have intentionally hurt her.

It had to have been her age. And so, when she came of age, the right age, she still wondered about him, telling herself that he was gone for good yet still wondering where he was, what he was doing, if things would be different if they ever saw one another again.

So silly. And immature.

This had been her mindset two years ago, as she'd been finishing up her degrees. That early entry to college and all of those hours and courses completed in high school had put her in a position to be ahead of the curve at twenty-two and in a secure career as she returned to the city she grew up in, took a job at the very same birthing center she had visited as a teenager doing research for a paper, and became a part of her parents' church again.

The church had grown even more in her absence. The staff had moved from a team of five associate pastors, led by her father, to a team of ten, and the young pastor leading the singles ministry was Craig Lucas, a guy straight out of the seminary in New Orleans.

He had only been at the church a few months when Faith moved back, and in that time, he'd sought her father out as a mentor, naturally becoming a part of the family. Grandma Trish loved him for his connection to New Orleans, Gracie loved him for his extroverted personality, and her mother loved him for his neverending compliments when he'd come over to eat at their house.

He'd been invited to one of those dinners two years ago on the very night that Faith came back into town, arriving when she was upstairs unpacking an overnight bag in her old room. She'd come down the stairs after everyone was already seated at the table, and Craig, when his eyes met hers, had stood at his place, his napkin falling from his lap to the floor, with a look of amazement on his face.

Love at first sight, he'd told her later. Much, much later, when she was in so deep that she couldn't remember how she'd gotten herself there.

He was a good guy. Better than a good guy. He was godly, focused, ambitious, and determined to win her over from the very beginning. As she'd settled into life back at home, finding her own place, beginning her career, and starting the rest of her life, he'd been there, giving encouragement, giving her all of his attention, and making plans. When Grandma Trish had gotten so sick and had passed away right there in her room, with her family gathered all around her, Craig had been the one to listen to Faith, to let her cry, and to offer solace.

It was inevitable that before long, the relationship Faith had regarded as casual had changed to something more. She had struggled with her feelings, remembering how it had felt to look up at Sam by the lake, back when she was sixteen. She didn't feel this for Craig, but there was certainly more substance to what Craig was doing, the plans he was making, and the life he was beginning than there had been so long ago with Sam. Good sense, logic, and responsibility mattered more in the long run than heart palpitations, butterflies, and feeling something just from his smile... right?

Even with all of this nearly confirmed in her heart, she had still been surprised when Craig had invited both of their parents to dinner, gotten down on his knee in front of them all, and asked her to marry him.

She'd said yes.

She still couldn't believe that she'd said yes. And when she'd heard about the clinic, about the opportunity, about the distance, a few months later, she'd jumped at the opportunity. Things had gotten tense between them since the engagement, and she'd reasoned with herself that distance would be good to clear her head.

Craig had been supportive, never guessing just how freaked out she was, telling her that there was no reason that he couldn't find a church in Texas if the job worked out and that's what they needed to do. She'd merely changed the subject every time he'd talked about resumes, wondering at what she was doing, acknowledging silently for both of them that something wasn't right with their relationship.

She thought of this as she answered her phone, preparing herself to speak with him...

"Hello?"

"Faith!" Not Craig. Just Gracie. Faith exhaled. "I've been praying all morning. Like, focusing and praying, for the past two hours, which isn't easy for me, you know."

Faith knew. Gracie was still, at twenty-three, as much of a mess as she had been back when they were tiny girls. "I appreciate it," Faith murmured. "Thanks for praying."

"Well?," she prodded. "How did the interview go? Can I stop praying?"

"Yes," Faith answered, pushing thoughts of Craig and marriage aside for the moment. "And I got the job."

"As if there was any doubt!," Gracie laughed. "Congratulations!"

"Thanks, Gracie," Faith said, smiling, thinking of her sister, back in Orlando, sitting on the couch in the living room likely, her phone to her ear, a huge smile on her face. She and Gracie had been in college together, had roomed together as soon as Gracie had gotten there, and just as soon as she'd graduated, she'd joined Faith back at home. Faith had never known life apart from Gracie, and even the thought of her dream job, in this new exciting place, had Faith swallowing back tears because Gracie wouldn't be with her.

Gracie seemed to be thinking the same thing. "I mean," she said, "it totally sucks that my best friend is going to be halfway across the country, but --"

"I know," Faith murmured. "I'm going to miss you."

"Okay, okay," Gracie said, exhaling loudly. "We'll save the goodbyes for later. Like when you actually leave Florida. When do you start?"

"Just as soon as I can get moved out here. Two weeks, tops," she said. "I've got a long list of things to start working on. Looking at some rental properties this afternoon, thinking of changing my flight and taking another day here before I go home to pack up everything. Do you think that'll end up costing me too much?"

"I wouldn't worry about the cost," Gracie said. "In fact, don't worry about changing your flight. Mom's already on it. And on changing your car rental."

"What? Why is Mom --"

"Are you up for a road trip?," Gracie asked.

"A road trip?," she asked, wondering what Gracie might have cooked up. "What?"

"Do you remember Thomas Fisher?," Gracie asked, her voice softer.

"Of course," Faith said, leaning up against the car, wondering at this. Thomas Fisher had been her father's mentor for the great majority of his ministerial career. There had been an Alzheimer's diagnosis decades ago, failing health... "Oh, Gracie. Did he pass on?"

"Hold up," Gracie said, whispering to someone with her hand on the receiver. Faith bit her lip and waited. "Thank you, Craig," she heard. "Are you sure you don't have any single brothers you can send my way?" Flirty giggles.

Oh, Gracie.

"Is Craig there?," Faith asked, her heart beating a little sporadically, knowing that he was there, listening. "Did he hear me talking about the job? I swear, Gracie, I was about to call him —"

"No," Gracie murmured. "He was just leaving. He spent the morning here with Dad going over church business for the week since we're going to be out of town for the funeral, and he'll be preaching all three services."

"Funeral," Faith said. "So, Dr. Fisher..."

"Yes," Gracie said softly. "Dad's having a really hard time with it."

"I can imagine," she murmured, thinking of the older preacher, how her father had admired him the same way that Craig now admired him...

"I think it would be helpful if you could meet us for the funeral," Gracie said. "Two days from now. In Fort Worth. Mom already has what she needs to change up all of your reservations to give you some extra time to do that. If you're okay with driving up from Houston."

"Why don't you fly out here and drive up with me?," Faith asked, imagining how much better the time would be with Gracie...

"I totally wish I could," Gracie groaned. "But they've already got me on the flight with them, straight into Fort Worth. Can you meet us, though? On the day of the funeral?"

She could do that. It would actually make things easier, having the time to get things done in Houston, giving her a couple of extra days to prepare herself for a talk with Craig...

"I'll be there," she said. "Text me the details, and I'll make sure I'm there."

Sam woke up with a gasp, opening his eyes suddenly, pushing out of bed violently, fighting against the nightmare he'd been having.

Home. He was home.

He took stock of it all quickly, with rapid precision, with his breath held, just to make sure.

There were his shoes by the door. His phone, wallet, and keys on the desk. His house, the house he was building, just out the window, across the field.

And there was his brother, Scott, sitting by the door, watching him with concern.

He was home.

Not in Afghanistan. Not the far reaches beyond Afghanistan that no one knew about, that Sam had known intimately, that he couldn't talk about, that he would never be able to forget, that he couldn't move past no matter how long he had been out of the Marines...

"Scott," he murmured softly, "was I screaming?"

"Yeah," Scott sighed. "Just like every morning."

Sam took a deep breath, blew it out and covered his face with his hands. "I don't normally wake you up."

"That's because I'm usually awake," Scott shrugged. "I get up with Nathan."

Sam thought of his nephew in the bedroom next to his, all of his short life so far spent with his crazy, tormented uncle screaming his head off every morning, dreaming about poverty, bombs exploding, people in pain, horror –

"Sorry," he murmured, feeling like a failure, like a man who would never move beyond this. "I'm so sorry, Scott."

"No need to be sorry," Scott said. "You have nothing to be sorry for, Sam. And no one's sleeping well right now anyway."

They weren't sleeping well. None of them. They'd gotten the call two days ago, telling them that their grandfather, Thomas, was passing away. Hospice had been called, and they'd given him three days. Scott and Sam had been packing bags, getting everything ready to leave, when they got the call an hour later saying that he'd already passed.

After decades of slipping away slowly, Thomas hadn't tarried a single moment when Christ came to take him into glory. Sam could imagine him even now, facedown before God in His glory, declaring that his whole life had been spent for just this moment, a moment that would now be lived out forever and ever, for all eternity.

A moment that was worth every pain and hardship along the way.

Sam had found solace in this, not just for his grandfather but for himself as well. Every prayer every morning every day of his life had been pointed towards a Lord who redeemed the past, who would one day show Sam the fulfillment of the faith he held on to, even after all that he'd been through.

"Any funeral details?," Sam asked, looking over to his brother.

"Tomorrow," Scott answered. "Ten o'clock. At Grace, of course. Visitation tonight starting at six. Told Mom we'd be down around lunchtime, but we'll have to get going soon to make that happen. You know. Baby, pregnant woman in the car –"

Sam squinted at his brother. "Is Marie pregnant again?"

"She was crying over a coffee commercial," Scott sighed. "I mean, I know we're all emotional and all. But coffee? Crying. *Scott, they were holding hands,*" he mock sobbed, in perfect imitation of his wife's voice, "*as they were this young couple, then with a baby in her arms, then a kid sitting on his lap, then with teenagers slamming doors around them, and an empty house, and little grandbabies, then by themselves again, Scott! Holding hands with their coffee cups! They were in love! They'll be in love forever, with their coffee, with each other! Just like you and me, Scott! Ek lief is vir jou,and --*"

"What does that even mean?," Sam grinned, thinking of Marie sobbing and falling into her second language without thinking.

"I have no idea," Scott shrugged. Then, grinning, "But I know it's good. Because she says it at some really great moments... *ooohhh, ek lief is vir jou, Scott, mmmmm...*"

"She'd kill you if she knew you were telling me this."

"She would," he laughed. "But you know what I'm talking about."

"Actually, I don't," Sam said.

"Yeah, you don't," Scott said. "You're a good man. A good, single, chronically celibate man."

"Which you obviously don't know anything about. How far apart will Nathan and this one be, then?," Sam asked, rubbing the back of his neck and yawning.

"Twelve months to the day or less as I'm figuring it," he said, smiling.

"Good grief, man," Sam muttered. "Did you jump in the bed with her in the delivery room?"

"Very nearly," Scott noted. "Irish twins. Just like you and me, brother."

Sam smiled at this. "Sam and Scott, Part Two."

"Yeah," Scott grinned. "Marie could be pregnant right this minute with a new version of me, ready to bless Nathan like I've blessed you all these years."

"Look out, Nate," Sam murmured. "Though you've gotten better with age."

"True enough," Scott nodded. "Have to name him Thomas, of course."

Sam swallowed at this, thinking of his grandfather. "Big name for a girl."

Scott gasped. "A girl... I hadn't even considered the possibility of a girl."

Sam smiled. "Better consider it, Daddy." Then, softly, "Thanks. For talking with me. Being here."

Scott simply nodded, then stood. "See you downstairs in a few, then."

And Sam began to get ready for the day. One of the benefits of having been a Marine for the majority of his adult life was that everything he did was defined by ritual, by habit, by a conscious movement towards completing tasks. Quickly made bed, bags packed efficiently, showered, then a stern look in the mirror at the beard he'd been sporting ever since the discharge. A long, laborious shave, and it was gone. And because he'd been distracted when he went in to get his hair cut earlier that week, he'd gotten the same cut he'd had for all of those years.

So, there he was, staring back at himself in the mirror. Sam the Marine. A face he'd known well enough but so different now. He looked away, swallowing heavily.

Once he was dressed, he made his way quickly down the stairs, his bag on his back, clearing his throat loudly just in case, as was often the case, Scott and Marie were making out in the kitchen. He hoped this would be sufficient warning.

It likely would have been, but nothing was going on, probably because Marie was alone, sitting in the big middle of the dining room nursing his nephew without any kind of covering.

"Oh, good grief, Marie," he managed, turning away from her with a grimace.

"What?," she asked.

"You're... you're not covered up."

"And?"

"I know, I know," he said. "Your house, your right to just bare all at the table —"

"it's what God made them for, Sam," she said.

He cringed at this. "Ugh..."

"But I'll respect you and cover up," she said. "And now Nate has the right to throw a blanket over your face the next time you sit down for a meal." A pause. "There. Decent again."

He glanced over at her warily, only to find her smiling at him, a yellow ducky blanket spread over her like a shawl. "You're so funny," she grinned.

And he couldn't help but grin back as he sat down across from her. She was just perfect for his brother, and she'd made this house a home, radiating the joy of Christ to all around her. He seriously doubted any woman out there would want to deal with all of the baggage he was carrying, but he had often thought that if God intended marriage for him, even after all that he'd been through, he'd want someone as godly as Marie.

"Funny and also super cute, underneath all that hair," she said, grinning even further, reaching out to touch his face. "Who would have guessed?"

He shrugged. "Been a while since I've seen this guy looking back at me in the mirror, but there was no way I was going to Grandpa's funeral without shaving."

"Samuel Thomas Huntington, USMC!," Scott shouted, coming into the kitchen from the bedroom. "Look at you!"

"Doesn't he look handsome?," Marie asked.

Scott stopped by her chair, looking at Sam critically. "Not as handsome as me, right?"

"No way, buddy," she said, reaching up and pulling his face down to hers.

Sam rolled his eyes at this, at the way Marie giggled as Scott loudly kissed her, as they acted like teenagers instead of --

"Why is my man Nate eating with a blanket on his head?," Scott asked, his lips still on Marie's.

"Because Sam is a really, really great guy," she said. "To the point of being ridiculous."

"Sam is ridiculous," Scott said, breaking away from her with one last kiss. "I already knew that."

"Yeah," Marie sighed contentedly. "Avert your eyes, Sam. Switching sides."

Before Sam could say anything to this, Scott moved on to more funeral information. "Just got off the phone with Mom," he said, sliding into the seat at the head of the table as Sam swiveled around to face him. "Grammy wants you, Seth, Jacob, Kenji, and me to be pall bearers."

"What about the rest?," Sam asked, thinking of their other two brothers.

"Preaching the service."

"Sean and Stu both?" Sam's eyes widened at this.

"Yeah, them, along with the guy who's pastor at Grace now, Uncle Josh, and Stephen Hayes."

Sam's mind settled on that last name. Stephen Hayes. And there in his thoughts, instantly, was a memory of Faith and the smile she'd given to him that morning right as his lips had left hers.

He'd had so much guilt in between saying goodbye to her and going back to Okinawa. He'd beaten himself up for not knowing the age difference, for acting so recklessly, for indulging in his feelings... for throwing her number away without giving any explanation at all. He'd considered finding her address, finding her number, finding any way to reach her again at least a dozen times as he was finishing up his leave, but he hadn't done it, not trusting himself to give an explanation and leave well enough alone.

He knew even then that he'd want to keep in touch if he'd contacted her, that he'd talk himself into continuing on with what they'd started. And what kind of pervert would that have made him, carrying on with a teenage girl?

He'd wrestled with a lot of "what ifs" between Texas and Okinawa.

And then, he'd left for Afghanistan. The triviality of social expectations, of happily ever afters, of simple mornings spent sharing kisses by the lake house had fallen away in the face of real issues -- life and death, right and wrong, getting through each and every day. And when things were bad, when they were truly awful, he'd thought of Faith. And he hadn't felt guilt in remembering her. He'd felt hope, remembering the way she looked at him, remembering the words of life she had spoken, trusting that there was good in the world, given by Christ and His redemption, knowing that he had seen it in her.

His mind had gone to her often and went to her now. Again.

"Five preachers," he murmured, as Scott and Marie watched him, given his long silence. "Wow."

"Yeah," Scott said. "I just might get saved all over again with all that preaching."

Marie laughed out loud at this, prompting Scott to grin over at her.

"Just a regular come to Jesus convention meeting," he laughed. "And the rest of the week is going to be more of the same. Aunt Em and Mom have jobs for all of us after the funeral, to help with all of the guests and everyone who's going to be coming into town."

Sam wondered for an illogical second if Faith Hayes would be included in the crowd. That was silly. She probably had her own life now, her own responsibilities, her own commitments... she wouldn't be there for the funeral of a man she had never really known.

"My parents tried to get back," Marie murmured. Her mother had been a member of their grandfather's church as a child, then as a young woman, up until she left for the mission field where she met Marie's father, married him, and had Marie. It was a coincidence that had been a real blessing to their family, that Marie had been connected to Thomas Fisher in this way, from the times he'd gone as a retired pastor to be part of what her family was doing on the mission field. She'd known him before she even knew Scott, and his passing was a loss even to her, not just as the mother of his great-grandchildren but as someone who had been influenced by him, all those years ago in Africa.

Thomas Fisher's legacy spread farther than any of them could fathom, likely.

"They weren't able to make it happen, though, were they?," Sam asked softly, as Marie wiped away tears.

"No, they couldn't get the flights booked with such short notice. But I can imagine if they were planning on it, there are probably hundreds of others making their way to Fort Worth right now." She reached out for Scott's hand, her voice heavy with tears. "All those people who he loved, who loved him."

"And we better join them," Scott said, leaning over and kissing her on the forehead, "just as soon as Nate's done."

"And as soon as I get some coffee," Sam said, wanting to relieve some of the sadness in the room. Looking at Marie, he pretended to get all choked up. "I mean, I'm so worked up about coffee that... well, I think I could cry about it, Marie."

She watched him, confused, while Scott pounded him on the back. "Very funny, Sam," he said. "Come and help me get the car loaded up."

Faith hadn't counted on the traffic. In either city.

Houston had been a mess to get through, and she'd thought the worst was out of the way as the freeways and busy mergers gave way to a scenic, flat Interstate drive. Actually, not scenic at all, as Texas from this perspective was flat and boring.

And then, traffic picked up again in Fort Worth, and she found herself worrying that she would get to the funeral too late.

Just as her phone buzzed with a text, she could see Grace Community Church on the horizon. She remembered it very faintly from her childhood and could feel the corners of her mouth turning up in a smile, even as she fumbled around for her phone.

A text. From Gracie.

Where r u?

She tossed the phone onto the passenger seat and accelerated even more, closing in on the distance between the car and the parking lot, which was quickly filling up. As soon as she'd found a space across the street, she parked, got out, and began making her way to the front doors of the church, texting Gracie back.

Here. Where r u?

"Right here, Faith."

And Faith clutched her hand to her chest very briefly as her eyes fell on her sister, smiling and standing next to a handsome young man.

"Gracie, you sneaky little thing," she murmured, reaching out to hug her. "Traffic was awful. Everywhere. I don't remember this about Texas, do you?"

"No, but I don't remember much," Gracie giggled. "Not much besides this guy!" She turned to the man who stood by her and smiled up at him.

He held his hand out, taking his eyes from Gracie for just a moment, a smile on his face as well. "Hey, Faith," he said. "Jacob. Jacob Morales."

Faith smiled as she took his hand, then pulled him in for a hug. "Oh, wow, Jacob..." She could well remember the evenings spent in the backyard with Jacob and Gracie both as their mothers and fathers, all in ministry in Fort Worth, had chatted inside. His sister, Sadie, had been too much older to enjoy playing with them back then, as Jacob himself had probably been. But he'd always tolerated Gracie bossing him around, getting him into trouble...

"He grew up to be a hottie, didn't he?," Gracie said in a whispered, singsong voice, purposely loud enough for Jacob to hear her, if the flirty little look she tossed over her shoulder at him was any indication.

He smiled at this, like he was having the best day ever... at his grandfather's funeral, no less.

Faith sobered immediately at this remembrance.

"I'm so sorry about your grandfather," she murmured. "He was such a great man."

Jacob nodded. "Thank you. Can't be too sorry that he's better off than he was, after all that time of being so sick."

"We know how it is," Gracie said softly. "Our Grandma Trish passed away just a couple of years ago."

"I remember," he said. "My parents went to the funeral. I wasn't able to get out there, though." His eyes traveled over Gracie's face. "Wish I had."

Faith raised her eyebrows at this, as Jacob and Gracie seemed to forget she was there, staring at one another and smiling.

"You guys have been getting reacquainted then?," she asked pointedly.

"Oh, yeah," Gracie grinned. "I came in last night, and Uncle Beau and Aunt Mel had Jacob and his parents over for dinner. And we've been having so much fun. Right, Jacob?"

"Well, yeah," he said. "Haven't been arrested. Yet."

"I already told you, that wasn't breaking and entering," Gracie said, "because we didn't technically break in. Just climbed a fence."

"Yeah," Jacob nodded, taking a breath. "So trespassing. And I had a weapon –"

"A shovel is *not* a weapon," she giggled. "We meant no harm. And it was *fun!*"

"Gracie," Faith cut in, imagining some horrible scenarios, "what are you talking about?"

"Another story for another time, Faith," she said, patting her sister on the hand.

"Yeah," Jacob said, looking over at the main doors into the sanctuary, "because we don't have time to tell it now. Funeral should be starting any minute now."

"We should go get our seats, then," Faith murmured, grabbing Gracie's hand. "We'll see you afterwards, Jacob."

"Oh, no," he said, "you're coming to sit with the family."

Before either sister could protest this, he was leading them to the choir room off of the sanctuary, which was filled, wall to wall, with people. Faith saw her mother, but before she could reach out for her, someone else stepped in the way. And just as she was turning around to tell Gracie to stick close so they could sit together out of the way of the real family members, a senior adult woman with a church name tag ran into her with a box of boutonnieres.

"Oh, I'm so sorry," Faith whispered.

"No, I'm sorry," the woman responded. "Running late. And it --" Then she gasped, looking at Faith, her hand to her chest. "Oh, my... Faith? Faith Hayes!"

Faith smiled at this, slipping right into ministerial mode. She had no idea who this woman was, but she was a church lady, obviously. So, just like she'd done her whole life, Faith smiled sweetly, accepted the embrace that came with the recognition, and glanced inconspicuously to the name tag the woman wore. Julia Stanley.

"Mrs. Stanley," she said softly, just as Gracie came to her side with the same sweet smile on her own face. "So good to see you after all these years."

"And there's Gracie," Julia said, reaching out for her as well. "My goodness. You girls are all grown up! How did that happen?!" She shook her head. "I still remember you coming into Sunday school that one time, Faith. All of six years old, and you told me, quite proudly, that it was okay for boys and girls to see each other naked if they were married because that was the way God had intended it, back in the Garden."

"Awesome," Gracie managed through a giggle as Faith blinked at this. "That sounds like you, Faith. Always ready with an answer from Scripture. On every subject."

"Sound theology," Faith murmured. "And at such a young age. And on a subject I didn't need to know anything about quite yet."

"Yes," Julia said. "Exciting Sunday, that one was." She looked down at the box of flowers that she held. "Could you girls help me by getting these on the pall bearers? They're lined up at the door over there."

And Gracie took the box from her with a smile and a "sure thing!" and pulled Faith along with her, taking the first one out and standing on tiptoe to pin it to Jacob's shirt as he smiled down at her. Faith picked up the next one and raised her eyes to... Seth. She smiled even as he smiled back, both of them recognizing one another despite the eight years that had passed since they'd last seen one another on that spring break trip.

One reunion after another today.

"Seth," she whispered.

"Faith Hayes," he laughed softly as she pinned the flower to his shirt. "Long time."

"No kidding." She held up the next flower. "Who's next?"

"I've got this one," Gracie said. "Kenji, right? Jacob told me about you."

The young man smiled and nodded at this. "And I have no idea who you are, but thank you for not sticking me with that pin."

"Thank me after I finish," Gracie answered. "You might jinx me."

"You get Scott, Faith," Seth said. And Faith looked up and gasped just a little. It was Thomas Fisher…. surely not…

"I know," Scott said. "I look like the guy in the casket, don't I?"

"Good grief, Scott," Seth muttered.

"Hey, I'm his living legacy," Scott shrugged as Faith worked on his boutonniere.

"Well, you look like him, at least," she offered. And with the four of them done, one flower remained. Faith picked it up and looked around for the missing grandson, moving gingerly between those that stood there, even as the door was opening for them all to go and sit down.

And in the close crowd, she was pushed forward and off balance, falling right into the arms of… Sam.

Sam Huntington.

He looked as surprised as she did, holding her in the choir room as the crowd around them dispersed. She backed away a second later as he blinked at her and seemed to struggle for something to say —

"Um, this," she whispered weakly, holding up the last rose. "Yours?"

He nodded just as weakly as she stepped closer to him and, with shaking hands, began to pin the flower onto his shirt. And even standing there, so close to him, even in a place like this, her mind and her body screaming at her, she had the fleeting thought that this wasn't anything like what she had with Craig.

Even the thought felt like treason. Especially since she hadn't heard one word from this man since he'd kissed her by the lake house, all those years ago.

She wasn't sure what felt worse in this moment as her heart pounded. Thinking of Craig waiting on her with such devotion or thinking of Sam, forgetting all about her.

Or not, since there was something there in his eyes as he watched her. Something so sad and empty, so different than who she had known back as a child, back at the lake house... back when she'd so sincerely and innocently loved him.

He was different. She could see it, and yet still, he was Sam... oh, Sam...

"Faith," he murmured so softly, so fully, something deep in his voice...

"I'm so sorry about your grandfather," she whispered, attributing the sadness to this, trying to push the thoughts out of her mind, glancing up at him.

And he watched her for a long, painful moment, his eyes so full... before nodding and looking around to see that they were the last ones to leave. He pointed at the door wordlessly, and she followed him out, into the church, and over to a familiar pew, where the last row of family members had squeezed in, leaving enough room just for two.

They sat down together, and Faith's mind rushed back to hundreds of Sundays spent right here... right beside Sam, just like this. As one preacher after another stood and talked about Thomas Fisher, she snuck quick glances to Sam, at his passive, expressionless face. When her father took to the pulpit to give the Gospel message, she heard Sam sigh softly.

She remembered how he had loved his grandfather and this church and knew the loss he must certainly have been feeling. She had felt the same way about Grandma Trish.

And so she didn't hesitate to brush her hand over his comfortingly. And when he closed his fingers around hers and held her hand in his, she left it there for the rest of the service.

Two hours later, his brothers, their wives, his sister, his parents, his cousins, his aunts, his uncles, and everyone else in the tristate area showed up, and general mayhem took over the Fisher home. Sam never lost sight of Faith, as she moved from one set of open arms to another, talking with all of the relatives, friends, and church members who obviously remembered her, but he hadn't had one moment of peace to talk to her alone since he'd been forced to get up at the funeral and let go of her hand.

Not that he had any idea what he'd say, since their last conversation eight years ago... well, had consisted of nothing but whispered proclamations of affection and adoration, followed by years of silence. His fault, of course, and based on the way Faith had avoided his gaze most of the afternoon, he could guess that she remembered the silence more than the sweet words.

His aunt, Emily, cornered him in the kitchen, as he mingled with the guests and kept watching Faith.

"Have you seen your brother?," she asked him.

"Which one?"

"Scott," she said. "One of the toilets is backed up. Mom should have had your father come out and check it earlier, but... well, you know how it's been."

He had. As ready as they had all been for this, as much time as they'd been given, they weren't prepared. Sam hugged his aunt close for a moment.

"Thanks, Sam," she whispered in his ear. "You always were the sweetest one of the lot." She smiled at him, running her hand affectionately over his cheek. She sighed, looking around. "Can you believe all these people?"

"Yeah," he smiled. "I expected as much, if not more. Grammy knows half the state."

"That's the truth," Emily murmured. "And beyond, of course. Have you gotten a chance to visit with Pastor Stephen? I know he and Chloe remember you boys with such fondness."

Sam shook his head. "No, haven't gotten a chance yet. But I got to talk with Faith for a few seconds before the funeral."

"Oh, my goodness," she said, looking at him. "Is she gorgeous or what?"

Sam looked over to where she was, affirming this with the adoration in his eyes, but Emily didn't notice as she continued on.

"You never met her, of course, but her aunt, Sophie? Always had all the men in the room, everywhere she went, staring after her. Probably still does, actually. And I swear, Faith looks just like her, except she has Stephen's genes, too, so she's –"

"More than beautiful," Sam agreed. And even as he said it, he saw Scott with Marie and Nathan, standing across the room, standing next to Faith, who was chatting with them and smiling comfortably. Her eyes met his, then flitted away.

She was more than beautiful. It was true.

"Oh, there's Scott!," Emily sighed. "Can you tell him to come over and get it fixed?"

"I'm sorry," Sam murmured, still watching Faith. "Fix what?"

"The toilet," Emily said. Then, she poked him in the arm. "Sam."

"Yeah," he said, turning to her as she gave him an odd look. "Toilet. You bet."

And Emily glanced back over at Faith and opened her mouth to say something. This was enough motivation to propel Sam to the other side of the room and away from her, where Scott looked up at him as he approached them. "Hey, have you met Faith Hayes?"

Sam nodded. "Yeah. We've met before." Understatement of the year.

"We were just telling her about Houston. You know," Scott smiled at her, "since we're going to be neighbors and all once she finishes up her big move."

Sam's heart raced at this. "Houston? Are you moving to Houston?"

"Yeah," Faith said softly, watching him warily. He was reminded again of the way he never called, never wrote, never acknowledged any of what had gone on all those years ago –

"New job," she said. "I didn't know that I even knew anyone who lived there…"

"And speaking of all that everyone didn't know, Sam," Marie said, smiling. "Did you know that Faith and I are cousins?"

He looked to Scott, a question in his eyes.

"Yeah," Scott said, grinning, "that makes her *my* cousin, too! But not yours, of course, so… good for you, Sam, if you –"

"How?," Sam asked, breaking off Scott's suggestive tangent. Faith said nothing as she watched him.

"Faith's mom," Marie smiled, "is my Tante Sophie's sister, you see. Of course, Sophie's not really my aunt by blood. But she's like my aunt." Marie grinned over at Faith. "Faith and I have been pen pals for most of our lives. Too bad Scott and I didn't have a real wedding here stateside. You two would have seen each other a lot earlier than now, and maybe you would have –"

"Well," Sam said, cutting off Marie as well. "That's… nice."

"I only say that, Sam," Marie continued on, a delighted smile on her face, "because you've been staring at Faith no matter where she's gone in this room, like some creepy stalker --"

"Marie," Sam managed, mortified.

"I'm sorry," she gasped mockingly. "Perhaps I'm being so honest and obnoxious because I didn't get my coffee this morning. And coffee makes me very, very emotional, which you've already heard all about." She looked over at her husband pointedly.

"And now I'm in trouble," Scott laughed. "Thanks, Sam. Thanks a lot."

"Complicated backstory," Marie said to Faith, smiling broadly. "But perhaps that's the word du jour with poor Sam here, huh?"

Complicated backstory made even more complicated, judging by the look in Faith's eyes as she glanced away from him.

"Hey," Sam said, looking to his brother, eager to make him and his wife disappear. "Aunt Em was looking for you. There's a toilet problem with your name on it."

"Hey, buddy," Marie said, patting her husband on the arm and moving their baby to her other hip, "that sounds like a whole lot of fun."

"Yeah, right," Scott laughed. "Hey, Faith, give us a call once you get settled in next month."

"Yeah," Marie added, smiling. "We'll take you out and properly welcome you back to Texas, okay?"

"Backed up toilet, man," Sam said, pushing all three of them out of the way so he could finally speak to Faith alone.

"Thanks, guys," Faith called to them as they walked away.

Sam and Faith watched one another for a moment, then both looked away at the same time. Just as Sam was gathering the courage to tell her that she looked amazing, that he still thought

about her, that she was the only hope he had most of the time...
well, she cleared her throat delicately and spoke first, saving him
from telling her everything and looking like a complete psycho.

"I had no idea that you left the Marines," she said.

"Oh," he sighed. "Yeah, last year, I had the chance to re-enlist
again, but... I didn't. I had seen the world, done my duty... all of
that, you know. I was ready to come back home and settle
down."

"So, are you?"

He looked at her distractedly for a moment. "I'm sorry... am I
what?"

"Settled down," she said softly. "In Houston. Working for Scott."

"Did he tell you I work *for* him?"

She smiled. "Yeah. Is that not entirely true?"

"Oh, it's the truth," he said. "I just always appreciate how he
phrases it that way. But, yeah, I'm settled down in Houston.
Working *for* my younger brother."

"Are you... do you have... a girlfriend?" Faith blushed even as she
said it. "Well, that sounded really stupid, didn't it?"

"No, it didn't sound stupid, but yeah."

Faith's face registered something that looked like disappointment.
And Sam wondered why, until he realized how she'd taken what
he'd said.

"Oh, *no*! No, I don't have a… no, I'm single. I meant that, yeah, I understood why you'd ask that. You know, as far as being settled down and all… settling down. You know."

Faith bit her lip. "Okay. Good. Because I'm not sure why I asked it."

Sam shrugged. "Maybe I understood it because… well, I wanted to ask you the same thing." He'd been wondering about it all afternoon, honestly.

"I don't have a girlfriend, Sam," she smiled at him.

"Ha, ha," he smiled back. "A boyfriend, then?"

"No," she said. "A fiancé, actually."

This took his breath away. And though it was completely illogical to feel this way about a woman he hadn't seen in years and certainly must not really know in any real sense, he felt as though he'd lost something significant.

Faith Hayes… engaged. To someone else.

"Oh," he offered a second too late. "Well. Congratulations." He looked down at her left hand, and sure enough, there was a ring. "Oh, well. Look at that."

"Thanks," she said softly, looking down at it herself.

He stood silently for a moment. Then, unable to think of anything else, he asked her, "Is he from Houston?"

She bit her lip. "No." She glanced up at him. "Though that would make sense. New job to be closer to the man I'm going to marry and all." Her voice caught just slightly at this, and her eyes darted around the room nervously.

Touchy subject, apparently.

"What's the new job?," he asked. "I mean, I don't even know what you do for a living."

She smiled at him, obviously relieved to be off the subject of her fiancé. "I'm a midwife," she said. "I deliver babies."

He raised his eyebrows at this. "I remember you saying that was what you were going to do. You know, all those years ago."

She nodded at this and seemed to consider saying something.

But she didn't end up saying it.

So, he filled the silence. "Hard work, huh?"

"Hard work for the women having the babies," she said. "Wonderful, rewarding work for me, helping them through it, celebrating with them once the work is done."

He nodded at this. "Witnessing what only God can do, sharing His grace with someone else in their moment of life change... you said that once."

And she tilted her head and studied him closely. "Did I?"

"You did."

"Wow," she murmured. "That's so profound. Are you sure I said that?"

He grinned. "I remember it." A pause. "I remember everything from that week at the lake house."

And Faith offered no words in response, lowering her eyes back down to her engagement ring.

Her heart was still pounding.

Sam's mother had come to get him ten minutes earlier, asking that he and his brothers come help carry in some more chairs from the garage, and he had said goodbye with a remorseful wave.

Why had she told him about Craig? About the engagement?

Well, that was a stupid thought. Perhaps the better question was why *wouldn't* she tell him?

She'd been a wreck all day, ever since she'd fallen into his arms in the choir room. Not that she'd been less of a wreck before, as life had made her very nervous and antsy as of late. Pre-wedding jitters, right? *Pre*-pre-wedding jitters, as they hadn't even set a date yet.

And now? She was even more nervous, with the move to Texas coming up, knowing that Sam would be there as well. She hadn't realized that he was even out of the Marine Corps, had imagined that he was still living abroad, moving every few years. She had no idea that he was in the same place she was coming home to, and so while she wasn't culpable or guilty for putting them, for the first time since she was a little girl, in the same place, she felt as though she had supremely betrayed her fiancé.

Who she wasn't even sure she wanted to marry. Maybe those feelings were what was betraying him…

... what was she even thinking?! *This* is what Sam Huntington did to her, simply by being here, prompting her to think more, hope more, want more, even though she had been done with him as much as he had certainly been done with her.

Because with or without Craig, there was that. In a perfect world where it would be okay to feel anything for Sam either way, she still had to remember that once upon a time, he left and never called, wrote, or even tried to explain himself.

She couldn't trust him. Not really.

And she certainly couldn't trust herself, standing here, freaking out, her mind making all kinds of crazy twists and turns, and –

"Hey." Faith turned to see her aunt, Melissa, looking at her. "You're ruining your fingernails, you know."

"Hmm?," Faith mumbled around her nails... which were in her mouth. "Oh, I know. Nervous habit. And after all the work Mom did on them so they'd look good for my interview."

Mel sighed. "Well, I wouldn't normally care. I mean, they're just nails."

"Fake nails at that," Faith agreed.

"Get out, really?," Mel asked, pulling her hand closer, studying them. "They look great!"

"I know, right?"

"Well, I was more concerned about why you were chewing them in the first place," Mel said with a knowing look. Then, she shrugged. "None of my business, of course."

"Just nervous about the big move, I guess," Faith mumbled. "Found out that Scott and…. well, Sam… um, well they live in Houston."

"Do they?," Mel smiled. "Is that why you and Sam have been staring at one another all afternoon?"

Faith blushed. "Aunt Mel, I –"

"I know, you're engaged… to Wonder Boy Preacher and all," she said, looking out over the living room.

"Aunt Mel," Faith chided. Her aunt hadn't been afraid to say what she really thought about Craig. That he was a good enough guy, of course, but that he was on a fast track to high profile ministry and that while she was sure that he loved Faith ("because what man wouldn't?," she'd said), she wondered if he had rushed things in his eagerness to have someone like her beside him as he climbed that great ministerial ladder of megachurch pastorates.

"I'm just calling it like I see it," Mel muttered. "Sam's a good kid." Then, tilting her head to the side, "Though I guess he's not really a kid anymore, is he?"

"No, ma'am," Faith replied, her nails going right back to her mouth.

Mel nodded. "Again, none of my business, but –"

"None of your business," Faith agreed.

Mel simply raised her eyebrows. "Then I won't say anything more… except that marriage is a big deal, and you don't have to do what everyone thinks you need to do, especially when most of us don't even think you need to –"

"Hey, Faith."

She sighed with great relief as her uncle, Beau, moved to his wife's side, kissing her softly, then reaching over to hug Faith. "Is Mel giving you a hard time about the move?"

Faith looked at her aunt, who exchanged a meaningful look with her. *Just remember what I said,* she could almost hear. "A hard time about the move?," Faith asked.

Beau smiled. "Yeah, we heard you were coming to Texas for an interview, and we got our hopes up. Thought you might be up in Fort Worth where we could see you all the time."

Faith shook her head. "No, but I'll be closer than I was. And thanks for the tip on the housing. You're saving me a fortune."

"No problem," Beau said. "It worked out well. The Gains get a free housesitter while they're abroad, and you get to stay in Houston in style."

Faith would be living in the home of her uncle's good friends, rent-free, as soon as she could move in, housesitting for them as they spent a year abroad. It was a great situation, in a wonderful neighborhood not too far from the clinic.

"Almost like God orchestrated that all, isn't it, Faith?," Mel murmured. "Like He wanted to get you out of Florida before you _"

And before she could finish the thought, Faith's phone buzzed. Mercifully.

"Gotta take this," she said, turning and walking towards the back door, out to the porch, where the roar of voices inside wouldn't interfere with her ability to hear whoever was calling...

"Hello?"

"Faith..."

Craig. Of course.

"Hey," she sighed, glancing around at the Fishers' backyard, her mind going through the conversation she'd had with Craig the night before. She'd told him about the job, about how it would be her ministry, about how she was certain this was something God was calling her to.

He'd been supportive. Because Craig was always supportive. It was hard to find any fault with him when he was always so encouraging, so positive, so... perfect. Faith had tried to find a reason for why she didn't feel what she thought she should feel towards him, what she felt towards Sam –

She took a breath at this. "I miss you," she said simply. And she did. She missed the certainty of him, the way she could count on him, the assurance that she was doing the right thing by committing to someone like him.

Someone like him.

"Oh, man, Faith, I miss you more," he said, his voice low and emotional. "I've been counting the hours since I dropped you off at the airport. And we're well past what it was supposed to be, with this funeral and all."

"I'm sorry," she murmured, sitting down on the Fishers' deck. "Been an unexpected change of plans for all of us."

"How's your dad doing?," he asked softly.

"He's fine," she said. "He did great at the service. Along with the other four preachers who preached."

"Wow," Craig breathed. "That's a lot of preaching."

It had been. But it had been too short, sitting next to Sam, like she had all those years ago...

What kind of a creep was she, having these thoughts while talking with the man she'd agreed to marry?

Agreed to marry. Not fallen in love with. Not *in love* with. Not completely head over heels, full of passion –

She could hear the difference even in her reassurances to herself.

"When I go on to glory," Craig said, never guessing the direction of her thoughts, "I want you to have two preachers do my funeral. But get two, young, first year seminary students. Tell them I went by the name Bob, that my passion was clog dancing, and that I was the crawfish eating champion of Lafayette."

"Craig," she sighed, smiling in spite of her feelings, "none of that's true."

"I know," he said. "But I'll be laughing from beyond watching those young guys try to pass it off as truth while everyone wonders if they've wandered into the wrong funeral. Make sure they each get an hour to exposit the Scriptures, too."

"Yeah, well," she sighed, biting her lip, thinking about Craig, years from now, together with him...

"Promise me you'll do that, Faith," he said.

And she said nothing for a moment wondering at the insecurity she heard in his voice. Something that had never been there before...

"Faith... promise me... you're going to be there, right with me, even that far into the future, right? We'll figure out the Texas Florida stuff, and you'll be there with me, right?"

And she swallowed and said, very softly, "Why wouldn't I be, Craig?"

CHAPTER FOUR

Two weeks later, life was back to normal for Sam.

As normal as it was going to get, likely.

He spent the majority of his days in class at the community college or working alongside Scott. Then, some days, he managed both. When he could steal some time away from those two commitments, he came back to the house he was building himself on Scott and Marie's acreage.

He had balked at the suggestion a year ago, when Scott had offered to sign the land over to him. Sam had told him that the last thing he and Marie needed was him with them for the rest of their lives, but Scott had insisted that he'd be doing them a favor, being close enough that they could send all the kids they were going to have over to their crazy uncle's house anytime he and Marie needed a break.

Sam had stopped arguing with them when Marie had insisted, with tears in her eyes, that this was what family was supposed to be, all up in one another's business and onto one another's property, pulling out the sad sob story of how far away her own parents were and how she didn't have any siblings and —

It hadn't been worth arguing. And the location was perfect. As was the house they were building.

He was working on it that morning, clearing out the weeds from the yard and waiting on Scott to do more of the work on the house, when a car pulled up into the dirt driveway they'd made. Sam squinted against the sun, raising his hand to shield his eyes, trying to figure out who was climbing out of the car, sunglasses on, pink scrubs, blonde hair pulled up in a messy knot, held together with a pencil —

"Faith?," he asked, recognizing her seconds later.

Sure enough, those were her eyes behind the shades that she pushed up onto her forehead. "Sam?," she asked, surprise in her voice.

"Hey," he said, wiping the sweat off his face and pulling on a shirt. "Didn't expect to see you here."

She smiled, self consciously, walking over to him. "Yeah, Marie called and asked me to meet her here. Something about some maps Scott has of the medical center? Which, you know, I'm in serious need of since I've gotten lost at least a dozen times already down there."

"It's confusing," Sam nodded. "Scott should be here by... oh, thirty minutes ago."

"Is he usually late like this?"

Sam shrugged. "Not most mornings. But since I work for him and am taking up the slack today, I guess he felt like he could sleep in."

Faith looked to the house in front of them admiringly. "This is beautiful, Sam," she breathed. "You and Scott built this?"

"Yeah," Sam said, taking a breath. "Well, we're still building it, but yeah. Ours completely, from the ground up."

"I'd love a house just like this one day," she said.

"I know the builders you need then," he smiled. "Of course, that's only if you're in Houston for the long term." He watched her for a moment. "Are you?"

"Am I... what?," she asked.

"In Houston for the long term," he said. "I mean, I know about the new job and all, but your fiancé..."

Why did he feel compelled to bring this up every time he got her alone? Stupid Sam...

She shook her head. "No, he's in Florida. Will be for a while."

"I figured," Sam nodded. "He works there then, huh?"

"Yeah," she said softly, touching her engagement ring and briefly meeting Sam's eyes before looking away again. "He's one of the associate pastors at my dad's church."

"Hmm," Sam murmured. "You'll be a pastor's wife, then. I can see that."

She frowned slightly. "It's an introvert's nightmare," she said, trying for a grin... and failing.

"You're not an introvert," he said.

"Oh, yes, I am," she said. "Meeting new people is torture. Talking with people, all the time... horrible."

"Surely you must talk to your patients," he said. "New patients, all the time."

"Yeah, but that's work."

"But you never had a problem talking to me," he said softly, thinking on this. "We stayed up all those nights at the lake house talking, and..."

He trailed off, not finishing the thought. Of course, his mind was always, here lately, on the lake house, ever since seeing Faith at the funeral, but there was no way she'd been thinking about him like that. And what kind of idiot was he for bringing it up again and again, when she probably didn't even remember –

"That was different," she murmured. "It was you. And that was the best week of..."

He watched her for a moment, surprised by this.

Not as surprised as she seemed, though, as her eyes darted from his nervously.

"Well," he said, "when's the big day? The wedding, that is." If this subject was getting these kinds of honest responses, he'd just keep going with it.

Faith looked at him. "I don't know. I haven't set a date yet." She cringed. "I'm probably the worst bride ever, because the actual wedding? Haven't even given it a thought."

Sam considered this for a moment. "And with him there and you here, just starting a new job and all... well, it'll probably be a while still."

"Yeah," Faith sighed. "I had a job back in Florida, of course, but I got the chance to come here and... I took it."

"The job here is that much better, huh?," Sam crossed his arms over his chest and looked at her.

She met his eyes for a moment. "It is." A pause. "But that wasn't all of it. I mean, I'm working at a birthing center that's like a ministry, which is incredible. But I think, given the right circumstances... well, I could've been happy where I was. Which begs the question *why* I would come all this way, right?"

Sam nodded, wondering at this.

"I don't know," she said. "I just... did it."

Before he could ask any more questions, they heard a truck heading their way and both turned to see Scott driving up the driveway.

"Hey," he said, jumping out and smiling brightly at Faith. "Sorry I'm running late. Big morning at the house right after you left, Sam."

"You two... you live together?" Faith looked between them.

Sam was about to speak when Scott spoke for them both. "Yeah, right over there."

He pointed to the house across the field.

"Oh!," Faith gasped. "That's probably where Marie wanted me to meet her!"

"Probably," Scott said. "But this works, too. And Sam and I are only living together temporarily. And I mean that. Seriously."

"It's no picnic for me either, living with you and Marie," Sam sighed. "Making sure everyone is dressed all the time and that I'm not walking in on something."

"Life is good in the Huntington house," Scott said, raising his eyebrows.

"Yeah," Sam rolled his eyes as Faith smiled, "but until I get my own house built, it's just easier to camp out in one of Scott and Marie's extra rooms. Which is, incidentally enough, right next to my nephew's nursery, so I'm treated every morning to a drum solo on whatever Nathan can get his hands on in his crib."

"He's got his mother's music talent," Scott laughed. "Oh, and by the way, the excitement this morning will totally affect you, brother."

"How so?"

"Well," Scott said, with a slow smile. "There's another drummer boy on the way."

"The coffee commercials proved true," Sam grinned. "And it could be a drummer girl. Congratulations."

"Oh, is Marie expecting?," Faith asked, smiling.

"Yeah," Scott grinned. "She's pretty excited. Called her mom and cried for a whole hour with her. I just left her on the phone with our mom, going on and on about baby names and morning sickness. And if I know Mom, she's already figuring out a way to add another high chair to the table." He looked over at Sam. "We're all doing our part to keep the grandkids coming, Sam. Except for Savannah. And you. Get to it, man."

Sam frowned at his brother. "I'm not even married."

"I know," he said. "And it's not like God isn't giving you some really great options." He nodded over at Faith very deliberately.

And Faith blushed, just as Sam shot his brother a look. "She's getting married, Scott."

"Hey, congratulations," Scott grinned. "And here I was getting on your case, Sam, and you've been getting things done –"

"Not to me, you nimrod," he said. "To... what's his name?"

"Craig," she said softly. "Craig Lucas."

"Well, that sucks," Scott said, simply. Then, not picking up on the tension, he pointed to the half-finished house in front of them. "Hey, Faith, what do you think about Sam's house?"

Faith, flustered, glanced over at Sam. "This is *your* house?"

"It will be," he sighed, thankful that Scott had changed the subject, "if we ever finish it."

"Working as fast as I can," Scott said. "Because the sooner I get you in here, the sooner you're out of my house. Not that you're much help these days, what with your academic pursuits."

"Academic pursuits?," Faith asked.

Scott slapped Sam on the back. Harder than necessary. "Sam is back in school again after a long, long, long break. Finally using the free education earned through all those years with the Marines to get a degree."

Faith smiled at him. "Sam, that's great."

"Oldest guy in all my classes," he said softly, thinking on how humbling this was.

"Oldest guy right here, brother," Scott added helpfully.

"Yeah, thanks for that," Sam muttered.

"Anytime," Scott smiled. "It'll be helpful to us once you finally finish and have your fancy business degree, though. The books are a mess, and my office looks like –"

"It looks bad," Sam said succinctly.

"Yes," Scott agreed.

"Organization isn't his strong suit, Faith," Sam added. "I'm pretty sure we're losing money somewhere because of some clerical oversight."

Scott shrugged. "Just have to work that much harder with my hands to compensate."

"And speaking of organization," Sam said, "do you know where the maps Marie promised Faith are?"

"Maps?," Scott asked dubiously. "Who knows? We could go back out to the house and search around to see if --"

"It's okay," Faith said, glancing at her watch. "I really should be heading back to work anyway."

Sam took a breath, regretting that she was leaving so soon. "I'll find them in his mess and... well, let you know that you can..."

Faith nodded. "Well, I can pick them up... or, you know, you can drop them off, or..."

"Yeah," Sam said, awkwardly.

"Yeah," Faith breathed out, just as awkwardly.

And they stared at one another for a moment.

"Well, okay," Scott said, looking at both of them. "This is weird."

Wow. It *was* weird.

Faith couldn't help thinking about the truth of Scott's words as she drove away, her face blushed and blazing hot.

It had been awkward (and exhilarating) enough to pull up to the house to find Sam half dressed and working so hard, the muscles in his back and his chest –

Her phone buzzed at her, causing her to jump in her seat. She fumbled to answer it. "Hello?"

"Faith, dear, where are you?"

Elaine Charles. Faith had been in Houston all of two days so far, and already, she'd fielded at least twenty calls from her boss.

When Elaine had said that her midwives were available twenty-four, seven, she'd meant it.

What Faith hadn't known was that she meant her midwives were available to *her* twenty-four, seven. She was needier than any pregnant woman Faith had ever known and ten times as crazy.

"I'm about twenty minutes from the clinic," Faith guessed, looking around at the beautiful countryside just outside her window, scarcely believing that she was actually in the city at all. It was like an escape from reality out here.

Or a rather harsh reminder of it, as her mind went back to Sam, to Craig, to all of the confusing thoughts swirling around her head.

"I'm hurrying to get there, Elaine," she said, forcing her mind back to the matter on hand. "Is something wrong?"

"Oh, no, dear," Elaine cooed. "Though we are swamped."

They were. Faith had picked up on that in her two days. The birthing center saw at least three times as many patients as the Florida clinic had with half the midwives to accommodate.

That many more people to share Christ with, Elaine had said, smiling, even as she and Faith were rushing to take care of them all.

Even now, Faith could hear the urgency and fast pace in the older woman's tone. "I have a patient coming in at ten, and I want you to take over her care." She lowered her voice. "Miscarriages. Three before this one. Second term, all of them."

"Oh, goodness," Faith murmured. "How far along is she now?"

"Twelve weeks," Elaine answered. "And nervous, of course, as you'd expect. Has been rather obsessively researching everything this time around, and when she came upon your biography on our website, she insisted on meeting you."

Faith frowned. "I have much less experience than you do, though."

"I know," Elaine said, merriment in her voice, "but it's not really about experience in these situations, is it, dear? Nothing either one of us can do to stop a miscarriage."

"No, there isn't," Faith managed, thinking of patients in Florida who had walked this road. "So, it shouldn't make a difference either way who her midwife is. Why does she want to meet me?"

And Faith could hear the smile in Elaine's voice. "I think it's your name, actually. Faith. Seems to already have given her some reassurance."

Faith exhaled at this. "No pressure on me, then, huh? To deliver some sort of miracle on the basis of my name alone, right?"

"Deliver indeed," Elaine said. "But you'll be a good friend to her. A good witness of the sovereignty of God regardless of what happens with this little one." A pause. "I'm praying that things will be different. Can you be praying as well, Faith?"

And she could. And she did, as she hung up the phone and drove the rest of the distance to the clinic, arriving in time to meet two other patients and perform their exams before she walked into the room where her ten o'clock appointment waited for her.

She was, Faith quickly assessed from a head to toe sweep, a woman in her late twenties, well off financially, physically fit, married... and stressed completely out. Some things were easier to determine than others, given the designer handbag at her feet, the wedding set on her left hand, the well-defined muscles in the arms that rested on the slight evidence of her pregnancy, clutching the child within almost protectively as she raised scared eyes to Faith.

"Good morning," Faith said softly, offering up a confident smile, along with her hand. "I'm Faith."

"Erica," the woman breathed out, taking Faith's hand in her own for a moment. "Thank you for making the time to see me."

Faith nodded, slipping her file onto the small counter in the room and moving to sit across from her. "My pleasure. Sincerely." She smiled again. "Twelve weeks."

"Yes," Erica said softly. Then, with great emotion, "Again."

"Your fourth child," Faith murmured, "right?"

Erica simply nodded, tears in her eyes. "I've done everything right. I thought I did before, too. But I've made sure this time to do it all right... more right than I did any of the other times."

Faith sighed, feeling such sympathy for the guilt in this woman's eyes. "It's not what you've done. I can tell you that, after looking at your file, your history, sitting here with you now, seeing your general health... it wasn't what you've done."

Erica wiped away a tear. "I sometimes wish it was," she said softly. "So I can do better this time. But then, I would have the guilt of before... as if I don't already have it."

Faith took a deep breath, offering up another silent prayer for the right words to say. "There aren't any easy answers for why things like this happen," she said. "They're all cliched anyway and wouldn't help you. You've likely heard them all."

Erica nodded. "Yeah."

"So," Faith said, knowing there was assurance in what she said, "I won't say them. What I will say is this. We're going to do everything we can to make sure you stay healthy. We'll monitor what's going on with the baby. But ultimately, we'll just have to trust that God knows what He's doing."

Erica bit her lip. "Like He knew what He was doing before? When those babies died?"

Faith swallowed, thinking through these harder questions that never got easier, that never had answers. "I think it's safe to say that God wept with you when that happened."

"But He knew," she insisted, a harder edge to her voice. "And if He's able to do anything, He could have saved them. But He didn't."

And Faith could only acknowledge this. "No, He didn't."

Both women watched one another for a long moment.

"No answers, then?," Erica asked softly.

Faith shook her head. "No. But if I was able to explain the intricacies of God and His purposes and plans to you in the time allotted for this appointment, then He wouldn't be much of a god, would He?"

Erica frowned at this. "I don't guess so."

"Then, perhaps the deep theology is better left for questions we can answer, things we can know with absolute certainty," she said.

"Such as?"

"That God has you here for a reason," Faith said softly. "That you're the mother of four children, one of whom you may experience life with on this side of eternity. And that He wants you to know Him better through this all, no matter what happens."

Erica blew out a deep breath. "I don't want to be angry, Faith. I really don't. Especially not now, when I think being on God's side might help me."

Bargaining. Grief. Hopelessness. Openness to anything that would make this story turn out differently. Faith could logically understand it all, could chart it all from a scientific point of view... but she was lacking when it came to understanding it at a heart level. Knowing what this must feel like, when it was all happening to you, when it was so intensely personal.

This is where medicine couldn't do much. Only belief and trust in God, who might not do things the way they prayed He would.

"I'm not sure that's how God works," Faith said. "And I think anger is a normal thing to feel. Though the stress of holding onto that probably isn't doing anything towards staying positive about this pregnancy, is it?"

"No," Erica said simply. "You know, I asked for you. Even though Elaine has been there for me through all the others. Something about you, about what you had in your introduction online, the certainty that you had about the goodness of God... I want to believe like that. I want Him to show me His goodness through this." She wiped her eyes. "I'm trusting that it'll happen. I'm really going to have faith this time."

And Faith wondered what would happen if it didn't turn out after all... and said a silent prayer that they wouldn't see the answer.

They'd gotten more work done that morning and afternoon than Sam had hoped they would.

The sun was going down, and Scott was nearing a stopping point, if the way he kept looking towards his own house longingly and grumbling about the heat was any indication. Sam stepped back from the work they'd been doing and sighed.

"What do you think?," he murmured. "Another month?"

Scott frowned at him. "I wish," he said. "This is like the house that won't be built. I feel like we've been working on it forever. And forever just won't end."

"Exaggeration," Sam said.

"Forever seriously won't end, Sam --"

"We'll be done sooner than you can imagine," he said confidently.

Scott shook his head. "Yeah, and you'd know, right? Since you've built zero houses, and I've built --"

"Shut up," he muttered.

"And with that," Scott said, "I don't feel bad at all about calling it quits before it's completely dark out here."

Sam nodded his assent, and wordlessly, the two brothers began loading up tools and supplies for the night, no longer needing to talk through the process after all these days, weeks, and months of working side by side on all of the different projects Scott's business had them doing.

This wasn't Sam's dream career, obviously. He would never have thought this was an option, and originally, he'd had no intention of continuing on like this for the rest of his life. He'd left the military uncertain of what was next, simply knowing that it was time to be done, time to distance himself from what he'd seen, time to try and forget as much as he could.

He had loved being a Marine. He'd never wanted to do anything else. But the reality of deployment and what he'd really been trained to do had changed everything. Plenty of men went through it all, came out stronger because of it, and he'd determined that he would be like the rest of them.

He lost friends there. He lost his sense of security. He had very nearly lost all of his hope. But he held onto the belief that there was still some good left in the world and that he would survive, get past this, and live a normal life.

And here he was, living a normal life... which included watching his brother work his way out of a pair of boots, catching a whiff of the smell of his own socks, and gagging visibly.

Not so different than life had been when they were seventeen and eighteen, right before Sam left for boot camp.

"Why are you doing that out here?," Sam asked. "We've still got to get to the house."

Scott glanced up. "I tracked a whole lot of mess into the house yesterday, and Marie told me I'd have to build yet another house for myself if I did it again, because she'd throw me out."

Sam frowned. "That doesn't sound like Marie."

"You bet it doesn't," he said. "As soon as she said it, excuse me -- *yelled* it -- she burst into tears and told me that she was sorry for being the meanest wife ever. Or so I assumed, since she wasn't speaking English when she said it."

"Wow."

"Yeah," Scott nodded. "And I guess she *really* felt bad because she came at me to make it up to me, if you know what I'm saying, and after she had worn me completely out, I made the suggestion that maybe she needed to take a pregnancy test because her mood swings were giving me whiplash." He shrugged. "I mean, parts of those mood swings are awesome, you know, but some restored sanity would be nice. Or at least some clarification as to why she's completely nuts." He sighed, a smile playing on his lips. "Now that she knows she's pregnant, a little self-awareness is sure to go a long way. But I'm still going to keep these boots out of her sight. Because I love her. And I'm honestly a little scared of her when she's so hormonal. Which is why I'm not waiting until we get right outside of the house to take them off. And you better take yours off, too."

"Good word," Sam said, sitting next to Scott and working on his laces.

Scott leaned over to work on his second boot. "So what was the deal with you and Faith this morning?"

And for the hundredth time that day alone, his mind went back to Faith, telling him how that week at the lake house was the best week...

Of her life. She hadn't finished her thought, but Sam finished it for her on his own. As discouraged as he been to come back home, he was seeing more and more good in being here, right here, right now, right where he was certain to see more of her.

She was engaged, though...

"There is no deal," Sam muttered, irritated by this remembrance.

"No," Scott said. "Since she seems scared to death of you."

"She doesn't seem scared of me – does she?" Sam stopped taking his own boots off to look at his brother.

"Yeah, she does," Scott said. "All tense and freaked out."

And it was true. She wasn't who she had been. But things were different. And maybe she was able to tell just how different he was now.

"Really?"

"Well, it's awkward with the two of you," Scott answered. "That much is true, at least. What did you do?"

"I kissed her," Sam sighed.

"Was it bad?," Scott murmured, staring at him. "I mean, you're probably out of practice."

Sam glared at him.

"Or not, because you're my brother after all. Good genes, you know," Scott shrugged. "So... how was it?"

"I'm not telling you anything," Sam said. "Besides, it was eight years ago."

"Eight years ago?"

"Yeah."

"When did you see her eight years ago? Did you even know her?"

"Not all that well," he murmured, thinking of how shocked he'd been to discover who she'd been. "We were at the lake. I was home on leave. You were off drunk somewhere, I'm sure."

Scott shook his head. "That was a while back, then. And Marie and Faith are the same age, so she was... in high school, right?" He stared at Sam incredulously.

"What? You're married to Marie now, right? Not such a big age difference."

"I wasn't kissing her when she was a teenager, Sam," he said.

"Yeah, I know."

"That's just wrong."

"Yes, I said I know!"

Scott watched him for a long moment. "Well. So, you kissed an underage girl. Which is not good, obviously. But she's not underage anymore."

Sam nodded, finally pulling off his boot. "Well, she's marrying someone else."

"Yeah, I don't think she's going to end up marrying that other guy," Scott said.

Sam looked at him. "What? Why do you say that?"

"You and her. The tension. More tension than a kiss years ago should warrant. There's something going on with you and her, and I'll bet it's enough to edge the other guy out of the picture."

Sam bit his lip for a moment. "I shouldn't want to edge him out of the picture, though, should I? I mean, she told him she'd marry him... and then, ran off to Texas and left him half a country away."

Scott laughed. "Wow, well I didn't know that part of the story. But there you go. What sense does that make?"

"Not a lot," he said, looking back down at his feet. "But it would be a lot for... well, you know."

"No," Scott answered. "I don't. What are you talking about?"

"It would be a lot," Sam said softly, thinking about this, "to expect that she could handle anything that... well, me. Or that she'd want to. I'm not who I was back when we knew each other at the lake house."

"Hey," Scott murmured.

Sam ignored him, knowing what was coming.

"Hey!," he yelled.

And Sam looked up at him warily.

"No more of that," Scott said sternly. "No more. You aren't who you were, but you're still a good man, Sam. And I don't know how many times it's going to take hearing it, but you're going to get past all that you've been through. God isn't done with you. And you need to stop thinking and acting like you're a burden to everyone around you."

Sam nodded.

"You hear me, right?"

"I do, Scott," he sighed. "I just... I don't know."

"You'll figure it out," Scott said, patting him on the back. "You'll figure it out."

The days turned into weeks.

And the patient list grew. Oh, wow. It grew.

Faith was convinced that half of the greater Houston area was pregnant and that each and every expectant mother wanted a midwife. Elaine Charles couldn't seem to say no or enough either one, and so Faith was on call every waking moment and most sleeping ones as well.

There were the women who were pros at this. Multiple births, all of them natural, so accomplished and accustomed to the waves of labor and the work of delivery that they could likely do the job themselves without Faith at all. She'd attended these births with ease and comfort.

Then, there were the newbies, with some lofty ideas about pain management, their ability to do this more quickly than science would allow, and the sheer magic of it all. And while some did well and got through it with only a few muttered words of exasperation and a few tears, there were those who screamed in Faith's calm, patient face, insisting that *this* wasn't going like she'd told them it would.

But the babies always came, no matter what. Babies to mothers who wore them in wraps, babies to mothers who carried them in car seats, babies who were put on sleep schedules, babies who were born in family beds and would stay there indefinitely, babies nursing, babies on formula, babies prayed over, babies dedicated to the Lord, moments after their first breaths, their names on Faith's lips.

She was doing exams, deliveries in the clinic, and home births, and her phone always seemed to be ringing with questions, concerns, and more patient names from Elaine Charles.

She was a pastor's daughter, of course, and knew that ministry, vocational ministry in a church, could consume all of your life if you let it. Who knew that delivering babies, when made into a ministry, could do the very same?

It had been weeks since Faith had even had a few hours to herself. Totally and completely to herself. She came into the giant house she was living in that night, finally off call for at least an evening, thankful for the time to herself.

As she put her things down and made her way upstairs to a shower and more comfortable clothes, she congratulated herself on fitting into life here so easily. She was exhausted, sure, but she was thriving, fulfilled, and content in a way she hadn't been in

Florida. Everything was working out just the way she'd hoped it would, she affirmed, as she took her jewelry off, and --

There it was. Her engagement ring.

Craig. She hadn't talked with him in a couple of days. Their last conversation had been tense, uncharacteristically tense. Craig, who was always supportive, always understanding, had been a little out of sorts as she told him about how amazing her job actually was, about how she was so busy now that she didn't have time to start planning the wedding or even pick out a date, honestly. And she'd likely be busy like that for a while. They could wait... right?

The insecurity she'd heard in his voice after Thomas Fisher's funeral had escalated in the meantime. She could hear it in his voice. And though he never raised his tone to her or spoke harshly to her, she could hear it all the same, the frustration there, and knew he was justified to feel this way.

They had to work something out. She had to figure out how to make this work. Because they couldn't be engaged forever. They'd be married... eventually.

She resolved to put it out of her mind as she kicked off her shoes, just as the doorbell rang.

Marie, likely. The two had met up weeks ago so that Faith could finally get those maps, and they'd been texting and calling back and forth ever since, when time allowed. The thought of a night alone turning into a night visiting with Marie, as she'd said they'd have to do, was a pleasant one to Faith, surprisingly enough. She'd appreciated Marie's friendship when they were pen pals separated by an ocean, and she was beginning to appreciate her even more as an adult, here in this new place.

With a smile on her face, she opened the door... and gasped out loud.

"Craig?," she breathed, dumbfounded to see her fiancé standing there.

His smile was brilliant as he took her in for the first time in over a month. "Faith, I've missed you so much." And he came in, uninvited, and swept her up into his arms, lifting her right off the ground as he did so.

"I didn't even know you were coming!," she said as he held her, surprised to hear the accusation and irritation in her voice.

"I know," Craig laughed, missing it entirely. "I was going to wait until we could make plans for a longer visit. But I was missing you so much that I was willing to come for just a day. What's the cost of a last-minute flight, if it meant I could see you, right? And you could see me... right?"

And before she could answer him, he brushed his lips against hers, respectfully, chastely, like he always did. There was more in his eyes, more in the way he held onto her, that suggested he wanted more, but he'd always respected the boundaries and signals that she unknowingly gave off.

She was glad for his consideration in this, at least.

"Are you glad I'm here?," he asked.

She was more concerned than glad, honestly, looking at the signs of stress in his eyes, the exhaustion in his smile, and the anxious way he watched her.

"Yes, of course," she said absent-mindedly, wondering at this. "Come on in. This is... home." She led him into the living room, noting the bag that he dropped next to the couch. "Are you... staying?"

"Yeah," he said. "Not here, of course. I got a room at a hotel a few blocks away. Took care of it all as I was waiting for the flight." He pulled her into his arms again. "It's really good to see you. I hate being away from you."

"Not so far away," she murmured, thinking of how it wasn't, not really --

"Fifteen hour drive," he sighed. "Three hour flight. Much too far away, especially when my hope was that we would have a wedding date by now and would be making plans to live in the same house, not just the same city, really soon."

"The job here is really amazing," she said to him. Again. This is what she'd said again and again, trying to convince him, to convince herself, that she'd gone away for the right reasons.

"I know," he said softly. "I get that. And so, I've been doing some work myself."

"Oh?," she asked, as he led her over to the couch and sat down with her.

"Yeah," he said. "I've put out my resume."

Faith felt her heart tighten a little at this. It just made logical sense, right? But they hadn't talked about it seriously, about him leaving Florida, about him following her here, about really pursuing this future she'd found herself bound to after his surprise proposal.

"Wow," she breathed. "Any interest?"

"Three churches, already," he said. "All in Houston, of course. I know people, from seminary, who were able to get me connected."

Three churches. Already.

"Anything you're seriously considering?," she asked.

"Considering them all," he said. "They're all a step down from where I'm at now, and I'll miss being part of your father's team... but it's worth it, right?"

And she nodded numbly, wondering at this.

"Faith," he said, simply, seriously. "I want to make this work. But I'm getting the feeling that you aren't on board with any of it. A new church, a new job... me."

"I told you yes, though," she said, clinging to this. She'd said yes. For some reason, she'd said yes and very nearly meant it.

He could see it. The doubt, the worry, the confusion.

"I know," he said. "So, it isn't too much to ask you to set a wedding date, right? I mean, if I'm going to take a job here, resign from the job I love, and move all the way out here... you can finally agree on a date, right?"

Her aunt's words went through her mind. About how she didn't need to do what no one even thought she needed to do anyway. She thought about the night she'd said yes to his proposal following months of dating him, valuing his friendship, convincing herself that love was more than fluttery feelings and attraction, that marriage to someone like this man was something any woman would want. She thought of how his parents and her parents had watched her as Craig had been down on one knee, how his parents had such hope in their eyes, her parents had such concern in theirs.

She'd said yes. What did it say about her ability to stay faithful, to keep a promise, to be a success at any kind of relationship from here on out if she couldn't honor the yes that she'd given him?

She wasn't sure. She really wasn't. But the thought of marriage, here and now, wasn't thrilling. And where was the commitment, really, when no vows had been made and no covenant had been established?

And she pictured the future, a calendar full of days to choose from, a future waiting to be lived... and she couldn't see him.

So, she found herself saying the words she'd hadn't been brave enough to say before.

"Craig... we need to talk."

It had been another long week for Sam.

He wasn't sleeping well at night. Worse than usual, actually, and he was worn out from the moment he started classes in the mornings through the afternoons he spent working with Scott.

He had it in mind to go to bed early that evening and try to catch up on the sleep he was always missing when he came home and checked the messages. Scott and Marie were still out, likely having dinner somewhere so that Marie could get a break from being in the house alone all day with a toddler. Sam couldn't figure how being out with a toddler was any less stressful, but Marie jumped at the opportunity most nights.

"Scott?" The feminine voice on the machine sounded urgent. Sam was about to skip over one of what was sure to be many calls from any number of clients needing Scott for various jobs, when her next words froze him in place. "It's Faith. Faith Hayes. I'm housesitting over on the west side of town, and... well, there's a leak in the kitchen. And I'm an idiot because I can't figure out how to fix it, and I was wondering, if it's not too much trouble, if you could talk me through it over the phone. Anyway, if you get this message, can you call me back?"

Sam pulled out his own phone and started pulling up Faith's information. One of the few good things about being in business with your brother meant syncing your phones together so that his contacts were your contacts. And never before had Sam been so happy to see that Scott had kept tabs on Faith.

There was a phone number. And even better than that, there was an address.

He'd go over himself rather than talk her through it on the phone. And so, with more energy than he'd had in weeks, he went back out to his truck and drove to the huge house that matched the address Faith had given.

She seemed more than a little surprised to see him when she answered the door.

"Sam," she said, biting her lip as her eyes trailed over him. "Um... hey."

"Hey. Got your message, about the leak," he said. "Scott's out, so I thought I'd come over and check it out."

"You didn't have to go through all the trouble," she said, flustered.

"It's no trouble," Sam managed. "Can I... come in?"

"Oh, yeah, sorry," she said, opening the door wider for him. "It's a leak in the kitchen, right below the sink. Probably something easy to fix, but I just have no clue."

Sam followed her to the kitchen and bent down to take a look for himself. "Okay... well, let me grab a few things out of the truck, and I'll be back."

He walked out, taking a deep breath to calm his nerves, and gathered up what he'd need. Back inside, he found Faith standing in the kitchen, nervously biting her lip, her arms crossed over her chest.

"You can go on and do whatever you need to do," he said. "It might take me a while."

"Can I do anything to help?"

He looked at the situation and... well, wondered what in the world he was supposed to do to fix this. Scott really was the how-to of this operation, but Sam wasn't about to let Faith know that.

"No, I think I've got it," he said. "Honestly, I'm sure there's a lot you need to get done."

She sighed. "There's always a lot to get done. But I'm just on call tonight. Waiting for the phone to ring and tell me someone's in labor."

He smiled at this. "Exciting life."

"Yeah," she said, a faint smile on her lips. "Something like that. Was hoping for a quiet night before that leak happened. I haven't had a break since I got here."

"No time off?," he glanced over at her, making himself comfortable on the floor in front of the sink.

"I had a night off last week... but I ended up having a visitor come into town and surprise me."

"Out of town, huh," he said, peering under the sink. "Someone from home, then?"

"Uh, yeah. Craig."

"Oh." Sam scowled at the pipes before randomly selecting a tool and contemplating some serious demolition. The thought of Faith with her soon-to-be husband wasn't pleasant, and —

"We... we broke off the engagement."

This bit of good news caused Sam's hand to slip, and the wrench flew right through the air, landing on Faith's foot with a loud clang.

She cried out, obviously, and Sam was on his feet in an instant.

"Oh, Faith, I'm so sorry!"

"It's okay," she managed, biting her lip. "Probably only broke a toe or something."

"I'm an idiot," he muttered. "Can you... should I..." He made a move to pick her up and carry her somewhere –

"No, no," she said, stopping him from offering assistance and making it worse. She looked down at her foot. "Well, I can move everything, so... no harm, no foul, Sam."

"You should probably get off of it, though," he said. "Here, let me help. I'm so sorry." And he helped her move from the kitchen to the living room, sitting her down on the couch and pulling her feet up.

"Thanks, Sam," she said softly. "Now I know why you told me to go on and do my work. You were trying to get me out of the way of flying tools."

He shook his head and laughed softly at this, his fingers brushing gently across the bruise that would be left from his clumsiness, bringing his eyes up to hers, then looking away again. "It probably wouldn't surprise you to know that I don't have any idea what I'm doing," he offered, meaning the tools, the home maintenance... talking with her like this.

"You know better than I do," she murmured. "I can't make much sense of anything these days. Pipes, time management, relationships..."

He looked her straight in the eyes. "You broke off your engagement?"

"Yeah," she said, holding up her left hand, where the diamond ring was missing.

"I'm sorry," he said, thinking that he wasn't sorry at all that Craig was gone. He was only sorry that she'd had to go through the process. "Was there a reason it didn't work out? None of my business, of course, but –"

"It's fine," she said softly. "It just… it wasn't going to work out. Life's just crazy for me right now, and Craig's in a very different place, and… well, I'm not sure my stress and job demands could have fit into what he had planned for us, and…" She sighed.

"Yeah?," Sam asked gently.

"It's just a mess. As is everything. I spend every moment of my life working."

"Hmm," Sam said softly, looking at her, pleased to find that she was watching him with tenderness.

"Why am I telling you all of this, Sam?," she whispered.

He shrugged, surprised to find his hands still on her feet, pulling them into his lap as he settled in next to her on the couch. "I don't know… but you can. You can tell me anything."

She sighed. "You're saving my life with that leak, you know. I don't have time for home repairs. I don't have time to do anything but check my phone in between running from one birth to the next."

"Do you want me to leave you alone so you can get some rest? Just go fix the pipe and let myself out?," he asked, praying that she'd say no.

"Oh… no," she said. "I need a break. I really, really need a break. Thought I was going to get to go down to Florida in a few weeks, but then Craig showed up here, and now, I *really* don't want to go down there and face everyone again."

"Florida is far, far away," Sam smiled.

She smiled back at him. "I'm well aware. As was Craig."

"I'm sure he didn't like you being here," Sam said, knowing full and well what it was like to be away from Faith for days, weeks, months, years...

"I think he would have been okay with it for a while, but... he couldn't get past my reasons for moving out here."

"What were those?," he asked.

"Honestly, I think I came all the way out here to avoid moving forward with him," she said. "Actually, I know that's what it was. Maybe I'm a... well, a commitment-phobe. Which makes no sense, right? I mean, it's not like I have a tragic backstory with marriage or anything. Since my parents are so perfect together, my grandparents were so perfect together, and..." She sighed. "I sound really messed up, don't I?"

"Maybe it's not a phobia of commitment. Maybe he just wasn't the right guy," Sam offered softly.

"Maybe," Faith murmured. "Though he was perfect on paper. And perfect enough that I said yes to him then just... broke his heart. And the whole time I was telling him, I was thinking to myself, really, Faith? Are you going to throw away your only chance to –"

And she cut off her words.

"To what?"

She shook her head. "To just... grow up. And stop believing in little girl fantasies. Or stupid teenage girl fantasies. About lake houses and men in uniform and..." She put her hands on her face and sighed.

Sam turned to face her, ready to tell her that he had been wrong, that he wanted to –

"Oh, just forget I said any of that," Faith said, looking at him with tears in her eyes. "I've gotten two hours of sleep in the past twenty-four. Two. Hours. I'm not even sure what I'm saying anymore. I'm just so exhausted. And I've been on the phone all night with a woman who's miscarried every baby she's ever been pregnant with, and it sounds like she's miscarrying this one, too. And it's like all of her faith and trust in God is hanging on this, and I just..."

He moved her feet to the floor and pulled her up next to him. And when her head rested against his shoulder, she started crying in earnest.

She was crying all over Sam Huntington.

Her logical, sane self screamed at her that this was probably a bad idea. The last time she'd been this close to him she'd had stars in her eyes and not a lick of sense, and it had ended with years of silence. The very last thing she needed was more of the same in terms of that heartbreak. *And*, her logical self continued to shout at her, *you shouldn't want anything anyway because you broke up just last week with your fiancé!*

Her emotional, exhausted self, though, told her to just shut up and cry on Sam because he was comforting, for some strange, inexplicable reason.

So, she just went with it. Everyone was leaning on her here. Elaine Charles, all of those pregnant women who had her on speed dial, Erica, who even now was certain that she was miscarrying, distraught that Faith had told her they could do nothing but wait and see.

She'd had so many hard conversations lately.

The conversation with Craig had been the worst. But she'd been honest. She'd told him how he'd moved towards marriage without preparing her, without discussing it with her, and without thinking that the way he proposed would have put her in a difficult position. Sure, she had to answer for her own response, but he'd been in the relationship, too.

But beyond how it had all happened, there was the truth of the situation. That something was missing from their relationship, from the way that she felt about him. And Faith was certainly no expert on relationships, on love, on the way this was all supposed to work, her only experience with any of it revolving around one week she spent by the lake as a teenager. But she knew something wasn't right.

Craig knew it, too, deep down. It was why he'd come all the way out to surprise her, to force her hand, to make her make a decision finally.

And the decision, in the end, had been to end it all. There had been relief in her heart, even as there had been heartbreak on his face, as she gave him his ring.

She was a horrible person. Because there was remorse, guilt, and pain for having hurt him.

But mostly, there was just relief, that she was free to live her life without dreading the next step.

She hadn't let herself grieve any of it. Until she was there with her head on Sam's shoulder.

"I haven't even *cried* about the fact that I broke up with him, Sam. He wanted to *marry* me, and I wasn't even moved enough by his heartbreak to cry about it," she said. "And I'm not even sure that's why I'm crying now. How messed up is that?"

He held her and let her carry on. She couldn't imagine why he'd waste his time here, but she didn't care. She remembered who he'd been back when she was a little girl, the kindness ever present in his eyes, the goodness there when she was a teenager, the godliness she'd known in the years they'd spent alongside one another so many years ago.

He was a good man. He loved the Lord. And he was discerning enough to know that there were no answers or solutions for what she was going through now.

And so he offered none, as he continued to let her talk and cry, until she had no tears or words left either one.

He let her cry.

For a long time, as she kept telling him her frustrations, her hurts, and her thoughts, he let her say whatever she wanted to say, hearing what she needed someone to hear. He would offer murmured comforts, holding her close, until he felt her relax against him, her breathing evened out, her shuddering sobs suddenly stilled.

Just as Sam thought that her tears were finished, just as he was about to apologize for all that hadn't been said between them all those years ago when he'd let her down, he chanced a look down at her face, expecting to be bolstered into bravery by the beauty there...

... and found instead that she was sound asleep.

Sound asleep in his arms.

"Oh, man," he sighed, regretting this opportunity lost but glad to see that she was getting some rest. Gently, he picked her up in his arms and carried her to the nearest bedroom, noting her shoes on the floor and her color-coded calendar on the wall, planning to leave her there, figure out a way to lock her door –

Well, that was a problem. He could fix the leak, take her keys, and leave a note about where he'd left them on her porch... that wasn't safe, though. Then, there was the option of just waking her up, but she looked so peaceful, curled up there, her cheeks flushed, her hair loosened all around her face, all of her delicate curves carefully detailed and on display as she sighed...

Sam needed to get out of here.

But before he could settle on the best option – hidden keys, waking her up, or throwing himself out her window – she reached out and pulled him right into bed with her.

Her eyes opened. "Sam," she sighed, sleepy and dreamy. "I'm so tired."

"I know," he said softly, desperately trying to move, even as Faith wound her arms around his neck. Oh, he really needed to get out of here.

"I think about you all the time. I always have," she murmured, closing her eyes.

His heart clenched at this, then even further at the way she snaked her perfect body around him, inching her leg up over his hip as she whispered her lips over his.

"You feel so good, Sam," she groaned, her eyes still closed as she moved even closer to him.

And Sam? Considered what he *should* do. Leave. Leave quickly. Get out of here. Do what he'd been doing his whole life with women whom he felt only a fraction of what he had felt for Faith Hayes, still felt for her as she pulled him closer and murmured, "Sam..."

Then, before he could make any kind of move of his own, thankfully, she began snoring.

"Faith... are you asleep?," he asked incredulously.

Another snore was his answer.

He sighed, closing his eyes and willing his body to calm down.

So, Faith was a sleep talker. And more. Oh, way more, he affirmed as she put her hand on his butt.

"How far apart are the contractions?," she asked.

"What?"

"Can you talk through the contractions?," she murmured, rubbing his butt, her eyes still closed.

"Um… yeah," he said.

"Five minutes apart, two minutes apart, like waves… crash, swell, calm… so natural… beautiful…"

And now, she was smiling. Sleeping and smiling, delivering a baby in her sleep.

"Mmmm," she murmured.

Watching her sleep so peacefully, he resolved to wait at least an hour before waking her up. That was something she needed, and he could do that much for her. As if agreeing with his silent decision, Faith snuggled up close to his side, muttering, "My Sam," as she did so.

"Your Sam," he whispered, loving the sound of that, settling in next to her, putting his arms around her, and drawing her close.

One hour, he yawned. He'd be up and out of her hair and her bed in one hour...

The next morning, Sam woke up to find his arms wrapped around Faith's waist, his fingertips just underneath her shirt, touching her soft skin, his lips dangerously close to hers.

And Faith, still asleep and dreaming, likely? Had one hand on his chest and the other still on his butt. She wore a peaceful smile that even now made his breath catch.

Oh, this was bad. Actually, it felt fan-freakin-tastic to Sam, which meant that it was *really* bad.

Careful not to jostle her as his heart raced, he took a breath, planning to check his watch and leave her undisturbed somehow, when her eyes opened. And rounded in shock.

She seemed horrified... or maybe not nearly as horrified as the situation warranted as her eyes flitted down to his lips. Which was a curious thing that brought up more questions than answers as they continued to stare at one another and...

... and she was still touching his butt. And he was lying there, enjoying it all.

She pulled her hands away suddenly and sat up, the movement so quick that she fell right out of her bed.

"Oh, Faith, are you okay?," Sam said, getting out of bed and coming to help her off the floor.

She stared at him, her eyes trailing from his hair to his face, to the hands that held hers.

"Sam, I... what..."

"I'm so sorry."

She stared at him. "Oh, Sam. What do you have to apologize for? What do *I* have to apologize for? What did I do last night?"

He shook his head. "You didn't do anything wrong. You were upset, crying, and you fell asleep. And I... fell asleep, too."

She bit her lip. "That's it? I didn't say or... do anything?"

Sam paused just long enough to cause her to put her hands on her face. "Oh, no, no, no –"

"Faith," he said, catching her shoulders in his hands. "You were asleep. It was easy to figure out that you didn't know what you were saying or doing."

Except it hadn't been easy. And he'd begun hoping, had allowed himself to be filled with such hope, as soon as the words had left her mouth... *my Sam...*

"Really?," she asked.

"I stayed with you. Brought you in here and didn't wake you up," he said. "I'm sorry. I just... you were just so tired."

She regarded him warily. "And then...?"

"Faith," he said softly, moved by the tears in her eyes.

"Oh, Sam," she began to cry in earnest now. "Did we...? Because I've never... never been with anyone before... and... "

"No... no," he managed, pulling her into a protective embrace, smoothing down her hair, not even thinking twice about it, especially as she put her arms around him. "I... me neither."

He realized that this was a very personal thing to share, but the admission of his own innocence, not just that night but all nights, seemed to be of some comfort to Faith, who sighed and brushed away her tears.

"Okay. I didn't think... well, I would know, surely... but... oh, Sam..."

"I would never," he said, holding her face in his hands as she blinked back the rest of her tears, "take advantage of you. Ever."

"Oh, I didn't think that, Sam," she breathed. "I just thought that... with you and me, and... oh, you know how it is. With us, with how we felt..."

He was about to ask for clarification, to ask if she still felt the way she had, the way he did --

But before he could, she gasped. "Did I ask you about contractions?"

He grinned. "Yeah, actually."

She regarded him with no small amount of horror. "Did I try to check your cervix?"

He frowned. "Do I... I don't have a cervix, do I?"

"Um... no," she said softly. "But I was asking about contractions, and work was on my mind, and... well..."

"I don't think you tried to check anything."

She breathed out a sigh of relief. "Good. Because you'd remember if I had... well, you know."

"I don't, actually," he said. "And I'm pretty sure I don't want to know."

"Effaced, dilated," she continued on. "It's all I think about these days..." She put her hand to her mouth. "Well, at least when I'm not unleashing all of my crazy on the man who came over to fix a leak. Sam..."

"Unleashing all your crazy," he said, smiling. "You didn't do that."

"No," she sputtered. "Just told you all about how I broke someone's heart, how everything's a mess, how my church back home probably hates me now --"

"Hey, I don't think that could be true," he said.

Faith seemed at a loss for words... then gasped. Again. "What time is it?"

He looked at his watch, "Nine."

"Oh, no, where's my phone?" She began rushing around the room, trying to find it, as Sam pulled it out from his pocket.

"Brought it in here last night when I brought you in... was going to set your alarm for you," he said, handing it to her apologetically.

"No missed calls," she murmured. "No appointments until noon, but... there's her number."

And Sam went and sat back on the bed awkwardly, unsure whether or not to leave now as she made the call. She asked several questions, then gave a small, relieved laugh, before saying goodbye.

She turned back to him and smiled. "Still pregnant, as best as I can tell from her description." She let out a long breath. "Maybe you're a good luck charm."

And she reached out and touched his face for just a moment, as he watched her silently.

"I'm so sorry," she said softly. "About last night and all that I said and... thank you for being here, for letting me talk. But lake houses and men in uniform… I said some really crazy things, didn't I?"

Before she was sleepy, honestly. And then more. Wonderful words about it all. Sam could remember every single one.

"Yeah," he murmured.

"Ugh," she muttered, covering her face with her hands. "So humiliating…"

"Hey," Sam stood up next to her, softly pulling her hands from her face, holding them in his own. "Let me take you to dinner tonight… to talk about all of this."

"You don't have to do that," she said, frazzled, her hand releasing his and going to her forehead. "Really, it's –"

"I want to," he said.

She bit her lip. "I don't really have time tonight. I've got a long list of appointments up through this evening, and –"

"Then this weekend?"

"Sam, do you really want –"

And Sam, wanting this frazzled, hectic Faith perhaps even more than the sultry, seductive Faith from the night before, leaned in and kissed her softly, tenderly. And just like she had all those years ago in the bright morning sunlight by the lake house, she responded by pulling closer to him, wrapping her arms around his waist, and sweetly sighing as though he was changing her world.

Little surprise, since she had forever changed his.

They parted, and he gave only one word. "Please."

She returned one to him. "Okay."

And Sam left that morning, knowing that he would do whatever he could to make Faith Hayes love him like she had.

CHAPTER FIVE

She'd slept with Sam Huntington.

Well, not like that. But she'd unleashed all of her crazy on him the night before, and rather than running for the hills, he'd stayed with her. He'd been with her. And the look in his eyes as he'd left her that morning had suggested that whatever nuttiness she'd exposed to him that night had only endeared her to him more.

Amazing, actually.

Kind of like that kiss he gave her, so much like the ones she remembered from the lake house. So different from Craig. So different from anything she'd believed she could hope to have one day. So different from what she'd expected from Sam that morning that it had rendered her incompetent to make a good decision, leading her to quick agreement to go to dinner with him.

"Really, Faith?," she whined, her hands to her hair. "Grow up. Grow up, grow up, grow up!"

If anything would force her to grow up a little faster, it would be a conversation with Gracie. The older, mature, big, bossy sister in her just naturally came out as soon as Gracie began giggling and talking about her own life, and Faith needed this. Gracie was also good, once in a blue moon, for completely honest advice that sometimes bordered on wise, and she needed this, too.

So, she went through her recent call list, touched Gracie's name, and waited.

Gracie picked up on the second ring.

"On my way to work, Faith!," she said. "Running late!"

This sounded like Gracie.

"And I just hit traffic. Uggggghhhhh," she groaned. "Why do we even have toll roads when they're all backed up like this?!"

"Well, at least you have some time to talk to me now," Faith said.

"I guess," Gracie muttered. Then, in a brighter voice, "And you're up early! Lots planned today?"

Faith glanced at her watch again. "Actually, this is late for me. And I have nothing planned but work. Like usual."

"Babies galore!," Gracie said. "Fertile, fertile Texas." She'd heard about all the odd hours and the odd patients, the stress and the challenges.

"Yeah," Faith sighed. "How about you?"

"Meet and greets all day," Gracie answered. "Had some pervy dad grab my butt yesterday and a hysterical toddler got ice cream in my wig, but even still, greatest job in the world, Faith. Seriously."

"I can't imagine," Faith murmured, thinking of Gracie working all day, flouncing around in her tiny little leotard, giving her flirty smiles to thousands of people, and kissing on infants.

She was Tinkerbell. No, really. She played Tinkerbell at Walt Disney World, just like she'd sworn she would back when she was a tiny girl on her first trip there so many years ago.

"That dad got his," Gracie said, "when I gasped and shouted that he was trying to get my pixie dust, all while I swatted him on the arm as hard as I could, and told him that he could take a little trip to Neverland. Tinkerbell is sassy like that, so she can get away with more, you know. Princesses can't be pulling that kind of stuff, but fairies can."

Faith smiled at this. "Such a smart girl," she said appreciatively.

"College degree," Gracie said. "I mean, it's a theater degree but still. And I ditched the wig after the ice cream fiasco and just pulled my own hair up in a fairy bun. Looked more like Tinkerbell that way than I do in the wig anyway."

"You *are* Tinkerbell," Faith confirmed.

"Sure am," Gracie said. "And the company knows it! They just released the promo material for the new year, and there's a three second clip of me in the intro, sitting under my toadstool on the parade float blowing kisses to the crowd and laughing at Mr. Smee."

"Awesome," Faith grinned.

"It is," Gracie sighed. "Living the dream. And I'm totally going to be talking about it all over church, trying to get everyone's mind off of your drama and your business."

Faith cringed. "Are they talking about it at church?"

"Hard not to," Gracie said, "when Craig spent all of Sunday sulking around like a dog that had been kicked."

"Ugh," Faith groaned, remembering the way Craig had looked when he'd left the week before. She'd hoped he'd be able to put on a brave face for church, weather the rumors and speculation, avoid causing more gossip...

... but apparently, that hadn't happened.

"And the girls!," Gracie yelled. "About ten of them from the singles class were following him around, trying to take advantage of his pathetic self."

"Really?," Faith asked, knowing that there had been plenty of women interested in him, even while they were together. It had been one of the reasons she'd wondered why she didn't seem to feel nearly enough for him. "Who?"

"Too many to name," Gracie said, "but the most aggressive one was Leah."

Faith nodded. "Leah Morrison. And she was my friend. Supposedly."

"Mine, too," Gracie said. "We were really great friends when we were younger!"

"You dated her brother for a while, didn't you?," Faith asked.

"Which one of her brothers?"

Faith frowned at this. "Well, you dated Lance --"

"Oh, that's right!," she giggled. "I always forget that! And I think I dated Ethan, too. Or... wait, did I?"

"That's really sad that you can't keep track of them all," Faith managed, thinking of her sister's long list of beaus over the years. "And that there's at least one pairing of brothers in your repertoire."

"Didn't even kiss either one of them," she said. "Never did anything I wouldn't have been okay with Jesus seeing, with *any* boy I dated."

"And I'm sure the astounding physical purity honored Jesus, even though dating half the youth group may have called to question your emotional purity."

"Hey," Gracie said, laughter in her voice, "someone had to take up the slack since you never gave anyone the time of day. Apart from Sam Huntington, of course."

Faith took a breath at this.

"What?"

Silence.

"Oh, come on, Faith," Gracie sighed. "It doesn't still bother you, does it? All that went on all those years ago at the lake house? I mean, you talked to him at the funeral, right?"

"I did," Faith said quietly.

"So, it's all good," she said. "Right? I mean, you moved on, with Craig. For a while, at least. You're over it, right?"

Faith remained silent.

"What?," Gracie demanded. "I said his name, and all of a sudden, you're all quiet."

"I'm quiet," Faith said, "because you haven't let me get a word in."

"Oh, no," Gracie said. "That's not it. It's him! You're still caught up in him! Even though you were engaged to someone else just last week!"

Faith blushed at this, feeling the guilt of it.

"So what?," Gracie said, sympathy in her voice. "Have you seen him since the move? Aunt Mel told me he lived down there."

Oh, yeah. She'd seen him.

"Yeah," Faith managed.

"And it's still weird?," Gracie said. "When did you see him? Where did you see him?"

"Well," Faith sighed, "this morning. In my bed."

And Faith heard a car horn and Gracie yelling, "What?!"

"Gracie," Faith began. "It's just --"

"Hold on," she said. "Getting back in my lane. Kinda shocked me back there, Faith. Almost got me killed. And now that guy's giving me a particularly juvenile one-finger salute." Faith could hear her raise her voice, probably yelling out the window. "I see you, buddy! You just flipped off Tinkerbell! Do you feel like a big man now?! *Huh*?!"

"Good grief, Gracie," she murmured. "He could be carrying a gun in his car, you know. Road rage, and --"

"Oh, please, this is Florida, not Texas," she said. "Okay... so what in the world?! In your bed?! What?!"

"Gracie," she groaned, "he came over to help me out with a leaky pipe. I wasn't even expecting him. I thought it would be his brother and his wife, Marie. You remember Marie, right?"

"Yeah," Gracie said. "But that doesn't explain why --"

"He came over," Faith sighed. "And we started talking. And he just... he was just so understanding, such a great listener, and I just... started talking. And I couldn't shut up! And then, I was crying, like a completely insane woman, more than I've cried in years, and I was telling him everything, and he was just holding me and..."

"And?," Gracie demanded. "And?!"

"I fell asleep," she said weakly. "And I woke up, and he was still there, holding me."

"Oh," Gracie said simply. "Well. That sounds perfectly fine. Innocent. Pure."

"Really?," Faith asked, great surprise in her voice.

"Yeah," Gracie said enthusiastically. "Except for the part where you were *engaged* just a week ago to someone else, and you're telling all of your secrets to a man who you hardly know and letting him see *all* of your crazy --"

"I know, I know," Faith groaned.

"What is it about him?," Gracie said. "It's like you're sixteen again, mooning over him and crying all night because he hasn't called and... good grief, Faith. Have you forgotten all of that? About how he took advantage of you back then --"

"He didn't," Faith said sternly. "He didn't." He hadn't taken advantage of her. She'd been sixteen, but it hadn't been like that...

"Same situation," Gracie said, hearing what she hadn't said. "Imagine that you have your own daughter one day. She's sixteen. And some twenty-six year old man takes her aside after only a few days of talking to her, kisses her, tells her how he wants to be with her... what would you call that now, Faith? Now that you're a grown woman and can see it for what it was?"

But it wasn't like that. It hadn't been... well, it hadn't, had it? She sighed. "I understand what you're saying. I really do, Gracie. But --"

"And," Gracie said vehemently, trying to reason with her, "apart from that, there's the fact that he never kept any of those promises! You have no reason to trust him now!"

"Maybe he did what he did because he was trying to be a good guy," Faith reasoned. "I mean, he probably didn't even know how old I was. He seemed so shocked. And we don't even know what happened after he left. He went to Afghanistan. There's no telling what life was like there."

"Still," Gracie said, her voice softening. "Faith."

"What?," Faith whispered, knowing that there was wisdom in what her sister was saying, what she was sure to say next.

"You just broke off an engagement," she said. "You need to be careful."

And Faith knew it was true. Had known it even before she picked up the phone.

"Thank you, Gracie."

"Are you mad at me?," she asked.

"No," Faith said. "You're right. And I appreciate you. I love you."

"I love you, too," she said. "Which is why I'm saying this."

"I know."

A long pause.

"You're going to see him again, aren't you?"

And Faith's silence was the answer.

"Well," Gracie sighed, "be smart, at least, okay?"

"I always am," Faith said very simply.

"No, I think this entire fiasco proves that you're not," Gracie said. "But... try, Faith. Try to protect your heart."

"I will, Gracie," Faith said, resolving that she would. "I will."

Sam drove home with a smile on his face.

That had been the first night he'd had in years where he'd slept without any nightmares.

He attributed it all to Faith who, rather than being a remembrance in his difficult nights halfway around the world, had been reality last night.

He'd been given another chance. And he wasn't going to blow it.

Scott was still at the house when he got there. Late morning, apparently, after an even later night. Sam took a deep breath, expecting the inquisition when he got in. He had stayed at Faith's house while she got ready, finally fixing that leak, tempted to call Scott himself for some guidance but avoiding doing so, knowing the questions once he got home would be bad enough even without a preface to the situation.

But Scott barely glanced up from where he was making breakfast. "Hey."

"Hey," Sam said, moving past him.

"Early morning?," Scott tossed over his shoulder.

"Yeah."

Scott nodded. "Not me. Making me feel like a slacker, already up and out this morning. Checked my messages a few minutes ago, and Marie and I are going to head out to Faith's house this afternoon to fix a leak. But the schedule's pretty clear otherwise."

Sam sat down at the table, yawning. "Already took care of Faith."

"Oh," Scott said, glancing over at his brother. "I take it then, that she's decided not to hate you. Either that, or the leak was just that bad."

Sam shrugged.

"You look awful, man," Scott added. "Didn't even bother shaving before you went over there, and –"

He stopped short, his eyes widening. Sam opened his mouth to say something, but Scott cut him off.

"You didn't go there this morning, did you? You were already there! Last night! That's where you were!"

"I was… well, I…"

Scott came to sit across from him. "Details. Now."

Sam frowned at him. "How do you even know I wasn't here last night?"

"Because I got up at three to take care of the baby. Looked into your room, saw that it was empty. And I thought to myself, 'Well, that's weird,' when I saw that you weren't here. But I assumed you showed up at some point, slept, then got back on the road early this morning." He leaned back. "But you were with Faith. You got her message to me last night. And you stayed the entire night with her, and –"

"It wasn't like that –"

"Well, then don't tell me if you don't want to. Let me just imagine how Faith managed to convince you to –"

"Scott, I swear I'll kill you with my bare hands if you don't stop talking about Faith like that."

Speculation was one thing. So were suspicions. But voicing any of this out loud, particularly when it involved Faith and her reputation, was off limits. Sam felt protective of her, even now.

Scott considered this for a moment. "I didn't mean anything bad. Just… well, she's engaged to someone else, like you said, and you –"

Mercifully, the land line phone rang, sparing Scott from mortal peril. Sam, glad for a reason to get away from his brother, stood to answer it.

"Hello?"

"Good morning, Sam," his mother trilled on the other end of the line.

"Hey, Mom," he sighed.

"*Hey, Mom!*," Scott shouted as he went back to making breakfast.

"Oh, I caught both of you at home! Taking a late morning?"

Sam ran his hand down his face. "Yeah. Late night. For both of us."

"Are you keeping Scott in line?," she asked, her voice lowered.

"Mom, he's a grown man, you know," Sam said. Then lowering his own voice, "And that's Marie's job now."

"Don't worry about me, Mom," Scott shouted from the stove. "I'm just a domesticated, old, married man. You should be worried about Sam. He's the one who spent the night with *Faith Hayes!*"

Even as his mother gasped, Sam picked up the only thing handy on the counter – a spoon – and hurled it at his brother's head.

"Ow! Mom, Sam hit me with a *spoon!*"

"I'll hit you with worse if you don't –"

"Samuel Thomas Huntington."

Aww, great. How old would he have to get before the Mom voice had no effect?

"Yes, ma'am?"

"You—"

"I'm sorry I hit Scott with a spoon, okay?"

"Oh, I don't care about that," she said, then speaking more softly, "It's just that Faith Hayes is... well, she's engaged."

"Mom," Sam sighed, "she and her fiancé broke up last weekend."

"Well, then, you need to be even more careful. You don't need to be taking advantage of an emotional woman and a —"

"Mom, nothing happened last night. And I can't believe I'm even telling you this because—"

"It's none of my business, I know," she said. "Honestly, I've tried to stay out of your business and your brothers' business, but Faith is —"

"I know, I know," he said. "I'm not that kind of guy."

"Sure isn't," Scott shouted, even as he covered his head with his arm, expecting another assault of flying silverware. "But I know he really likes her, so it's possible that —"

"I will kill you, Scott," he warned.

"Sam," his mother said softly, breaking his attention from his brother. "I know you're a good guy. But Faith? She's in a new place, so young, and now with this breakup... And I don't know why you were with her all night, but —"

"Nothing happened," Sam said again.

"Yes, Sam, I got that," she said, "But for Faith? Having your attention all night? Well that was probably something very big to her, especially with this breakup."

Sam swallowed hard, thinking about this. About how it was something big for him, too.

"Just don't hurt her, okay?," his mother asked, concerned.

"I don't have any intention of doing that," he said.

And he didn't. And as soon as he got a chance, he began making plans.

She spent the next few days steeling herself against feeling much of anything for Sam Huntington.

Dinner. Just dinner. She could do this. And if she felt inclined to go beyond dinner, to go beyond allowing him this, to go beyond what she should feel in the wake of the biggest breakup of her life...

... well, she'd remember waiting around for a letter. For a phone call. For any sign that he had meant what he said back by the lake, all those years ago.

He'd insisted on picking her up, rather than meeting her there, as she'd suggested. It was chivalrous, thoughtful, just exactly what she would have expected from him.

What she didn't expect was the call from Carmen Hastings, a patient in active labor, an hour before Sam was scheduled to come by.

"I'm really re-thinking this whole thing," Carmen managed, a laugh in her voice.

Faith smiled, even as she glanced at her watch. "Too late for that. How long have you been hurting?"

"Well, it was pleasant enough for the past few hours with just mild contractions, but now... well, I've been feeling some significant pressure for about thirty minutes now."

Faith's eyes widened as she went into action, gathering up her supplies. "Pressure? You should have called me sooner," she said. "Are you by yourself?"

"No, I've got the two older kids in here with me," she said.

"Carmen, I meant Paul," Faith said, thinking of this woman's husband, capable and well instructed for just such an unexpected turn of events like this. "Is Paul there?"

"On his way," she sighed. "He went into the office for just a few minutes, and... oh, here comes another one, Faith. Hold up."

Faith counted in her head, fishing her keys out of her purse and leaving the house at a light jog.

"Carmen? How are you doing?"

She heard nothing but a very loud breath. Then, "Okay. Officially not fun anymore."

Faith smiled, even as she sat down in her car and started the engine. "Wasn't it like this with your first two?"

"I had the epidural done so quickly that I didn't feel anything with either of them," Carmen managed. "Why didn't I do that this time around?"

"Because," Faith said, pulling out into the road, "this is going to be far more wonderful, doing this naturally, at home, than you can imagine."

"Not wonderful, Faith," Carmen managed through gritted teeth.

"Another contraction," Faith murmured, even as she glanced at the clock, noting that she wouldn't be at home when Sam came by. "Breathe through it, and I'll be there in a few minutes. Keep talking to me, Carmen. Keep talking to me..."

He arrived at her house five minutes early.

And she wasn't there.

He had only a moment of standing there at her door, wondering at this rebuff, before his phone rang in his hand. Faith.

"Hey," he answered.

"Hey, Sam," she said softly. "You're at the house, aren't you?"

He glanced at his watch. "Yeah... you changed your mind, didn't you?"

And there was a pause. Then, a softer, "No... I had a call from a patient."

"Oh," he said, feeling relief at this. "Everything okay?"

"Better than okay," she said, and he could hear the smile in her voice. "An eight pound baby girl. After only five minutes of pushing."

He thought about this. "Is that quick?"

She laughed quietly. "Yeah. That's really quick," she said. "I was here just in time to catch her but still five minutes before the proud daddy arrived. Just stepped out of the house to give them some privacy."

He sat down on the porch, imagining her doing the same wherever this delivery had taken her. "Does this happen often? Getting a call just in time to catch the baby?"

"All the time," she said. "And would you believe it? It usually happens on my off hours."

"Babies," Sam chided. "Can't they keep it to office hours?"

She laughed at this. "I wish." And a long pause. "Totally ruined dinner plans, didn't I?"

"You didn't ruin anything," he said. "I'm talking to you. That was the extent of my big plan for tonight, honestly."

He could hear her sigh softly. He closed his eyes at this, content to sit here just like this on the phone with her all night if need be...

"And I'm starving," she said. "Didn't get lunch earlier because there was another patient. Thought she was in labor, but it was just a false alarm."

"Did you go over to her house, too?"

"Yeah," Faith murmured. "Spent two hours sharing Christ with her, talking about how He numbers our days, how He knows when her baby's days here with us will begin. She's spent her whole life turned off to any mention of God, but something about a baby... about expecting, about knowing that there's life inside of you... she's receptive. And I'm not going to waste a minute."

Sam swallowed at this. "Amazing," he said, thinking on the truth of what she'd said, on how he knew it, too, how God knew every day Sam himself would face, every thing he'd see, what it would do to him, how God would still restore him...

Silence. "Sam, I'm sorry I ruined tonight." She took a breath. "I'm sitting out here in a sundress, all fixed up for dinner, looking like an idiot, and you're across town, probably regretting that you ever asked me out at all."

"I don't imagine you look like an idiot," he managed, thinking of how she must look. "Are you going to be back tonight?"

"Yeah," she murmured. "Going to wait another hour, at least, just to make sure everything's okay. You should just go on, Sam. Honestly."

"Well, we'll definitely miss our reservation," he said, thinking that he didn't really care about the strings he'd pulled with some clients, posing as Scott, securing them a table at one of the nicest restaurants in the city.

"I'm sorry again," she said softly. "I'll see you... well, I'll see you again sometime, I guess."

And he smiled even as he reassured her, "Yeah, Faith. I'll see you soon."

Long day. Hard day. On top of a hard week.

Five births the day before, with hard, long labor for the mothers, hard, long hours for Faith, who felt so sympathetic to all that they went through, then as triumphant as they were once the infants were in their arms.

So rewarding. Just like that day, with an unexpected birth and all of those words about Christ, about redemption, about sovereignty.

And Sam.

Faith sighed a little, regretting that their plans had been dashed like that. She had talked to him on the phone, imagining him sitting on her porch, irritated by the inconvenience of her work, of her inability to keep to their plans.

Well, good. Because if he was irritated, like any normal man would be, it would be easier to not feel anything either way... or at least not feel what she was so inclined to feel for him, even now.

She wouldn't be on call for another twenty-four hours. Her big plan was to slip into some jammies, kick her feet up on the coffee table, and watch mindless television while eating up warmed up leftovers, way past a sensible dinnertime.

The plans changed, though, when she pulled into her driveway, her headlights washing over Sam, sitting on the tailgate of his truck with a bag of takeout and a bouquet of flowers next to him.

Why was he still here? Why had he waited for her like this?

The answer was there in the smile that he gave her, even as she got out of her car and watched him for a moment.

With Craig, she would have found herself annoyed. With Sam, she just felt touched, moved, amazed that he'd stayed and waited for her.

"Hope it's okay that I picked up dinner," he said, almost shyly to her.

And she couldn't figure out why this man felt like home, but she rejoiced that he was here. And, at the same time, she warned herself, again, against feeling too much. "Yeah. It's great. Thank you."

He watched her for a long moment. And then, with disbelief in his voice, he whispered, "I bought you that dress. Years ago."

She broke her gaze from his and looked down at it. He had. She'd known the significance of it when she'd slipped it on earlier. And though she's sworn that this -- Sam and Faith -- wasn't going to go anywhere, she'd hoped, oh, she'd hoped, that he would recognize it, that he'd remember, that he'd say something...

"You did," she said softly.

He took a breath. "Still beautiful," he said. "All these years later. You're even more beautiful than you were."

And she wondered at how wonderful these words were, even as she forced her mind past them. "Come on in, Sam," she said, turning towards the house and whatever came next.

She'd heated up dinner as he watched. And she'd talked. A lot. About the day. About the delivery. About the conversations she'd had all day long on the phone with patients who had no idea that this was her day off.

Sam had listened. And they'd talked more over dinner, sitting at the small table in the breakfast nook, Sam's knee brushing against hers every time she moved.

They were both aware of that, as evidenced by the way their eyes kept meeting, recognition passing between them, remembrances of another time just like this...

And then, just as they were finishing up, Sam finally said it.

"I had no idea you were sixteen."

She wiped her mouth and watched him carefully. "You didn't remember me."

"No," he shook his head. "Not until that last morning. I mean, at one point, I remembered you, earlier in the week... but you were so different that I figured you couldn't have been the same little girl I'd known."

She could understand this. "The same silly little girl."

"Silly?," he asked. "I don't remember you being silly."

She frowned at this just slightly. "Silly because I spent my time thinking that I was so much older than I was, hanging out with a teenage boy, imagining that we were friends."

"Well, we were friends," he said. "That wasn't just your imagination."

"You were probably just humoring me," she said simply.

Sam smiled. "I only humored you when you told me you were going to marry me."

Faith rolled her eyes. "Yeah, well, I wish you would just forget that. Because I was six when I said it and didn't have any idea what it meant."

"But I remembered," he said, "so it counts."

"Sam," she sighed.

He looked intently at her, vulnerability in his eyes. "I think about that last morning at the lake house every day of my life, Faith."

And she wondered at the wisdom of offering him anything... but offered it anyway. "Me, too," she said softly.

"I should've called you afterwards."

And he should have. She'd said it a million times. But how could he have done it? What would have happened?

"You broke my heart," she said softly, looking him straight in the eyes as he linked his fingers through hers on the table.

"You were sixteen," he said. "What was I supposed to do?"

Even now, she could remember who he'd been. A good guy, a man of integrity, a strong believer who wouldn't compromise any of his commitments to Christ. She could picture how he'd rushed to get her a shirt that one morning, his eyes never glancing at the bikini she wore. She thought of how he'd treated her with respect the whole week, going out of his way to honor her. She remembered how he'd even asked for permission before kissing her.

Hearing that she was sixteen had prompted him to do the godliest thing of all -- leaving, even though he likely didn't want to.

Faith looked down at their hands. "I was old enough to really feel the way I felt. And I would've understood if you had told me it wasn't the right time."

He looked at her doubtfully but not without kindness.

"Okay," she admitted. "So, I wouldn't have understood then. But today? Right now? When I'm all grown up? I would understand. And I would have appreciated how you tried to protect me even then."

"I'm sorry, Faith," he murmured. "There was no way for me to win, you know."

She knew it was true. And that's why the rejection had hurt so much. Because in its very essence, it had shown what a good guy he was, refusing to be with her when she was so young.

"Samuel," she sighed, knowing that he'd won her over already.

"Yeah, that's exactly how you always said my name," he smiled. "And so, in my head, even now, I'm hearing your tiny little girl voice say my name, all while I have this clear mental image — all these years later, mind you – of you at sixteen, and I'm sitting here with you now, and you're even more beautiful than you were. And I want *you* to know that I certainly don't see you as a little girl anymore. Or even as a teenager. I mean, you're... you."

"Yes," she said, simply.

"But you can see why I freaked out back then. Because I have a hard time reconciling all I feel for all of – well who we are and have been. Does that make any sense?"

"I think so," she murmured. "It's hard to forget that once upon a time, you were eighteen when I was eight."

"Yes. Exactly. But I'm going to just get over it, Faith. Because you're *you*, and I'm not going to miss my chance to be with you. Because I very nearly missed it once already with Craig in the picture."

And she could hear what he was clearly saying, and she wanted what he was offering, what he was declaring. But she remembered Gracie's words and vowed to protect her heart, to be smart about this, and to tread carefully.

"I just broke off my engagement," she said, noting that her hand was still in his, even as she said this. "I need time to... just heal from that."

"I understand," he said. "I just want to hang out with you."

"Hang out," she murmured.

"You seem like someone I would enjoy being around. I always did, back when we were kids, back at the lake house..."

"I don't even think we really know each other," she said to him, weakly, wondering at how he could make her feel like this without any good reason. "I mean, what do you even really know about me from the very brief moments we've spent together?"

He smiled at her. "I know you're Faith Hayes."

"Actually," she smiled back at him. "My name is Sophia Faith Hayes."

"Well, you've proven your point already, since I don't even know your name," he leaned back in his seat. "Should I just give up now?"

"No," she said, looking down. "Maybe, though, this is a good place to start." She smiled, nervous about starting this without having any idea where it would go, how it would end. "Hi. My name is Sophia Faith Hayes, but you can call me Faith."

He smiled back, reaching out for her other hand and holding it there on the table as well. "Samuel Thomas Huntington. You can call me Sam."

CHAPTER SIX

The months passed by quickly.

Faith moved her membership from her father's church in Florida to the same small church where Scott, Marie, and Sam were members, and before long, it was a lot like it had been, so many years ago.

Faith Hayes and Sam Huntington, sitting together in the pew, him slipping her a piece of cinnamon gum during the sermon. She'd narrowed her eyes at him the first time he'd offered, and he'd grinned after a moment, no longer bothered by the age difference, seeming to enjoy the memories.

They'd fallen into an easy friendship. Easy except for those moments at night when he'd say goodnight and leave her house, where he'd stand by the door for a few minutes afterwards, wanting to say many unsaid things, wishing for the time back, wondering if she was standing inside, just on the other side of the door, thinking the same things.

He wondered sometimes when she'd look at him and he could only think of those days at the lake house.

He went up to the birthing center to pick her up for lunch on a day Scott had cleared the calendar at work.

Scott's reason for doing so became obvious when he, too, stepped into the waiting room where Sam sat surrounded by pregnant women.

"What are you doing here?," Scott asked, grinning and spotting his brother immediately.

Sam watched him warily. "Well, the better question is what are *you* doing here?" He indicated the very disturbing diagrams and pictures on the walls.

"Pregnant wife, remember?," he said, pointing back towards the exam rooms. "Excused myself to go use the restroom... but I really just wanted to avoid the conversation. Have you been listening to any of the talk between Marie and Faith? It gets kind of gross."

Sam considered this. "I stop listening when the topic of conversation is Marie's body. Honestly, Scott."

"Well, can't fault you there," Scott murmured. "Marie wants to bypass the hospital gig on this one. Very nearly talked me into a home birth, so when she found out what Faith does, she started coming here." Scott smiled. "Which is why you're here. To see Faith."

Sam nodded. "Yeah."

"So, when are you going to finally make a move, Sam? Marie and I are placing bets on when this Sam and Faith thing is finally going to happen --"

And the door opened, and Faith and Marie stepped out, in the middle of a conversation.

"Which is probably why your milk supply has been down," Faith concluded, then stopped abruptly when she saw the men.

Their presence didn't deter Marie from speaking, though. "That's a relief," she said. "And the pressure and the heaviness, Scott?" She turned to her husband. "Faith says it's just... how did you say it, Faith?"

"Um," Faith said, looking over to Sam with a smile, then back to Marie, "just pressure on your cervix as your body readjusts to pregnancy. It can happen, especially when you get pregnant so quickly after your last delivery."

"Who knew, right?," Marie said, smiling at Scott and wrapping her arms around him.

"Pressure on the cervix," Scott said. "Fascinating."

"Yeah," Marie laughed. "Wondered why you disappeared after your bathroom break. Was it to avoid the conversation, or was it because of Sam?"

"Oh, it wasn't to avoid anything," he said. "I just love, love, love hearing all about the intricacies of this pregnancy. And your cervix."

"Scott," she continued on, ignoring him, "Faith talked me through a whole bunch of exercises I can do to strengthen those muscles. May make delivery easier. And quick. Like your mother says her deliveries were." She looked to Faith. "Do you think Scott's mother worked out her cervix like that, too?"

"And now," Scott said, turning to Sam, "they're talking about our mother's cervix. Awesome."

"I'm not even sure what that is," Sam muttered, his face blazing as Faith glanced over at him.

"Well, maybe Faith can explain it to you," Scott said, kissing Marie.

"Did you tell him the good news?," Marie murmured, smiling brightly at her husband.

"Oh, I'm sorry, was that good news?," he asked, laughing.

"The best news of your life," she said. "It's a girl, Sam!"

"Congratulations," Sam said, trading a smile with Faith over this.

"I'm not even sure what to do with that," Scott said.

"You'll figure it out as we go along," Marie said to him. "And we need to get back home. Mrs. Jones from Sunday school is watching Nate and will completely ignore him when Wheel of Fortune comes on."

"Wheel of Fortune," Scott murmured. "See you later, guys."

And as he and Marie left, talking animatedly about the baby, Faith turned to Sam. "Come on back with me to my office," she said, leading him that way. "I need to close out a few things, then we can get going --"

And a flustered, grinning woman with glasses on her head and papers under her arms, papers in her hands, and papers on the ground behind her came up to them as she made her way down the hallway. "Faith, dear, are you taking a lunch break today?"

"Yes, Elaine," Faith said with a small nod. "A short one. But I'm getting out while I can."

"Smart girl," Elaine murmured. Then, she looked to Sam. "Well, hello. Which little mother do you belong to?"

Sam raised his eyebrows at this. "Um... ma'am?"

"Your wife," she clarified. "I can help you find the right exam room if you --"

"Oh, he's with me," Faith said. "I mean, not with me, but --"

"Sam," he said, holding out his hand to the woman. "Sam Huntington."

Elaine smiled at him, even as Faith followed up with, "Yes, my... friend."

"Oh, lovely," Elaine cooed. "How did you meet our sweet Faith?"

And Sam glanced over at Faith, as she looked up at him with a smile in her eyes. "Uh, well, we knew each other years ago," he said. "Grew up together."

"Really?," Elaine asked. "You look... well, quite older than her."

He did. He knew this. He watched as Faith visibly flushed at this.

"Elaine," Faith began. But Elaine carried on.

"Wonderful, though," she said. "And what is it that you do, Sam?"

"Kind of in between careers at the moment," he said. "I build houses with my brother."

"That must be hard work," she noted. "Kind of like delivering babies. Watching something beautiful take place by the work of your hands. New homes, new families. Same line of business as Faith then, huh?" She smiled over at Faith. "And what did you do before?"

"I was a Marine," he said.

"A... Marine?," Elaine asked, confusion on her face. Then, realization. "Oh! The service! Combat, killing people... that kind of thing."

Sam's eyes narrowed just a little at this, at the implication in what she'd just said and the boldness in her saying it at all. "Well, yes."

Faith bit her lip at this, even as Elaine recoiled just a bit. "Oh. Well. That's... not like building a house. Or delivering a baby. Nothing about life involved in war and --"

"Elaine," Faith said with some authority to her voice, "I'm taking lunch now."

And the two women traded a silent look. Elaine gave her a tight grin, even as she put her glasses back on and pulled out one of the files that she carried under her arm.

"Well, okay," she said, smiling up at Sam. "Nice meeting you, dear," she said before scurrying down the hall, even as Faith reached back for Sam's hand and pulled him to her office, shutting the door behind them.

"Well," he said, holding her hand in both of his now. "That was... interesting."

Faith rolled her eyes. "You would think that given this ministry she's running, the conservative bent of her theology and all," Faith hissed, "that she would be more conservative politically as well. But... she's not, obviously." She met his eyes. "I'm sorry for that."

"For her pacifist political views?," Sam grinned, squeezing her hand.

"For her inability to keep her mouth shut," Faith clarified... still holding his hand.

Sam shrugged, not caring a bit since it had given him this opportunity to stand here with her like this. "Can't have a parade welcoming back the veteran everywhere I go, I guess."

"But still," she said, "that was uncalled for. And I'm apologizing on her clueless behalf."

"I appreciate that," he said softly.

"She's a good woman," Faith said. "And there's good work that goes on here. Even if I don't agree with every ideology she has." She took a breath before letting go of his hand and making her way around the desk. "So, what are we eating today?"

"I was thinking Mexican," he said.

"And now I'm thinking you're a genius," she said, smiling at him.

Well, he loved hearing that. He'd spent part of the morning in class then part in the library working on a paper for his English class, barely refraining from banging his head on the table in frustration.

He knew that in this world, a degree of some sort made you someone. He was nearly the oldest in his family, and yet, he was behind all of his siblings in this regard. They were all being heralded as accomplished by the world's standards with their educations, their careers, their aspirations that fit in with what was considered enough in terms of achievement and worth.

And Sam was struggling to get through a class where all of his classmates were barely legal adults, and he couldn't even write a paper. He knew what he wanted to say, but it could never come out written like he intended it.

Kind of like how he had so many things he wanted to say to Faith and couldn't, because she needed to heal, all these months, all this time...

"Well," he managed, "not sure about that genius part. I can't seem to get a paper written for Freshman Composition."

She looked up at him from the laptop she was working on shutting down. "How long have you been working on it?"

"Two weeks," he said. "It's due next week, and it's not going well." He sighed. "It's like being back in high school, struggling through it."

"I could read it," she said. "I could help. I made great grades in English."

She likely made great grades in everything. "Really?," he asked.

"Yeah," she said. "Is it saved somewhere online? I could read it later, then you could come over tonight, and we'll work on it."

That sounded like a great idea. Paper or not, any excuse to spend more time with her was great. So, he found what he'd written online, sent it to her, and smiled as she promised to have some notes for him tonight, closing her laptop and letting him lead her out of her office as she began asking how his day had gone so far.

She had her feet in his lap that night, and they were laughing.

They'd been laughing for the past half hour, as Faith had gone over his paper, a red pen in hand.

"Sam," she said, giggling, as she fanned out the pages in front of her, "it's like English isn't even your first language!"

She'd struggled to understand it earlier, as she'd read it alone without him, and as soon as he got to her house that evening, he'd explained it ten times better verbally than he'd written it. She couldn't understand the disconnect.

"I'm a poor writer," he said, grinning at her. "I told you that --"

"The ideas are great," she said, studying the notes she'd made. "Really deep, well thought out... or what I can understand of it. But the writing is really distracting. We're going to be here all night editing this."

He didn't seem at all upset by the mention of spending more time with her, working through this. "I'm dyslexic," he said. "You're lucky that it's not worse."

She grew silent, even as he continued to laugh at himself... so silent that he looked up at her, concern in his eyes.

"What?," he asked.

And she felt remorse that she'd laughed at all, knowing that this wasn't his fault, writing like this, struggling like this. She'd spent her whole life trying to be so perfect, and she'd learned, through the breakup of her engagement, through her hard adjustments to Elaine Charles and the busy center, through all the changes that had come so suddenly... well, that she needed to leave some room for her imperfections. Being honest about her own failings, her own weaknesses, had given her more grace towards others, more apathy...

And with Sam, there was more tenderness. To the adjustments he had made, certainly, in coming back to the US, in all that he was trying to redefine about himself, in all that he hadn't shared with her about his past.

"I'm sorry," she said. "I wasn't laughing at you."

"I didn't think you were, Faith," he said. "I'm laughing at myself. I'm thirty-four, and I can hardly pass Freshman Composition." He smiled at this. "Maybe college isn't for everyone."

"Oh, you'll pass it," she said with certainty. "I'm going to edit every last thing you have to write for that class. You're going to make an A, Sam."

"Thank you," he grinned.

"But," she said. "You're right. College isn't for everyone. And if you're doing this just because everyone thinks you need to... well, you don't." She took a breath. "Everyone at the church, except for my parents, thought that I needed to marry Craig, and you see how wrong they were."

She was surprised to hear herself admit this, especially as Sam watched her with interest. But if she had learned anything in these months since the breakup, in these moments spent with Sam, it was that she was much happier now, more content, more certain of who she was in Christ, than she had been in the years she'd spent in a relationship with Craig. She was more content in being who she was, rather than trying to be who she thought she had to be.

There was something to be said for that.

"I'm not sure if anyone expects it," Sam said, leaning his head back on the sofa and biting his lip as they watched one another. "It was just the logical next step after I came back home."

And she knew it was personal, all that he hadn't said, but she felt close enough to him now that she thought he might share it with her. And so she mentioned it finally, after wondering for so long.

"You never told me why you left the Marines."

"It was time," Sam sighed, smiling over at her sadly.

"I remember the stories you told at the lake house that summer," she said. "Impressive career with the Marines, being a hero – all very exciting stuff to a sixteen year old who had never been anywhere too far from home."

"It was exciting," Sam said softly. "And when I went back, they deployed me... to some places that weren't as exciting."

He looked down at her feet, his hands running over them softly, something distant in his eyes. "I was enthusiastic and optimistic about it all. Certainly at the lake house, before I left, you know?"

She remembered. "Yeah," she said.

"And then," he sighed, "it just..."

He said nothing for a long moment.

"Sam?," Faith said softly, touching his arm.

He looked over at her. "It was hard," he said. "Not the work but the emotional aspect of it. And I told myself, you know, that I just needed to man up and keep on... and I did, for a long while. Until I wasn't sure who I was anymore. And I had given my time, had given more than most give, and decided when it came time to re-enlist that it was okay if I left, gave myself time to heal, and figured out who I was now."

She said nothing for a long while, then reached over and touched his face softly. He caught her hand in his after a moment and held it in his own.

"That makes sense," she said softly. "And I can understand. I had wondered, Sam. I prayed for you, a lot of the time, all those years you were there."

And she silently prayed for him now, even as he watched her and took a breath to tell her more.

He could believe it, that she had prayed for him, even as he was remembering how her face had been in his thoughts, in his heart, half a world away. How her words, her teenage words, about Christ had ministered to his heart, even then.

She watched him with tenderness, her hand still in his, her eyes warm with affection for him.

He could see that. Even with the other images in his mind, the disturbing recollections, and the painful memories, he could still see her affection.

He could still see her.

"You know, there are seasons," he said. "Seasons where faith is easy, and devotion is second nature. And then, there are those seasons where it's really hard to see what God's doing and why He's walking us through some really difficult times. But I've held onto the truth that He's not just watching from the sidelines. That He's walking through every one of those difficult times with us, even when our faith is small, and that He's doing it because what we're walking through is going to make us more faithful, more devoted, more hopeful in Him, in what He offers apart from our broken world, our broken selves, you know?"

He had seen it. A broken world, hopelessness... hope still in Christ.

She nodded at this. "I haven't been through much," she admitted.

"But you see people who are going through more than they think they can bear," he said, recalling the stories she'd shared with him about Erica, who even now he prayed for with her. "All those babies lost. Where is God in that? He's got to be right there with her, hurting for the loss as well."

"Even though He could have stopped it?," Faith whispered.

"Even though," Sam responded softly. "And we don't have the answers. Never will on this side of things. And I don't have the answers for that, nor for all that I've experienced, but I know that

God leads us out of seasons like that, into better seasons, and that we can look back and see what He's done and know, without any doubt, that He's used every tear, every heartache, for eternity, to give us hope for something more."

Faith wiped away a tear at this. "That's true. And so good, Sam. Thank you."

And Sam thought about how, for the first time since leaving the Marines, he felt like he was finally in a new season as well, considering what God had brought him through, how even he could offer hope to others and a newer, stronger faith in Christ because of it all.

And maybe something more, with this woman who even now, understood his heart because she had been there with him, all along.

She talked him into a trip down to the beach after church that next week.

His words had been playing through her mind. She'd shared some of them with Erica, had seen her encouraged in the light of his wisdom, and had prayed peace and a better season for her and this new child.

And as she thought through seasons, she'd considered that perhaps it was time to move into a better season herself.

It had been months since Craig. She felt at home here finally... at home with Sam.

So she was okay with whatever happened next.

He had no idea what she'd been thinking as they'd peeked in the shops in the small coastal town, as they'd eaten a huge seafood dinner, as Sam had walked her down to the beach, where she frowned at the brown water.

"Florida is better," she said to him.

He'd grinned at this. "Better but far away. But this is nice, too... right?"

And she heard what he was implying in the look he gave her, in the way he reached out for her hand and laced his fingers through hers. He'd been patient, careful, thoughtful...

"Yeah," she said, meeting his eyes. "It's very nice."

He smiled, looked over the water again, then turned to her with clear intent in his eyes.

"What?," she asked.

"I like you," he said simply.

She could feel herself blush at this. All grown up. Still blushing. "Well, one would hope, with all the time we've been spending together."

He grinned at this. "You made a big deal about it, though. Months ago. Eons ago."

"It's felt like decades since then," she sighed, feeling precisely the same way he was feeling. Or so she assumed, judging by the way he moved closer to her.

"Yeah," he murmured. "You said that I didn't really know you, that we didn't really know each other. But all this time later? I feel like I do. And you know what?"

"You like me?," she asked, a smile playing at the corners of her mouth.

"Yeah," he said. "And I've decided something."

"What have you decided?"

"I want more," he said.

She took a breath at this, thrilled to hear the words, still so conflicted, hearing her own warnings about the lake house...

"You want... more," she said.

"Yes."

"I think we have a lot," she said. "I mean, I spend more time with you than I spend with anyone else, honestly. So, you're getting my time."

"Yeah," he said. "And I want that, obviously."

"And you have my friendship, of course," she said. "I figure I'm one of the best friends you have, Sam."

"The very best," he affirmed.

Wonderful. So wonderful.

"And there's my extensive knowledge on all things relating to pregnancy and childbirth, which any normal, single man would find helpful," she said with a laugh in her voice. "I mean, really."

198

"Yes," he smiled. "There's that."

"What more could you want?," she asked.

"This," he said softly, taking her hand gently, pressing a kiss to her palm, then putting her hand on his chest, moving to do the same with her other hand. "And this."

She held her breath, even as she ran her hands up the rest of his chest, over his shoulders, and up and into his hair, as he pulled her closer. She'd imagined doing this so many times...

"This, too," he murmured, putting his arms around her waist, drawing her even closer.

"That's something," she murmured back.

"Something," he whispered, his lips inches from hers.

"A lot," she managed, her eyes falling shut, melting against him. "It's a lot, Sam."

"Too much?," he asked softly, his hands moving gently on her back, the feel of his breath on her cheek.

"Oh, no," she sighed. "Just right... just... just perfect."

"Enough?," he asked.

"No," she breathed. "I want more, too."

And he gave it to her, putting his mouth to hers and kissing her at last.

CHAPTER SEVEN

Marie invited her over for lunch that weekend.

Sam was reluctantly going hunting with his brothers. Reluctantly not because he didn't enjoy these trips with them but reluctantly because it took him away from her. They'd been together every day since they'd become "more," in Sam's words, and she'd dreaded the separation as much as he had, as she spent every waking moment with him or thinking about him or reliving his kisses...

But still. She assured him that she'd spend most of the time working, and that when she was on call, she and Marie would probably spend a good portion of the weekend together discussing cervixes, labor, contractions, breast milk, and any number of other topics that he would have no interest in anyway.

She hadn't guessed that lunch with Marie would include all of the sisters-in-law. Apparently when the men went away, the women all got together as well.

They were all talking, all over one another, all at the same time, when she walked in. She recognized all of them from the funeral but couldn't recall having formally met any of them before, with the exception of Marie, of course. And Savannah, who sat in their midst with a tablet, around which they all sat and pointed.

As soon as she shut the door behind her, all of them stared up at her.

Faith was tempted to look behind her to see just what they were staring at so intently, certain that it couldn't be her.

Marie smiled at her and made her way over to the door, leading Faith in after a quick hug. "I'm so glad you came over! Savannah's showing us some pictures she took at the end of the summer and resisting our suggestions."

"Because they suck," Savannah said very simply, rolling her eyes. "Hey, Faith."

"Do you and Savannah already know each other?," Marie asked, as Faith took the seat next to her.

"Oh, yeah," Savannah said, glancing up and smiling. "We grew up at church together for a while, of course, then we met up again years later for spring break once. Which is where, I believe, you got reacquainted with my favorite brother."

"Favorite?," Marie said. "You told me Scott's your favorite."

"Yeah, well, I've said the same to every other woman here, about their husbands." She looked at Faith and lowered her voice. "But seriously. Sam is my favorite. Because he stays out of my business."

Faith smiled at this and looked around at the other three women who were watching her quietly. One of them smiled brightly at her and held out her hand enthusiastically. "I'm Jennie," she trilled. "I'm married to Sean, the oldest."

"Sean," Faith murmured. "The one who did part of the funeral message?"

"Yes," Jennie beamed. "Didn't he do great? I told him that he really left people feeling positive and upbeat about the whole thing."

"As upbeat and positive as one can be at a funeral," another one of the women said, watching Jennie with some concern.

"Always hope," Jennie said to her. "There is *always* hope. *Especially* in death. If you're in Christ."

"Well... yeah, but it was a funeral, Jennie," she said.

"I know that!"

The woman shook her head and turned to Faith with a smile. "I'm Abby. I'm married to Stuart, the other guy who preached and probably didn't leave everyone feeling positive and upbeat."

Faith nodded, remembering the more sobering truths and the overabundance of Scripture that one of Sam's younger brothers had given.

"Still encouraging, though," she said. "So much Scripture. So much truth from Scripture."

"That's all Stu has," Abby noted, smiling. She turned to the woman next to her, "And this is –"

"Chelsea," she said, reaching out and squeezing Faith's hand. "I've got the youngest brother, Seth. And I'm actually the oldest woman here. Ironic, huh?"

"Everyone else went for younger women," Abby said, looking back down at Savannah's tablet.

"Some much younger than the rest," Jennie noted quietly. All the sisters-in-law looked at her reproachfully. "Well, I'm just saying..."

Before Faith could take any offense at what she wasn't even sure was an offensive comment, Abby looked back up at her with a smile. "And all of our children are with our mother-in-law. *All* of them."

"Yeah," Jennie grinned. "That's the best part of this weekend. Jess said she could handle the whole lot. Rented a van to get her through, had Nick cancel all of his projects, and is likely right now pulling all of her hair out." She smiled. "Awesome mother-in-law."

"They're all there?," Faith asked, wondering at the insanity of so many small children all under one roof.

"All except Nate," Chelsea said. "Because Nate lives connected to Marie."

Sure enough, between greeting Faith and joining the group at the table, Marie had managed to pick her son up from the pack-n-play in the living room and was even now nursing him while eating a snack herself.

"You should get him on formula," Abby said to her. "I mean, I know it's not as good, but —"

Jennie gasped out loud. "Abby!," she said, scolding.

"Here we go," Savannah muttered.

"Just think of all the benefits of nursing exclusively," Jennie continued on. "Aside from what good it can do for babies, obviously, think of the benefit to the mother. Hormone regulation, less risk of cancer, helps you lose the pregnancy weight faster..."

And all eyes lifted to Marie, who was halfway through a handful of cookies. "What? This extra weight I'm carrying is because of the second pregnancy. I'd be tiny and cute otherwise, right?"

"You're cute as is," Chelsea grinned. "And while I agree with Jennie –"

"Thank you, Chelsea!"

"I think Abby was right to choose what worked for her and Stu," Chelsea concluded.

"And I preferred to keep my sanity and let Stu feed the babies at night when I had to be at work early the next day," she said.

"And for the love of all that is good and right in the world, *please* don't start the debate about working moms versus stay-at-home moms," Savannah groaned. "If you do, I'm officially done with these get-togethers." She pointed the tablet towards Jennie. "What do you think about your hair in this one?"

Jennie studied the picture for a second. "Looks better than the other shading." Then, with a laugh in her voice, "Oh, Abby, look at Chance! He's standing just exactly like Stu is! Just like a little teensy weensy copy of him! So sweet!"

"Yeah," Abby murmured, smiling. "And he doesn't have a second head growing off of his neck because his mother fed him formula. Imagine that." She grinned up at Jennie.

"That he doesn't," Jennie answered, laughing.

"You two need to be nice to each other," Marie muttered. "And stop being such hurtful, vengeful, old biddies."

Abby and Jennie frowned at this, while Savannah shook her head with a smile.

"What?," Marie asked.

"Well, that was a little rude," Abby said. "We're both over here laughing, and you just --"

"I'm pregnant," Marie said. "I get a pass for saying things like that because I'm pregnant, right?"

"Your house, your rules," Chelsea noted. "Are you like this to everyone or just women engaging in neverending Mommy wars?"

"Hey!," Jennie and Abby exclaimed together.

Marie sighed. "I'm like this to Scott. Like, all the time, lately. I told him the other night that he was chewing his boerwoers too loudly."

"What's boerwoers?," Faith asked.

"It's amazing," Marie said. "But I overcooked it, and bless his heart, Scott was still eating it and acting like it was wonderful. And after I jumped all over him because he was chewing like a cow --"

"Eww," Savannah muttered.

"Well, he was," Marie murmured. "Gave me a headache. Everything gives me a headache lately with this pregnancy. I'm irritable, crabby, tired..."

"Only gets worse, you know," Jennie said, shaking her head. "I mean, you know how it is with a newborn. But at least you can sleep when he sleeps."

"Theoretically," Abby piped up.

"Yes, well," Jennie said, grinning. "Once you get the new baby in, there will be *no* sleeping either way because Nate will be up! And it'll take *forever* to get them on the same schedule. Trust me. Ezra and Nehemiah couldn't get it straight between the two of them before Esther came along, and then, before I could freak out about that, I was pregnant with Jonah! Not to be discouraging or anything, but I haven't slept in *years!*" She let out a nervous laugh at this.

"Thank you, Jennie, for that disturbing recollection of Bible characters and that horrifying testimony to the curse of motherhood," Savannah muttered.

"You're so welcome!," Jennie grinned. "And then, apart from the babies, there are all the problems you yourself incur after giving birth over and over and over again. Seriously, my jeans will never fit like they once did."

"At least you don't pee every time you cough," Abby noted. "And I've only been pregnant twice. I would need to wear adult diapers if I had another child."

"Eww," Savannah managed. "Chelsea, do you have anything to add to this discussion? Because my ovaries haven't completely shrunken up and withered away quite yet. A few more words, and I think you could seal their doom."

Chelsea smiled at her. "I won't say a word," she said. "But that's only because I don't want to scare Faith off completely."

"Faith is a midwife," Marie said, smiling over at her. "She's heard much worse."

Faith smiled. "Yes. All very... interesting," she said. "These kinds of conversations."

"Yes, well, hopefully they're all done," Savannah said, turning the tablet towards her. "What do you think of the picture, Faith?"

And Faith looked at it for a long moment. All of the Huntington brothers and Savannah, all the wives, all their children... and there was Sam, sitting to the side by himself, smiling, looking just a little different than the others.

"Beautiful," Faith murmured quietly.

"Savannah took it the week of the funeral," Chelsea said. "She's planning on putting together a book for her grandmother, her mother, her aunt, and her uncle, with old pictures from her grandparents' house as well."

"And she took pictures of all their families, too," Abby said. "Along with a giant picture of every descendant of Thomas Fisher."

"So many people," Faith said.

"And everyone managed to look happy in the picture," Jennie said, smiling. Then, softly, "Well, except for Sam. But he's been so messed up since coming back from —"

And she stopped talking as all the sisters-in-law turned their attention to her. "Oh, I'm sorry," she whispered. "Are we not supposed to talk about how Sam went crazy?"

"Seriously, Jennie?," Savannah asked, shooting her a look.

"What? You all remember how he was before," she said. "Or at least those of us who knew him before."

And Faith had been one of those. Sam had been more easygoing, more carefree before Afghanistan certainly, but there was something more to him now, even with the sadness. A new depth, a greater faith, a sincerity in Christ, and a stronger hold on Him. Faith had seen it because he'd let her see it. She doubted that he let many people in like that.

She was thankful for all that he had shown her.

"Well," Marie said, attempting to lighten the tension, "he certainly seems happier these days than he has in all the time I've known him."

"That's true," Jennie said. "All praise to God. We've been praying for him."

"We all have," Abby affirmed.

"And some of us have been praying very specifically that as God works out all that he's going through, that He would bring the right woman to him," Chelsea added, smiling at Faith.

"And," Marie added, reaching over to touch Faith's hands, "some of us have been praying even more specifically for you, Faith. And here you are."

"Here I am," Faith said, looking around as the other women smiled at her, imagining herself here in this group for years to come.

Nights on call for Faith meant staying in. And staying in meant eating at the house, sitting around talking, and hours and hours of long, slow kisses.

Sam loved nights on call. He figured he'd love them even more once they were married.

That was the plan, of course. His plan. As soon as he could ask her father for his blessing, he was going to get down on one knee, tell her that she had brought so much joy to him, and ask her to be by his side forever.

"Sam," she murmured underneath his lips. "Sam, sweetheart?"

"Mmm," he murmured back, pulling her closer.

"I'm buzzing," she said, putting her lips back to his.

"Me, too," he smiled, kissing her again.

"My phone, Sam," she laughed. "On the side table. Could you hand it to me?"

He backed away with a smile. "Yeah," he said, reaching over to grab the phone, handing it to her even as he went back to kissing her neck.

"Sam," she said a second later, concern in her voice. "I've gotta take this."

And so, he sat up next to her, as she dialed the number. "Who is it?," he asked.

"Erica," she murmured. "Thirty weeks. Sounds like she's in labor."

He watched as Faith bit her lip, holding the phone to her ear. "Erica," she said, her voice tense. "I just got your text. Tell me what's going on."

She listened intently for a long while, then took a breath, her eyes roaming around the living room nervously.

"Okay," she said calmly, though her face was panicked. "I'm going to need you to do something for me, Erica," she said, certainty and serenity in her voice, even as she stood and went over to her purse. "I need you to go to the medical center, not the birthing center." She listened for a moment. "I know. I had my heart set on it, too. And I could do the delivery at thirty-two weeks myself, but my concern is for the baby, obviously. I want the baby to come in a place where they can get him to the NICU." She closed her eyes, then opened them to look at Sam, grief on her face, even as she pulled him closer and put her head on his chest. "Thirty weeks," she said with assurance, even though her shoulders sagged and he could feel her pulse beginning to speed up, "isn't impossible. Not at all. The survival rate is good."

And she listened again, holding Sam tighter, even as he kissed the top of her head.

"It was nothing you did," she said confidently. "You did so well, Erica. You're such a good mother. Already. And this is a good day." Another pause. "I'll be there soon, okay?"

She didn't say much on the drive to the medical center.

When she hung up with a very distraught Erica, she'd looked up at Sam helplessly, and he'd wordlessly led her out to his truck, where she got in and he drove her to her patient.

"I wish I could do more," she said into the silence.

He acknowledged this with a nod. "You've done a lot for her."

"Not everything," she said. "She's so scared."

"It won't end up like it did before," he said.

"No," she said, looking at him. "Not a miscarriage. This will be a birth. Though, what will happen past that is up for question, isn't it?" She sighed. "What was wrong with the other babies? Do you think that's what's causing her to go into labor now? Did I miss something in all of those checkups? Did I not get something right? Did I —"

"Hey," Sam said, a hand to her knee. "You have to let go of this idea that you can do what only God can do."

"I know," she said, weakly.

"I know you live your life being better than everyone else at almost everything," he said. "But some things even you can't control, Faith. And that's okay."

And she agreed with him, putting her hand over his, praying for Erica and her baby as they continued driving.

Once they got there, she was told what she'd known, that while the hospital could appreciate all the prenatal work she'd done as Erica's midwife, she was, after all, a midwife, not an obstetrician, and they couldn't have her in the delivery room, especially with concerns for the infant.

So, she and Sam prayed in the waiting room. They prayed together, they prayed on their own, and they prayed silently as they sat and watched the doors, waiting for a word.

Seven hours later, it came. And Faith was allowed back to see Erica who was lying in the bed in recovery, shivering.

"Hey," Faith said, going into a mode that was more relational than professional, more nurturing than authoritative. "Congratulations, Mommy."

"You're here," Erica managed softly. "Jerry went to go check and see how the baby's doing." She bit her lip. "Faith, the baby is so tiny… and he wasn't even crying when they took him."

"They know what they're doing in the NICU," she said. "Pediatricians, pulmonologists, all checking him out, right now, getting him what he needs." She took a breath, putting her hand to Erica's forehead. "All while you recover back here on your own. You've been through a lot today, too."

"Yeah," she said, weakly. Faith pulled the blanket from the end of the bed and pulled it up around her shoulders, assessing by touch alone that the fever was normal as was the look of shock on Erica's face.

"Are you still hurting?," she asked.

"Uh… yeah," she said. "Not like I was, but some. I didn't let them give me anything."

Faith smiled. "Good for you," she murmured. "Though there would have been no shame in doing so."

"I know," Erica said. "But I wanted to experience it all. And, wow. I did."

Faith laughed softly. "I'm proud of you. Wish I had been here to encourage you, but I'm sure Jerry did a great job with that. And the OB on call, of course."

"They were great," Erica said.

"Once they get you to your room for the night," Faith said, "you need to start pumping. They'll be able to use the milk in the NICU eventually, and it'll help with the cramping you're feeling."

"Will it make it less intense?"

"It'll make it more intense," Faith grinned. "But that's what your body needs. Everything functioning the way it's designed to. God made it so your sweet baby could help with your recovery while you care for him."

Erica took a deep breath, tears springing to her eyes in the silence that filled the recovery room. "Where is God in this, Faith?," she whispered.

"In the birth of your baby," Faith said confidently, "after all these weeks of praying for it to be just as perfect as you wanted it to be."

Erica nodded. "I should be thankful that he's here. That we even got to this point. But there are no guarantees. We don't know that this will turn out differently at all. And... I just don't know where God is in this."

And this had been the question all along for this woman. Where was God? Where had God been all along?

"Right here," Faith whispered. "He's right here. With you. And with your son."

"It was going to be perfect this time," Erica cried. "Everything was going to be different... perfect."

And Faith put a hand to her face comfortingly, tears in her own eyes, and whispered, "It doesn't have to be perfect to still be amazing."

Elaine Charles came into the waiting room while Sam was there, waiting for Faith, sitting next to the coffee and breakfast he'd picked up for her in the cafeteria.

"Hello, Mrs. Charles," he said uncertainly, standing, wondering if the woman would recognize him.

She was flustered, like normal. At least like the few occasions where he'd seen her before. She appraised him quickly then breathed a sigh.

"Oh, goodness, there you are," she said. "Which means that Faith is here, right?"

Sam nodded. "Yeah, she went back about ten minutes ago."

"I lost my phone!," Elaine shrieked. "Totally lost it in my kitchen, which was no big deal because Faith was the one on call, of course. And then, this morning, I went looking for it, and would you believe where I found it, dear?"

Sam raised his eyebrows. "Uh... no. Where did you find it?"

"In the freezer!," she exclaimed. "What was I thinking when I put it there? I have no idea. I was probably looking for ice cream or something. Anyway," she said, heaving a great sigh. "I found it, and it still worked, all praise to God, and I saw the messages. Thirty weeks!"

"Yeah," Sam said. "Faith's been here most of the night. And the baby was born about an hour ago. In the NICU, obviously."

Elaine dabbed at her eyes with a tissue. "This work is so hard sometimes," she said. "By God's grace we'll survive it, but nights like tonight? You just can't do anything."

"That's what Faith always says," Sam said. "But she says it's rewarding."

"Yes," Elaine said. "And that's what we've got to remember. Work like this is rewarding, even still. Not even like work." She watched him for a moment. "What is it that you do for a living again, dear?"

And Sam was about to remind her of Scott's business, of the fact that he was in school, when she interrupted him.

"Oh, that's right!," she exclaimed, her hand to her hair absent-mindedly. "In between careers. Military... and something else I can't remember. And Faith. So many years of study and hard work and... brilliant." She glanced over at Sam again, her mind obviously in so many places. "You know?"

And Sam couldn't explain why this stung, but in his mind he remembered Faith, laughing over the paper for his English class, then going to work correcting his childish mistakes.

She hadn't been laughing at him, of course. She'd said it. And it hadn't bothered him then. Really, it hadn't.

But now, watching as he was assessed, as Faith was assessed, as he came up lacking... well, it did. His mind went back to class, where he always felt like the dumbest one there, where he felt judged for not being as far along as everyone else, when he'd been working his entire life towards a career that he left because it was all too much.

Before he could say anything else, Faith came out of the maternity ward, with an adoring glance his way and words on her lips, as Elaine swept her into a bear hug, and they began talking through terms Sam didn't know, didn't understand, and likely never would.

Because he wasn't like them. And though he was working towards a normal life, his normal life would probably never be as important or meaningful as...

... well, as Faith's.

Elaine had told her that she *had* to take a week off.

Erica was doing well and had been discharged from the hospital, even though she spent most days up in the NICU with her son who was, by all appearances and reports, thriving and growing stronger more and more every day. Erica's faith had increased through the trial, and she'd had hopeful words for the first time ever on her last checkup with Faith just the week before.

Sam had been uncharacteristically quiet as they'd driven back to the house after that long night, but Faith had chalked it up to exhaustion. And when he'd get quiet when they were alone together, she'd assume it was more of the same with Sam, all the memories from combat, all the things that weighed him down. So, she sat with him in silence, knowing that no words were sometimes the best to offer, willing him out of whatever he was battling.

They'd been talking through plans for her week off. She'd pulled him out of the silence he'd been in by suggesting that she tag along to his classes in the mornings, spending her time in the library while he went to his lectures, then to wherever he was working with Scott, helping out by handing him things.

She'd done plenty of that already at his house, on those odd weekends where she had a few hours to herself that she'd always choose to spend with him. They'd make an afternoon of it, building the house, small piece by small piece, watching it come together as they talked through nothing, anything... everything.

"We should take a road trip," he said, talking through the possibilities of her week away from work. "Who needs school when you can take a road trip?"

"To where?," she asked, lacing her fingers through his, kissing the back of his hand.

JENN FAULK

"Back up to the lake house," he said. "We can take Scott, Marie, and Nathan, too. So we're well chaperoned and all."

"Mmm," Faith murmured. "My parents sold the lake house. Years ago."

He groaned his disappointment. "Why didn't you tell me?"

"It was just a place," she answered. "The significance was what happened there. Not the place."

"The significance was you," Sam said simply, smiling, back from the dark corner he'd retreated into.

She was thankful to have him back.

"I really like you," she whispered to him, right before she leaned in to kiss him.

He kissed her back. "And I really love you," he said, his hand on her face. It was the first time he'd said it, and Faith didn't miss the significance of it.

She seemed to shine ten times brighter as she considered this. "Me, too, Sam." Then, touching his face, biting her lip as she considered it. "Hey, let's forget the road trip. Let's fly instead."

"Fly where?," he asked.

"Florida," she said.

He moved so as to look at her more closely. "Your first trip back since moving here, huh?"

"Yeah. Come home with me, Sam. Seriously, blow off classes. No big deal, right?" And she grinned at the remembrance of when he'd said the very same thing to her all those years ago at the lake house.

"No big deal," he affirmed, remembering it as well. "You really want me to go with you?"

"Of course I do," she smiled. "I want you to meet my family. Even though, well, you've known my parents longer than I have."

He smiled. "Yeah. I will, though. Yeah."

"No big deal," she smiled against his lips again.

"No big deal," he laughed.

And she knew, even as she kissed him again, that everything about all of this was a very, very big deal.

CHAPTER EIGHT

He hadn't been on a plane since coming back to Texas for the final time, after years of traveling to places where he dreaded the arrival, where he knew things wouldn't be easy.

But this time was different. He was looking forward to getting there, Faith's hand in his, her eyes reassuring as she'd smile over at him.

It was more of the same when the cab finally pulled up to the modest house tucked into a cul-de-sac in a busy neighborhood. She assessed him one last time calmly, anxiously, clearly a little nervous.

"Don't think they'll like me?," he asked.

"Oh, no, it's not that," she said. "They've loved you your whole life. I just want everything to be perfect."

And while he figured that nothing in life is ever perfect, he hoped it would be for her sake. For his own sake. For both of them.

"It will be," he murmured, leaning in for a kiss.

Just a few moments later, they made their way inside, where Faith called out, "Mom? Dad? Gracie?"

Around the same corner at the same moment, two blonde heads popped out. Sam recognized them both instantly and smiled.

Faith's mother was on the phone and held up a finger to the newcomers, apology in her eyes. "Well, I was just making sure," she said. "Wanted to know where you were, just in case. It's not safe to be driving across the country when no one even knows where you are, you know." A pause. "Okay, well, Grant's sister knew. But I didn't, Maddie, and you know me. Have to be in the big middle of everyone's business."

Gracie, who had been watching Sam with a smile, nodded at the truth of this, even as she finally closed the distance between her and Faith, pulling her sister in for a hug.

"Gracie," Faith said softly. "I've missed you."

"Well, of course, you have," Gracie laughed. She glanced over at Sam. "Hey, Sam, remember me? Faith's cuter, smarter sister?"

"I do, actually," he said, taking the hand she held out to him. "How are you, Gracie?"

She grinned, watching the two of them. "Just great. Sorry that Mom's on the phone. It's totally distracting her now from being a great hostess, of course, but it sure didn't stop her from peeking out the window with me earlier, where we saw the two of you making out in the driveway, and —"

"Gracie," Faith murmured, warning in her voice.

Gracie grinned even wider. "Just surprised, Faith, that's all." She looked up at Sam. "She doesn't get this way, you know. Like *ever*, Sam. So, I'm figuring that you're –"

"Okay, Maddie," their mother continued on, still on the phone, coming into the room with them at last. "Speaking of other people's business, I need to let you go. Faith just brought home… well, *him*." A pause. "Yes! Him!" Another pause as she smiled. "I'll tell you the details later. Just like you'll tell me all of your details, okay? Okay. Be careful. Let me know when you get back to Fort Worth. Love you, too. Bye."

And she turned off the phone and handed it to Gracie, her eyes immediately going to Sam.

"Sam Huntington," she said appreciatively, reaching up to hug him. "Welcome to Florida."

"Thanks, Mrs. Hayes," he murmured, his hand on her back, glancing over at Faith who watched him with a smile.

"None of that Mrs. Hayes stuff," she said. "I think you're old enough now to call me Chloe."

"Chloe," he said. "Thanks for having me."

"Oh, we've been looking forward to it for a long, long while," she said. "Longer than you would believe probably."

And before he could say anything to this, she looked to Faith and moved to hug her. "I was just on the phone with Madison Smith," she said, embracing her daughter, then holding her out to look at her. "Your hair looks great, by the way. Still not coloring it?"

"No need," Faith said.

"Dodged your father's gray genes," Chloe smiled. And, glancing at Sam, she added, "And Sam's not gray at his age, so your kids will hit the gene lottery on that one, unless --"

"Mom," Faith warned.

"Unless," Gracie piped up, ignoring her sister and smiling up at Sam, "the recessive Hayes genes make an appearance. Been coloring my hair since I was seventeen, Sam." She gasped. "Mom, Sam and Faith's babies could get Uncle Beau's bald Thibideaux genes, and --"

"I know, right?!," Chloe gasped right back. "I thought about that! And it would --"

"Oh. My," Faith managed, looking horrified.

"I know!," Gracie exclaimed. "Can you imagine?! Bald babies are one thing, but when a boy is starting to lose hair on his head just as quickly as he's growing hair on his back, just like Uncle Beau, it's --"

"I meant the talk," Faith interrupted. "About Sam and babies..." She looked up at him. "I'm so sorry."

He wasn't. "You probably heard worse when you hung out with my sisters-in-law."

And Faith blushed at this, making him wonder at what they all talked about when they got rid of their men –

"So," Faith said, trying to change the subject. "Maddie. On the phone. How's Maddie?"

"In love," Chloe grinned. "Head over heels in love. Came out here to pack up everything so she can be with this guy, Grant, and just as she was getting ready to leave, who should show up, after jumping on a last minute flight to come and make his intentions known, but –"

"Grant," Faith and Gracie said together. Gracie grinned and added, "So predictable."

"It is," Chloe shrugged. "But still sweet. They left last night, have been driving since, and are almost back in Texas. And I had to call and make sure that they made it safely."

"You're a good mom like that," Faith answered. "Though not a good enough mom to show up to the airport. We had to take a cab."

"I know!," Chloe groaned. "I totally got the times all mixed up. Believe me, it was a shock to see you already here and out in the driveway!"

"And it was really, really shocking, like I've already mentioned, because that's where you and Sam were –"

"Gracie," Chloe interrupted, "let me see your phone again so I can call your dad and get him here!"

"Where is he?," Faith asked, moving them farther into the house.

"At the hospital," Chloe said. "Praying for someone as they go into surgery. Told me he'd be back in plenty of time, but that time was the wrong time, obviously, as you've already figured out, Faith."

"No big deal," Faith answered, glancing over at Sam with a smile. He felt the warmth of that smile from head to toe and reached out for her hand, smiling at her as well, nearly forgetting everyone else there.

"Just glad to be here," Faith said, joy in her voice.

And Chloe beamed at them both, the phone already back to her ear. "And we're so glad you are."

Dinner was over, but they all continued to sit around the table, where Gracie was, by all appearances, falling in love with Sam herself.

"Seriously?," she giggled at him.

"Seriously," he said, great amusement in his eyes. "There's a pattern there. Every multiple choice test. Natural pattern to the answers. You can figure it out if you think about it long enough."

Gracie sighed. "Where were you when I was nearly flunking out of every class my first semester of college?"

"Afghanistan, likely," he said. And Faith was surprised to see that he could say this with a smile even still.

"Academic probation, Sam," Gracie said to him. "That's what ended up happening to me. And I was pledging that semester, very nearly certain I wouldn't be initiated, all because I don't test well. I mean, I can learn the information, memorize everything, and know my stuff, but you put a test in front of me? And it all goes flip flying out the window."

"Me, too," Sam said. "It stinks, doesn't it?"

"Yes!," she exclaimed. "Do you enjoy your classes, at least?"

Faith wiped her mouth, waiting for him to launch into a discussion about how much good it was doing, getting this degree for the business he was growing with Scott. She smiled in anticipation of hearing it, her pride in what he was doing, even though it was a struggle.

"Not really," he confided to Gracie. "But that's life, right?"

"Preach it, brother," she said. "Just something to get through. But if I can do it, you can, too."

And before Faith could wonder at how Sam was shortchanging himself, offering this, and how he was refraining from talking about his goals and how college was a help, her father cut in.

"You stay pretty busy, then, huh?," he said, smiling. "School, work, church..."

From the moment her father had come home, going immediately to Sam, who he welcomed in warmly, they'd been talking about all that Sam spent his efforts and energy doing. As far as inquisitions went, it was less obvious than it could have been, but Faith still felt the scrutiny of what her father, her very accomplished, very capable father was asking. Or so she assumed it was scrutiny, based on how she regarded Sam nervously, hearing him just admit to a man with a PhD that he really didn't want an undergraduate degree at all.

The last man she'd brought home had been very different, obviously. She wondered if anyone was comparing the two of them. She was surprised to find that she cared either way.

"Yeah," Faith cut in before Sam could speak for himself. "And he's actually taking on more responsibility at the church. He was nominated to be a deacon last month." She smiled at him, even as he regarded her with just a hint of surprise.

He'd told her that he wasn't even sure he was going to be pursuing this. Faith had omitted that part.

"Oh, Sam, that's wonderful," her mother said. "I can see you serving well in that way."

"Thank you," he murmured. "I haven't decided officially whether or not I'm going to go through the process, though."

"Why is that?," her father asked, a question in his eyes.

And Faith took a breath, ready to explain this away, to make Sam sound better to the ears around the table, but before she could interrupt him again, Sam spoke up.

"I've been studying Scripture on it," he said. "My brother, Scott, has been nominated as well, and we've been studying together, really asking ourselves questions about whether or not this is a time in our lives when we can give our all to being there in that way in our church." He shrugged. "I mean, we do a lot of the work that deacons are called to even now, without the titles, but we know once we take on the positions that we'll be held to a higher standard. To a vow and a covenant promise to be more available than we are even now. And Scott," he smiled, "is well on his way to having a house full of children, so I think he has to be wise about where his time is invested. Can't serve others when your own children are starved for your time, you know."

Her father nodded at this. "Well said. And I really get that, more than you can probably imagine."

Sam nodded. "Well, you figured it out, sir. Obviously. And the proof is in the fruit of this family... your daughters."

And Faith watched him, glad to hear these words, knowing that he'd said the perfect thing, even as Gracie grinned at him.

"Obviously, right, Sam? Because we're totally awesome," Gracie affirmed.

"But you yourself, Sam," her father continued on, studying him. "Your time is more flexible than your brother's."

"Yes, sir," Sam said, glancing over at Faith... then looking her father straight in the eyes. "But I want to be careful, from the start of other obligations and joys God might be calling me towards, to be mindful of what should come first."

And his meaning was implicit, to Faith, at least, who felt him take her hand underneath the table and squeeze it in his.

It was also clear to her father, who smiled and nodded upon hearing it. "Very wise, Sam." He took a breath, raised his eyebrows at her mother, both of them smiling at one another, and said it again. "Very wise."

Her mother stood at her place rather abruptly with a euphoric glance over at Faith. "And now, the girls and I are going to get to clearing up all of this."

"Thank you for dinner," Sam said, standing in his place. "I can help clean up."

"Oh, no," she said, waving him away. "You and Stephen go out to the porch and enjoy our great weather. We'll be out there in a bit."

And Faith watched him as he gave her a confident smile and followed her father outside.

The weather was great.

Back home, it had already started getting colder, but here in Florida, they could sit out on the porch in shorts and imagine that they were in the midst of summer. Sam waited for Stephen to sit down before he lowered himself into the chair across from him.

"It was good of you to come all the way out here with Faith," Stephen noted, leaning back in his chair as he watched Sam.

"I was glad to do it," Sam said. "I wanted to speak with you, and I prefer doing this in person rather than over the phone."

Stephen smiled. "Speak to me about what, exactly?"

Sam swallowed, thinking about this. "I wanted to apologize," he said.

Stephen seemed to be caught off guard at this. "For what?"

And the guilt Sam had felt, the guilt that was just a memory now, returned as he thought about how he would feel with a daughter, a sixteen year old daughter, looking at the man who had seen her as more than he should have.

He wanted to make this right before he moved on and dared to ask for more. Absolution, forgiveness would have to come first.

"Back when Faith was sixteen," he said, "when we were all at the lake house that spring break, I showed her attention that wasn't appropriate, given her age." He paused for a moment. "It's no

229

excuse to say that I didn't know. But I didn't. And while I didn't do anything that dishonored Christ, I certainly intended more towards Faith in my heart than was right at the time, given the fact that she was so young. And I've apologized to her. But I want to apologize to you as well. And to Mrs. Hayes, of course."

Stephen watched him for a long moment. "I appreciate that," he said. "We figured it was a misunderstanding at the time. And Chloe made an excellent point about it all to me, even as it was happening."

"Oh?, Sam asked, surprised that they had talked about it so long ago.

"Yeah," Stephen said, leaning forward, his hands clasped between his knees. "She said that while your age certainly wasn't ideal, we couldn't be sorry that Faith, a girl who had never shown any interest in any boy, had fallen for one who was everything we had prayed for in terms of godliness and integrity. And when you never called or wrote, I suspected that it was your integrity that drove you to that decision, not that you had been toying with her heart." He shrugged. "And here you are, all these years later, making good on any promise you must have made to her back then. So, that must have been it. Your integrity. Your unwillingness to follow through once you'd thought through it all."

Sam exhaled at this, relieved, so thankful that he got it. "That was exactly it, sir."

Stephen smiled. "She seemed a lot older, didn't she?"

Sam nodded, thinking about it. "Yes, sir. Seems older even now than she actually is."

"Yeah, I know," he said. "Rushed through school and got to this place in her career where she's only a step from the top, years before she needs to be there. And I don't know what she intends as far as serving underneath this woman at the birthing center indefinitely, but I figure eventually, she'll want to branch out and have her own center. Do you see that?"

Sam had, especially when Elaine Charles spoke to him, showed some of her ideologies, and didn't line up with what Faith thought was right.

Faith wasn't hard to get along with, but she had her own way of looking at things. Sam knew it. Sam had seen it. And people like her either learned to accept imperfections in others or they steamrolled completely over everyone around them.

"Faith has this thing, you know," her father said, following Sam's line of thought completely, "about being perfect, about everything needing to be a certain way. And she really struggles when things veer off from the way she thinks they should go."

"I know," Sam said, thinking of her struggle to leave her patients in God's hands, to show herself grace, to forgive...

"But I'm encouraged," he said, smiling, "to sit here with you, to hear that you have so much clarity, so much awareness, such an ability to discern and accept that life isn't perfect. That you aren't, either. As evidenced by your apology for something that happened and was forgiven years ago."

Sam nodded. "Well, that awareness was hard-earned." His mind went back to combat, to reality, to God's grace through it all.

"I imagine so," Stephen murmured. Then, he smiled. "This isn't the first spiritual one-on-one conversation we've ever had, Sam."

"It isn't," Sam said, remembering the only other time.

"You were the first person I baptized as senior pastor of Grace," Stephen said, leaning back in his chair and smiling over at him, remembering it as well.

"Was I?"

"And the youngest person I've ever baptized, honestly," he said, looking out over the yard. "Your mother was none too pleased that I gave the green light either. Thought you were too young for such a big decision. But you had marched yourself to my office, sat me down man-to-man, and told me that you had decided to live for Jesus. And that was that. And you don't tell a five year old that he doesn't know what it means to live for Jesus, especially when he seems so serious about it."

"I remember going to your office," Sam said. "And the picture you drew to explain what it meant to be separated from God and to trust Christ. Still use the same kind of picture when I'm sharing the Gospel with others."

Stephen nodded. "You understood. I knew you understood. And all these years later? Well, the proof of faith is definitely in the life you've lived." He smiled at Sam. "I'm proud to know you."

Sam heard what he said and felt it was the best moment to say what he'd been meaning to say all along. "I want to marry Faith."

Stephen sighed, the smile still on his face. "I want you to marry her, too."

Before Sam could thank him for this blessing, the sliding door between the kitchen and the porch opened and Chloe and Faith stepped out. Faith looked between the two men cautiously, biting her lip.

Had he said something wrong earlier? Because she looked unsure, uncertain, unhinged just a bit –

But he caught her eye, and the uncertainty was gone as quickly as it had come. She smiled at him and made her way over to him, where she reached out and put her hands to his shoulders, even as he looked up at her.

"Stephen," Chloe said, coming to sit next to her husband, "you and Sam have the whole week to catch up. He and Faith have to be tired after a week of work and the travel out here."

Faith smiled at Sam as he looked her way. "Maybe a little tired," he murmured.

"Sam spent all morning before the flight working on his house," Faith said. "Got so much work done on it, too."

"You helped," he grinned.

"Handed you what you needed," she said, "after making you stop, come over, and show me all that you tried to describe."

"Doesn't know anything about tools, does she, Sam?," Stephen asked.

"Not unless she needs them to deliver a baby, no," he affirmed, fighting back a yawn.

"Come on, then," she said. "I'll go show you where the guest room is."

And they said their goodbyes and made their way up the stairs, where Faith would stop every few steps, turn, and kiss him again, until finally they were at the door to the room where he'd be staying, where he wanted to pull her in with him, and –

"You've been great," she said, her hands on his chest.

"How so?," he asked.

"Meeting them again, answering all their questions... putting up with Gracie." She grinned at this last one.

"She's nothing like you," he stated simply, smiling as he said it.

"No, but I love her," she said. "And I love you, Sam. I really, really do."

He put his forehead to hers, closing his eyes at this, resisting the urge to just get down on one knee right here, right now.

He'd waited so long for this moment. He would wait a little longer so that it would be perfect.

"I love you. And I'm going to be counting the minutes until I see you again."

"You'll be sleeping through them all," she said, taking one last kiss. "Goodnight, Sam."

And he watched her as she made her way back down the hallway.

She left him at the door to the guest room, stepping into her childhood room, closing the door behind her, and then gasping when a hand closed around her arm.

"Good grief, Faith," Gracie giggled, holding onto her sister and pulling her into a hug. "You're a little on edge."

"Not tonight," Faith murmured, kissing her on top of the head. "I was feeling perfectly at peace tonight... until my sister snuck into my room and grabbed me!"

"I was waiting for you," she said. "Come on!"

And she took Faith's arm and dragged her over to the closet, mainly empty now, given how Faith hadn't lived here for a long while.

Faith smiled as Gracie sat down on the floor, getting down with her, both of them sitting knees to knees, grinning at one another.

"You know," she said, "I think we could stay up and actually talk in the room. Mom's not going to come in and get onto us for staying up and talking at our ages. No need to hide out in the closet."

"Plenty need," Gracie said. "For old times. Just like it was."

"Yeah," Faith murmured. "Except the closet is a lot smaller than it was, right?"

"Either that, or our butts have gotten bigger," Gracie said. "And let's hope they have, since we're grown ups now, right?"

"Just as long as they don't get too big," Faith grinned. "Well? What do you think?"

"About what, Faith?" She grinned even wider. "Butts?"

"No, you goober. Sam," she said. "You've been itching to give your opinion all evening, clearly."

"Will it make any difference what I think?"

Faith thought about this. She loved Sam. Entirely, completely, wholly. It wouldn't make a difference what anyone thought, not even Gracie, her confidante, her best friend, her sister in Christ all these years...

"Wow," Gracie breathed. "I see it in your eyes. This is real. Who cares what I think!"

"Sorry," Faith mouthed.

"Oh, don't be," Gracie said, waving her away. "I abdicate my role as your number one, handing it over gladly to Sam. And I only say that because I like him."

Faith clapped her hands silently, then grabbed her sister's knees as they both laughed. "I had hoped, you know."

"Oh, I know," Gracie answered. "Because someone's gotta help you plan the wedding, and that'll go a lot better if I'm actually excited about the groom you've picked --"

"Getting ahead of ourselves," Faith said cautiously. "Like you always do! And you drag me with you--"

"Totally not doing that this time," Gracie swore, holding her hand up.

"Good," Faith said.

"I did find some great maid of honor dress possibilities on your laptop, though. Bookmarked them on your browser so that you're ready when he --"

"You're so funny," Faith laughed, watching her sister laugh along. "I've missed you. Every day, Gracie. And with all of this happening, and life changing... I just... I wish I could drag you back to Texas with me."

Gracie swallowed at this, her eyes wet with unshed tears.

"Don't cry," Faith said, her own eyes filling with tears. "Or I will, too!"

"Good grief, Faith," Gracie muttered, waving her hand in front of her face. "Let's talk about something else, then."

"Okay, okay," Faith said, both of them now waving their hands and blinking back tears. "Are you dating anyone right now?"

"I was," Gracie muttered, then grinned. "A guy from costuming."

Faith frowned. "Was he..."

"He most certainly was straight," Gracie said. "A rarity at work, I know."

"And how."

"Yes, and he talked a great talk about faith and loving Jesus, once he found out what I was really about. But it was all pretty much a farce that ended up with my green fairy slipper up where the sun doesn't shine, if you get my drift."

"He made a pass at you?," Faith gasped.

"Pretty much," Gracie nodded. "But I showed him. He called me a tease."

"Noooo," Faith murmured.

"Which, you know? Maybe he was right," she sighed. "I mean, I want to be married and have a family so bad sometimes that I let myself show attention to any guy who even remotely sounds like he might be a good guy. Boy-crazy, just like I've always been. Although, I guess now, it should be called man-crazy." She grimaced. "I don't want to be man-crazy, Faith."

"Just trying to find the right one. But none of them are," Faith said simply.

"No," Gracie said. "And those who seem to be... just aren't right, after I give them a few weeks, a few dates. I mean, none of them seem to want something long-term. Nothing as serious as what I want." She sighed. "Do you think I'm wrong for wanting nothing more from life than to be a wife and a mother?"

Faith smiled. "No," she said softly. "That's one of the best things about you. That you're so honest about wanting that and nothing more. And there's gotta be someone out there who will want to be the one to give that to you."

"I hope so," Gracie said. "And I'm so happy for you, Faith, that you've found the someone who was out there for you."

Faith looked at her hands, right on top of Gracie's knees, where she squeezed them. "Thanks, Gracie."

Gracie pulled her sister close. "I was wrong back when this all started," she said. "Wrong about him and the whole thing."

"Really?," Faith asked, softly.

"Yeah," Gracie smiled. "It's right. You and him, Faith. This is right. Just exactly what God's been doing all along."

Later that night, he heard her voice.

As images replayed themselves in his dreams, like they did so often, he heard Faith, calling to him, pulling him out of the nightmares.

His eyes opened with a gasp, and he saw her, sitting next to him on the bed, watching him with concern in her eyes.

Oh, no. What had she heard?

"Hey," she said softly. "Sam... are you okay?"

He swallowed, then blew out a deep breath. "Yeah." He moved to sit up slowly. "Yeah... I'm fine."

She watched him warily, compassion there in her eyes even still. "You were yelling."

"Was I?"

She nodded softly.

"Well, I don't... sleep well, obviously," he managed, his racing heart slowing again.

"Dreams?," she asked. "From... you know."

"Yeah," he said simply. He watched her silently for a moment, at how she was dressed for bed, her hair down, a sleepiness to her eyes...

"I woke you up," he said. "I'm so sorry."

"Don't apologize," she said. "I was glad for a reason to come and see you before sunrise." She smiled at this, leaning forward to give him a long, slow kiss.

And his heart began to race again.

"I'm surprised I'm not seeing the whole family again," he said, trying to get his mind back to where it needed to be. "Did I wake everyone else up, too?"

"Just me," she said, scooting closer to him. "You should lie down. Get a few more hours of sleep."

And so he did, watching her curiously as she laid down with him.

"Mmm," she smiled, leaning her head against his chest. "I'm glad you're here."

"I'm glad I'm here with *you*," Sam said softly, wondering at the wisdom of this, even as he put his hands on her face and tilted her lips up towards his. Not because it was smart, of course. But because she was here. And he wanted to. "I think I could get very used to always being with you." He kissed her again.

She pulled back very briefly, just long enough to whisper, "me, too, Sam," against his lips before she pulled him close again.

And it felt so good, being here with her, the nightmares so far away now, as she slipped her arms around him and traced the lines of the muscles in his back. He groaned slightly at this as she continued touching him, and she clearly took it as unspoken permission to slide closer to him, pressing every one of her curves to him.

"Faith," he whispered, right before she deepened their kiss. She rolled to her back, pulling him with her so that he was over her, prompting his mind to go where his body certainly wanted to —

Sam pushed himself back, just far enough to see her face clearly.

"We... we can't do this," he said softly.

"Sam," she sighed, more than a little breathless beneath him, clear intent in her eyes, "I want to."

And though he desperately wanted to as well, he made himself stop. His convictions, his commitment to leading a Christ-honoring life, had been enough up until this point to keep him from crossing this line with any woman, and as his mind affirmed to him again that these were convictions worth honoring, he was amazed that a new conviction gripped his heart as he watched Faith, staring up at him with hope, trust, and desire in her eyes.

It wasn't just about honoring Christ. He wanted to honor her. All that he felt for her to this point seemed to pale in comparison to the depths of what he felt now, as he saw her as the treasure she was, to be honored, protected, and kept, until the right time.

So, the decision wasn't difficult. Okay, so it *was* difficult. But Sam made it anyway, knowing that Faith was worth waiting for and that he would do it gladly.

"I can't," he whispered to her. "Believe me, I want to. But... I want to do things right."

She pulled him closer. "But I feel like I've been waiting for you forever. You're here. I'm here. And I'm so in love with you, Sam, and —"

"I love you, too," he choked out, his resolve weakening as she rose up to press her body against his. "But I can't feel good about doing this." A pause. "Okay, so I would probably feel really good. But I know we need to wait. Can you wait, Faith?"

She had never ever felt like this.

And the way she felt had her forgetting the very good reasons why she guarded her heart, why she'd kept her mind and her body pure, and why she was saving herself for the permanence and blessing of marriage.

She'd all but forgotten them entirely lying there, looking up at Sam, loving him, knowing him, trusting him, desiring him...

But he'd said no.

He'd stopped her. He'd told her no. And when she went so far as to tell him yes, he still told her no.

While she could agree with her logical, well ordered self that this was right and good... the rejection still stung, deep in her heart, deep in those places where she was, like it or not, still that sixteen year old girl waiting for him to call.

She sighed and dropped back down to the bed, covering her face with her hands. "So embarrassing," she muttered.

For a moment, Sam said nothing. "What?," he asked.

"Ugh," she groaned, moving out from underneath him, pulling at her clothes self-consciously, not daring to look at him. "Just forget that... that this happened."

"Hey," he said softly, turning her to face him, desperately trying to look into her eyes even as she studiously did her best to avoid his. "You shouldn't be embarrassed."

"Yeah," she breathed out sarcastically, "because getting in bed with you then being all out rejected isn't at *all* embarrassing."

He watched her warily for a second. "Is that why you came in here?"

She shook her head at this. "Well, no. I came in because I was worried about you."

"Oh," he breathed. "Okay. I thought maybe when you said that..."

"No, Sam," she sighed, even more embarrassed. "I came in to check on you, then... well, you know. Just kissing you, touching you... just got caught up. Or at least, I hope you were feeling some of the same things before you pushed me away."

"I didn't push you away."

She swallowed. "Okay. Rejected. Is that better?"

"This was soooo not a rejection," he said, leaning forward to turn her face to his. "Just a... deferment. Until later. Until... well, until you're mine to have."

She glanced up at him, slightly relieved to see the adoration in his eyes.

And she knew it was wrong, but she tried again, to see if she could change his mind, to see if he honestly thought of her beyond the little girl she'd been...

"Will I be yours to have, Sam?," she whispered against his lips, pulling him closer, even now. "Whenever, however you want me?"

"Oh, yeah," he barely managed to croak out. Then, forcing himself back, "I promise you, Faith."

And she very nearly believed the sincerity in his voice, the way his eyes stared into hers...

But it was familiar, this look that Sam wore. She had seen it so many years earlier at the lake house. And what had come of her trust then? Silence. Years of silence. Rejection. Not unlike this right now.

"I better go to sleep, Sam," she said, softly kissing his lips so as to avoid looking him in the eyes again. "Busy day tomorrow, if I know my mother and her plans."

"Faith," he said, following her to the door, "are we okay?"

"We're fine," she smiled at him, pushing down the anxious thoughts that were creeping back into her mind, long after she was certain that they were gone forever. And she went back to her room, suddenly feeling like she was sixteen again, waiting for a phone call that would never come.

Chloe was waiting for him the next morning when he came downstairs.

"Good morning," she said brightly, peering up behind him, looking for Faith. "She's still asleep, huh?"

He certainly hoped so. At least one of them should have gotten a good night's sleep, and it clearly hadn't been him, as he'd been awake most of the night, praying against the great need he'd felt to go to her room and tell her he had been wrong, spending the rest of the night doing exactly what she had wanted him to do, what he wanted to do. It had taken a lot of prayer and perseverance, and he had welcomed the dawn when it came, as the rest of the family woke up and made it impossible for him to betray himself. He had been tempted to peek into her room that morning, just to see if she was okay. Okay, probably more than just see if she was okay. But –

"Yeah," he said, absentmindedly. "I'm assuming so. Her door was still shut."

"Good," Chloe smiled at him, lowering her voice. "Stephen told me about the talk you two had last night, and… well, I'm thrilled, obviously." She stood and rushed to his side, reaching up and hugging him exuberantly.

"Well, she hasn't said yes yet," Sam said, smiling himself.

"Oh, but she will," Chloe said. "And," she sighed, going back to the counter and picking up a small jewelry box, "she will likely say yes and cry when she sees this." She opened the box to reveal an astronomically huge diamond ring to him.

"Wow."

"You, of course, don't have to give her this," Chloe said. "But this was my mother's."

"Grandma Trish," Sam said.

245

Chloe smiled. "She's told you all about her, of course. And about how close they were. Seems only fitting that Faith should be the one to get this, then."

Sam took the box as she stretched it out to him. "I don't remember this... well, she wasn't wearing this when..." He didn't want to say Craig's name and invite his memory into this moment.

Chloe seemed to understand. "No. He never asked us. So he never knew that this was waiting for Faith, whenever she met the right guy." She smiled. "Which, you know, she did years ago, back at Grace."

And as if on cue, at the mention of Grace, Gracie came down the stairs with serious bed-head and a look of uncensored euphoria as she saw what Sam held in his hand.

"*You're going to marry Faith*!," she shouted, jumping up and down.

"Gracie, lower your voice," Chloe admonished. "And you *have* to keep this a secret!"

"Can do," Gracie smiled, embracing Sam as she squealed.

"Let's hope so," Chloe winked over at him.

He had put the ring in his luggage where Faith wouldn't be able to find it. And as he was leaving the room to go downstairs again, her door opened, and she stepped out looking twice as beautiful as she had the night before.

He had done the right thing. But, wow, he doubted his own sanity for doing it.

"Hey," he whispered, catching her by surprise.

"Hey," she echoed, smiling at him shyly.

And it was enough of an invitation for Sam to pull her into his arms again and lower his lips to hers for a kiss that reawakened everything from the night before.

"I want you so much," he choked out, just as she pulled away from his lips. "Faith, you make me –"

"Um... excuse me." Sam looked up to find Pastor Stephen, already dressed for a full day at the church, ready to leave the house, trying to inch past them towards the stairs.

"Oh... uh... yeah. Um... sure," Sam mumbled, moving aside, then letting go of Faith a moment later, his face blazing as he did so.

No one appeared more embarrassed than Stephen, though, who didn't say another word but simply walked by them, then down the stairs and out of sight.

Sam looked back at Faith, only to find that she was biting her lip nervously.

"That went well," Sam whispered.

"Mmm," Faith agreed. "He should've been there last night."

"What?"

He could see the hurt in her eyes. "Last night. When you sent me away. That would have been something he would have appreciated seeing."

"Hey," Sam said, "I thought we were okay."

She sighed. "Oh, we're fine," she said, smiling tightly at him. "Just fine."

And because Sam didn't know any better? He believed her, leaning over and kissing her again.

"Let's go see what's on the schedule for today, okay?," Faith asked, turning to go before he offered an answer either way.

River Fellowship was a big church.

Faith could remember coming here for the first time when she was eight, with seven year old Gracie proclaiming that this looked more like a shopping mall than a church.

It did. It really did. And it had only grown during her father's pastorate. Sixteen years in the same pulpit, while the church around them had changed so significantly. From liberal to conservative, from inward-focused to outward-reaching, from a place that Faith felt foreign in to a reassuring home.

She felt like she'd hugged half the church before the service began, and after it ended? She felt like she'd hugged the other half.

She'd done a good job of trying to forget the night before. She'd been ashamed enough when she saw Sam in the hallway, remembering what she'd done, yet still irritated with him, upset with him for reasons that made no sense anyway. She respected him. She knew he was right.

But still. She found herself shying away from the very innocent kiss he tried to give her as she slid her hand in his after the service as the church cleared out around them.

Let him feel rejected, she thought, feeling a little justified by the look in his eyes, feeling like –

"Faith."

She felt her eyes, which were still on Sam and his hurt expression, widen just slightly at the familiar voice.

Craig.

Oh, my. She hadn't thought about running into Craig here. Which she should have, honestly, but she was thinking more about being in love, about being with Sam, about starting this next chapter in their lives, then about the rejection, the hurt feelings, the lake house...

"Craig," she said, turning to him, noting that Sam glanced at him as well when he heard the name. "How are you?"

Craig watched her for a few moments. "Oh, I'm just great," he said, no inflection in his normally bubbly, energetic voice. "And this is?" He glanced up at Sam.

"This is Sam," she said. "My boyfr... um, my... manfriend." Well, that sounded stupid. Curse Gracie and her talk from the night before...

"Manfriend," Craig said, raising his eyebrows and looking at Sam. "Hi. I'm Craig. Surely you've heard something about me." He held his hand out.

And Sam took it, gripped it firmly, and said, "Good to meet you, Craig."

"And just where did the two of you meet?," Craig asked, looking back at Faith expectantly. Harshly. Rudely.

All justified. Faith tried for a smile… and failed. "Uh, well, we knew one another from church, back in Texas. Back when we were kids."

Craig opened his mouth to say something about this when Gracie popped up on the other side of Sam, after rushing back from meeting up with friends.

"Craig! There you are!," she exclaimed. "I was looking for you earlier! You're late for the meeting!"

Faith exchanged a thankful look with her sister, just as Gracie winked at her.

"Meeting?," Craig asked. "What meeting?"

"The meeting to plan the trip to Atlanta," she said. "Big conference, Craig. You were the one who set up the committee, remember?"

He nodded. "That's right," he sighed. "I remember setting that up. But, wow, Gracie. That was months and months ago. And so much has happened since then." And here, he cut his eyes at Faith. Again.

All justified. Again.

"Yeah, well," Gracie said, "the world just keeps on turning, doesn't it? Despite the soap operas we find ourselves in, right?"

"And we have to move on past silly drama," Craig concluded. "Just like Faith here has moved on. With Sam. How nice."

Faith felt the need to apologize, but she kept her mouth shut as Sam put his hand inconspicuously on her back, silently acknowledging the difficulty of standing here, hearing this --

"And speaking of moving on," Craig said brightly, finally sounding like himself again as he turned to Gracie, "you look absolutely gorgeous today, Gracie."

Her sister. Practically her twin. He was checking out Gracie, clearly trying to make her jealous. Faith very nearly gasped at this, at how far he'd fallen to get to this point of pettiness, while Gracie simply raised an eyebrow at him, grinning.

"I'm sorry... what?," she asked.

"Can't I tell you that you're beautiful?," he asked, glancing over at Faith.

"You can," Gracie said, "but you never have before."

"Well, maybe I've been distracted," he said with a tightness in his voice. "And maybe I'm finally seeing clearly and can see which Hayes sister was the real catch all along."

Gracie stared at him for a moment... then, she burst into giggles. "Bless your sweet heart, Craig. Are you for real?!"

"Yes, and it --"

"Can you believe this?!," she asked Faith, giggling.

Faith couldn't, but before she could tell Gracie either way, Craig cut in again.

"I'm being serious, you know," he said.

"Oh, no, you aren't," Gracie said, shaking her head at him. "And that's a low thing to do. You just might hurt my feelings, pretending like that."

"Not pretending," he scoffed.

"Okay, that's it," Gracie continued, very nearly advancing on him as he stood there watching her. "You keep using me to get back at Faith and I'll have to kick your butt, even if you are my pastor, and --"

"Hey, Craig," Sam said, pulling Gracie back by her denim jacket, "it was nice to meet you."

"Yeah, whatever," Craig muttered before turning and walking away.

Gracie turned to Faith with a huff. "Unbelievable!"

Pretty much. Faith sighed.

"Has he ever acted like that before, Faith?!"

"No," she said, reaching out and putting her arm around Sam's waist, leaning into him as he put his arm over her shoulders. "That's not him. Not the way he was. Don't hold that against him."

"Oh, I won't," Gracie said. Then, with a grin, she added, "And if he's not too embarrassed the next time I see him, post-outburst like that, I may take him up on the suggestion in what he said."

Faith rolled her eyes. "Oh, good grief..."

"Can't help myself, Sam," Gracie said, grinning up at him. "Man-crazy even when the man in question is crazy. Right, Faith?"

"Something like it," Faith murmured.

"And he's actually a decent guy, even though you couldn't tell it today, Sam," she said. "He's back in school on Dad's suggestion. PhD. Fancy, fancy."

"Really?," Faith asked, thinking about how Craig had never expressed a desire to go back to school, to go beyond the education he already had. "But he didn't care about school. About going back. Like, ever."

Gracie grinned. "Well, things change, don't they?"

And Faith noted that they did, as Sam squeezed her shoulders, even as she moved her arm from around him and distanced herself just a little more as she thought about the night before...

Things did change. A lot.

Sam had picked up on a difference in Faith that morning. A distance in the way she looked at him, in the way she halfway listened to all that he said, in the way her eyes flitted away from his, in the way that she turned from his kiss there in the church that morning.

Well, she'd turned away because of *him*, obviously. Craig. Dr. Rev. Theologian Craig Lucas, with his BA, MDiv, soon to be PhD, and who knows what else.

He could see the respect in Faith's eyes later on that day, as she asked her father about it, as they talked about the program, as he told her about what it would mean in the longterm for Craig as he sought out bigger pastorates, more responsibility, and his own church.

Sam could clearly, so very clearly, see the respect in her eyes.

And as the week continued on with little affection and even less warmth from her, he wondered at what she saw when she looked at him.

CHAPTER NINE

They came back at the end of the week, and he'd driven her home from the airport when their flight got in late, stopping at the door after he'd brought in her luggage, reaching out for her.

"Hey," he whispered, feeling as though they hadn't talked, really talked, in a week, "are you okay with me?"

She put her hands to his chest and nodded, biting her lip. "Yeah."

He bent down to look in her eyes, to make her finally meet his gaze. "Really?"

And she looked at him. Finally. "I said yeah, Sam."

"I only ask because you've been..."

"What?," she asked with just a hint of annoyance. "What have I been?"

"Different," he said simply.

"Just being me," she said softly, a hint of something in her eyes as she continued looking at him. "Maybe I'm just nervous about the banquet tomorrow, huh?"

The banquet. The giant fundraiser banquet that Elaine Charles held once a year to fund her clinic, to raise awareness for what they were doing, to continue to gather support from like-minded believers who had invested in it all.

Sam and Faith had come back in time to be there so Faith could give a speech, so Faith could mingle, so Faith could be there to impress all of the very important people who would be there.

He was going to be her plus one, dressed in the tux she'd picked out for him, prepared already with what he needed to say when asked about the center, when asked about the ministry.

"It's going to be great," he told her. "I'm so proud of you."

And for a moment, she was like she'd been, winding her arms around his neck, standing on tiptoe to press her lips to his. "I can't wait to see you all dressed up."

He smiled underneath her lips. "Would you believe that of all the reasons I'm looking forward to tomorrow night, *that* is the number one? Me, wearing an itchy, uncomfortable, completely impractical suit?"

She laughed at this, pulling him closer. "You should really be looking forward to what *I'm* going to be wearing, Sam."

"Really?," he murmured, kissing her again. "Sneak preview before I head back to the house?"

"Nope," she sighed. "You'll have to wait until tomorrow night."

He groaned a little. "It'll be all I can think of until then."

And they'd said goodbye, and she'd not returned the "I love you" that he'd given. But he hadn't lingered on the oddity of this, chalking it up to the strange mood she'd been in, his mind already on something else as he drove away from the house.

What either of them would be wearing, what they would be discussing at the banquet, what would happen under Elaine Charles's watch, was *not* at the front of his thoughts as he headed towards his house.

No, the most exciting part of the night to come was what Sam had planned for afterwards.

He got back to Scott and Marie's thirty minutes later, and as soon as he walked in, Marie met him at the door, smiling.

"Welcome home," she whispered, reaching up to hug him.

"Thanks," he said.

"Good week away?"

"Great," he said, smiling. "And we're whispering because...?"

"Nathan is asleep," she said. "Won't last long, but I'm hoping to get in some rest myself in the meantime."

"I'll leave you to it," he said. "And I won't go upstairs. Maybe he'll stay asleep longer if I stay down here for a while."

"Thank you," she murmured. "Scott's down at your house."

"This late?," Sam frowned, glancing at his watch. "How can he work in the dark?"

And her grin told him what he wouldn't have guessed.

"No way," he whispered. "He wired the house while I was gone?"

"Yeah, and he very nearly lost his religion while doing it," she giggled softly. "Had to call in an electrician. Really wounded his pride, but he got it done, all while staring over the poor guy's shoulder so he could do it himself the next time without any help."

"I should've been here, staring right along with him," he murmured. "He didn't have to do all of that for me."

"He wanted to," she whispered. "Wanted to surprise you. We both did." She sighed, tears in her eyes. "You'll be able to move in before we know it. I'm going to miss you, Sam."

"I'm going to be right across your backyard."

"But still," she cried, still whispering.

And he leaned over and kissed her forehead. "You're my favorite sister," he said. "Don't tell Savannah. But it's all you, Marie."

"Oh, I already knew that," she cooed, hugging him. "You should go down there and see what Scott's done."

So, he did, making his way across the yard, smiling to see the lights on, smiling even more when he opened the door and saw Scott, packing things up for the night.

"Hey, welcome back," he said.

"And what a great welcome it is," Sam grinned. "Look at all of this."

Scott nodded, a proud smile on his face. "Getting you out of our house sooner than I had hoped," he said.

"You're going to miss me," Sam said. "You'll cry into your pillow every night."

Scott laughed out loud at this. "Not hardly. How was Florida?"

"Okay," Sam said.

"Just okay?"

Sam's mind went back to the coldness, the distance, the odd feeling that something wasn't quite right.

"Hard on Faith, I think," he said simply. "Being back and away from work, probably. Made her a little on edge with me, but that's probably normal."

"I can see that," Scott said. "First time Marie and I went back to Namibia, she wanted to kill me."

"Really?," Sam asked, wondering at this.

"Oh, yeah," Scott said, waving away this information like it was truly no big deal. "Justified mostly, though."

"And what wasn't justified?"

"Well," Scott shrugged. "Forgiven and forgotten. That's marriage, though. Dealing with bad moods and dumb decisions, sticking together even when you don't particularly like one another."

Sam frowned. "That's depressing."

"Shouldn't be," Scott said, smiling. "Because sticking it out together makes you like one another even more. I mean, look at Marie. She can't keep her hands off of me. And I've done a lot of dumb things, and she's full of nine months of bad moods. Again. Still love her. Still like her."

And Sam took this as great counsel and further confirmation for what he knew he would do no matter what, in this very place the next night.

"I need your help," Sam said.

"Have I not helped you enough by doing all of this?," Scott said, indicating the house around them.

"You have, but I need something else."

"What is it?"

And Sam reached into his pocket where he'd put the ring box, pulled it out, and opened it.

Scott studied the ring for a long moment. Then, with a glance up at his brother, he said, "Well, I'm flattered. But I'm already spoken for. And you're a dude, so --"

"This isn't for you," Sam said, laughing.

"Of course not," Scott said, taking a closer look. "Good grief, am I paying you too much, Sam?"

"No, you're not paying me nearly enough," Sam murmured. "It was her grandmother's."

"You got it from her parents," Scott said, grinning. "Which means that you're serious about doing this. About proposing."

"Yeah," Sam said. "I am."

"Even with her being on edge with you?," Scott asked.

And Sam thought on this, recalling everything that had happened over the past week, remembering how she'd treated him.

But it didn't change the commitment he'd already made to her in his heart. It didn't change his resolve to covenant this. Regardless of how she acted, how she treated him, how she did things -- he loved her enough that one week of coldness was hardly worth noting.

"Even now," Sam said. "And I've got a plan, but I'll need your help."

"Whatever you need," Scott answered, smiling. "Marie's going to cry when she hears, you know."

"What else is new?," Sam asked.

And they both laughed as they began to make plans...

She'd had a delivery early that next morning because babies never respected office hours, of course.

It had been a joy, though, to jump back into work, to feel herself refocused, to be reminded that she was someone who did something important in this world.

The week in Florida had been a roller coaster of emotions. She found herself drawn to Sam like normal, like she'd always been drawn to him... then, distancing herself from him because of that one night, the night he'd turned her away. Then, there were the things he'd said about school, the baffling way she'd felt when she found herself making excuses for him, the puzzling thoughts that had crossed her mind as they'd heard about Craig's ambitions, as she'd wondered why Sam wanted nothing more than just to be who he was, and --

She loved him. She loved him apart from what he did, apart from whatever degrees or education he accumulated. She loved him for the integrity he had, even if it had been what made him turn her away.

So, why did she find herself frustrated? And why did her frustration get mixed up with the way she felt, so much so that she didn't know whether she was pulling him closer or pushing him away?

She closed her eyes as the thoughts tumbled around her mind. It made no sense, and she resolved to herself even as she opened her eyes and looked at her reflection in the mirror, that she wouldn't let what she couldn't understand ruin what she knew for certain. She loved Sam Huntington.

And loving him was enough. No matter what.

She got ready for the big night, for the big, fancy fundraising banquet, fielding calls from expectant mothers in between fixing her hair and makeup, silently praising God when it appeared that no one was actually in labor.

She slipped on the little black dress she'd told Sam about, turning in front of the mirror, admiring the way it hugged everything just right, proclaiming to all the world that she wasn't a child anymore, not even a sixteen year old girl, and --

And she frowned at herself, at this errant thought that she fought back even as she slipped on her shoes and heard the doorbell.

Grabbing the small purse that held the notecards for her speech, she made her way to the door and opened it to...

Sam. Looking absolutely amazing.

And looking at her as though she was everything.

She sent away every crazy, errant thought from the week before as he pulled her close, breathed in deeply at her neck, and managed, in a deep, low voice, "Whoa..."

She smiled even as her eyes fluttered closed, her arms around him as he kissed her neck. "Told you," she said.

"You," he said, bringing his face up to hers, his eyes intent on hers, "are incredible. Have I said that before?"

"A few times," she managed, resolving to think of nothing but this, of this look in his eyes, for the rest of the night.

And after a long, lingering kiss and another disbelieving look of appreciation, he put her arm through his and led her off to her big night.

She was incredible.

He had known it before, of course, but as he watched her make her speech, impressing the crowd with her knowledge, inspiring them with her emotion, and charming them with her smile, he felt himself sit taller and taller, feeling so proud to be with her. As she made the rounds with him, then with Elaine Charles, then by herself, he watched her still, with a smile on his face, counting the minutes until they'd be done here, when he could take her to the house, get down on one knee, and --

"Hey." He heard her whisper just as she laid her hand on his shoulder. Before he could get up and give her his seat, she settled into his lap and leaned up next to him, whispering in his ear.

"How do you think it's going?"

He looked up at her, tucking a strand of her hair behind her ear. "I think it's going well," he said softly, smiling.

"Really?," she asked. "I feel totally inept, working the room like this." She released a short breath.

"Introvert's nightmare, huh?," he asked, sliding his arms around her waist.

"Yeah," she murmured, reaching over to the table and picking up his drink. "Do you mind?"

"No, go ahead," he said, as she took a drink. "Do you want me to get you another one?"

"No time," she said, putting the glass back down and lowering her voice. "The gentleman heading our way... very important. Dr. Stan Jones. Chief of Medicine at a hospital up in the northwest part of the city. Widely respected and a huge contributor to what we're doing here. He'll want to hear less about the evangelism, more about women's power, feminism, all that."

"Okay," Sam nodded, recalling all the conversations he'd already had, the hints Faith had given him about which direction to take them all, how to do what he could to be her support here.

"Do I look okay?," she asked.

"You look perfect," he assured her, just as she stood and he stood with her, ready to shake hands with --

"Dr. Jones," Faith said, holding out her hand confidently. "We're so glad you were able to come tonight. I'm Faith Hayes."

"Oh, I remember your name," he said, smiling at her. "Hard to forget anything about you after that speech you gave."

Something about the suggestion in the way this man looked at Faith rubbed Sam the wrong way. But he pushed aside the minor annoyance as the doctor looked over at him, a question in his eyes.

"Dr. Jones, this is Sam Huntington, my guest for the evening," Faith said, barely glancing his direction.

Yes, that was another annoyance. He'd been her "guest" all evening. *Boyfriend* sounded juvenile, though, and *manfriend* sounded odd, so he'd reasoned it away. But still.

"Stan Jones," the doctor said as he shook Sam's hand. Then, his eyes went right back to Faith. "Elaine has been telling me about the work you've been doing. Increased the productivity of the clinic. Doubled the patient load. All on your own."

"Yes, sir," Faith said. "It's been a wonderful six months. So many empowering, natural births for women, giving them greater choices and options for their prenatal care and their deliveries. Which you know all about, I'm sure, given your experience in the field."

"In obstetrics," he said, smiling. "But I've been intrigued by what you're doing here. Have been for years. And now, after hearing your speech, hearing about the women you've impacted in even this short while, I'm even more inclined to continue on, helping as I can."

She smiled at this. "Thank you," she said, so sincerely, so sweetly.

The doctor glanced over at Sam. "Quite a young lady you have taking you as her guest... what was your name again?"

"Sam," Sam managed, really, really disliking the way this man was looking at Faith.

"Sam," the doctor said, grinning at Faith again. "Are you in medicine, Sam?"

"No, sir," Faith said, speaking up for him, as though he couldn't answer for himself. "Sam's studying business."

"Ahh," the doctor murmured. "MBA, perhaps?"

"No, actually," Sam said, "I'm just trying to get my undergraduate degree."

This prompted a puzzled look from the doctor... then another smile. "Well. That's nice. Starting a little late, but... well, good for you."

And he had just about turned his attention back to Faith completely when Sam saw Faith blush. She was embarrassed. Embarrassed of him, of who he was, of what he'd done.

So, before the doctor could move on to more compliments in Faith's direction, accompanied by more looks and likely suggestive overtures, Sam spoke again.

"I'm starting a little late because I was out earning my way," he said simply.

And there it was. Panic. All over Faith's beautiful face.

"Oh?," the doctor asked, his eyebrows shooting up. "How so?"

"I was in the military," Sam said. "US Marine Corps. Sixteen years of active duty."

"Well," the doctor managed. "And what was it that you did in the military?"

"Combat," Sam said. "I wasn't trained to do anything but combat."

"Hmm." The doctor looked at Faith. "We in the field of medicine wouldn't know anything about combat, would we, Faith? Because our objective is to save lives, not end them."

Faith opened her mouth to speak to this, and Sam interrupted her before she could say anything, certain that he wouldn't be able to bear the apologies she'd make for him.

"Sometimes saving the lives of many involves ending the lives of a few," he said.

The doctor narrowed his eyes at this. "Killed a lot of people, then, Sam?"

And Sam said out loud what he'd never said to anyone before. "A few, sir."

He saw the horror on Faith's face, and he couldn't figure out if it was for what he'd been through himself or what he'd just put her through.

And what was it all for anyway, what good had it done, as the doctor simply shook his head, thanked and praised Faith again for being her brilliant, amazing self despite her poor choice in dinner dates, and left.

And Faith, with one last helpless look, walked away from him, too.

The ride back was quiet.

She noted the direction he was driving, back towards his own house, back towards the start of their bright future together, and she said, with terseness in her voice, "My place, Sam. Take me to my place."

He glanced over at her. "I was hoping to take you by to see the work Scott did on the house."

"Not tonight," she said, the familiar coldness to her voice. So distant, so angry, so far away from him...

"Great," he muttered.

"What?," she asked, daring him to say more as she cut her eyes at him.

"This," he said, waving his hand at her. "This attitude. I'm not sure what I did to make you so mad all the time, but --"

"You told a donor that you *killed* people, Sam!"

Yes, he had. And he could get the anger over that. But before this. The week before. This was more of the same. This shortness.

"I get that," he said. "And I should've censored my words --"

"Yeah, you should have," she said.

And he could hear it in her voice. This talking down to him. This lack of respect.

"Sam, those people are important," she pleaded, condescension in her voice even as she did so.

He got that. Oh, he got it. Everyone was important in this world, Faith most especially. Self-important, every day of her life, even as she iced him out as though she was too good for him. As she made excuses for why he wasn't more like Craig, for why he'd done what he'd done for his country, for who he was --

"Are you even listening to me, Sam?," she shrieked, just as they pulled into her driveway.

He turned around and faced her.

"Were *you* listening, Faith?," he said. "To what that man said to me?"

She sighed. "You started talking about politics!"

And like that, she made it his fault. It was *always* his fault. Just like whatever he'd done to her last week was *his* fault, making the rift between them *his* fault, making *everything his fault.*

"Tried my best not to, but he asked me what I do, and I couldn't very well leave it at the fact that I'm a middle-aged man enrolled in freshman level courses at the local junior college, now, could I? Not when I'm with the most brilliant woman in the room."

"Get over it, Sam," she said. "Who even cares that you don't have a degree?"

"*You* do, Faith," he swore, thinking of the way she'd looked at him in Florida after talking with Craig, after hearing him agree with

Gracie that school was awful... at the way she had to be thinking of him every time Elaine said something. Just the way he was always thinking of it.

"I told you," she said, honesty in her eyes, "that you don't need to do anything because you think people are expecting it. Especially when they aren't even expecting it. I told you that, Sam."

And she had. But he didn't care. He was so tired of being talked down to like this.

"Well, you're always telling me something because you know so much more than I do, don't you?"

She took in a sharp breath at this, hurt in her eyes. This didn't stop her from preparing to launch into another complaint, though. He cut her off before she could get it out.

"I told him about my career, Faith," he said. "My real career. What I spent all those years working towards."

"And you let it get political," she said.

"It wasn't my fault," he said severely.

"Sam," she groaned, "I've already told you that they think differently. And that we don't have to agree with them to do ministry here. And you know it. You *know* how Elaine thinks, how her board members think. And yet, you went and made everything political. He respected me, and you just ruined it. Just put Elaine and the work we do in jeopardy with the men who fund the center!"

"This wasn't my fault!," he yelled.

She shook her head. "I should've known this would happen if I brought you."

And he heard what she didn't say.

"You don't respect me," he said. "You're ashamed of me." He thought of his brothers with all their fancy degrees, their ability to sleep all night without horrific nightmares, their very normal lives.

She wanted someone like them. He knew it. He'd always known it.

"Samuel," she said severely, "I have *never* been ashamed of you. I've been so proud of you, every moment we've been together, ever since I was a little girl." She rolled her eyes. "Not like I want to talk about that, though. Because I'm a grown up now, even if you can't see it."

"What are you even talking about, Faith?," he asked, done with the attitude she'd had all week.

"I'm talking about how you still treat me like a child," she spat out. "How, in the back of your mind, you're still seeing me as a child. All the time. You've said it before, how you're hearing my little girl voice, seeing me at sixteen, letting that keep you from wanting me --"

"I want you," he said hotly.

"Or so you keep saying," she muttered. "But what does it matter, right? Still just a kid to you, as clearly evidenced by how you apologized to my parents –"

"How did you know about that?," he asked. And, he refrained from asking, why would it matter that he had done it anyway?

"My dad," she said. "He told me how wonderful it was that you would go out of your way like that, to apologize for the past, to make things right. With him." She frowned. "Like I'm someone under the authority of her father, even still, when I'm a grown woman. I'm not a child, Sam."

And this was so petty, on top of so many other petty things she'd done all week long.

"Hard to tell," Sam said, "when you've been acting so childish lately."

And before he could take the words back and apologize because he'd said them in anger, she threw angrier words back at him.

"Must have been why you sent me away that night," she said, tears in her eyes, her teeth very nearly clenched as she stared at him.

He felt as though the air had been knocked out of him. "I did the right thing," he said, slowly, evenly.

"Yeah," she muttered, "because who am I but some sixteen year old you promised everything to then left behind?"

This. Always this. And suddenly, it didn't matter if she was ashamed of him or not, because it always came back to this. And even if he went on and was as brilliant and successful as the other man she'd turned away, as brilliant and successful as she herself was, it still wouldn't be enough. Because it always came back to this.

"You know," he said, surprised to find that he could still be calm, that he could still keep his anger in check, even now, even as she was watching him with the same coolness and bitterness in her eyes that she'd been unable to mask all week, "you've got to start believing the best about me. You've got to come to our disagreements, our conflicts, and our issues in the here and now, Faith. You can't keep going back to what's done. You have to believe the best about me *now*. You have to want who I am *now*."

"Who you are now?," she said. "The man who just went and shocked someone tonight, just because? Not for any good reason? Because Sam, I was with *you* tonight. I chose *you*. And you went on and --"

"I'm not perfect," he said, regretting at least part of what he'd done tonight. "And I didn't intend to put you in a bad position. But he was --"

"Sam," she cried, "can you not just apologize?"

And he said nothing for a long moment. Then, softly, "Yes. I'm sorry. For trying to shock him without any thought of how it would hurt you." He looked at her. "But you've been hurting me all week. And it doesn't make it right, what I did... but it points to a bigger problem."

"And what problem is that?," she asked, wiping her eyes.

"That you can't see me for who I am," he said. "That you can't be content with who I really am. You have to want who I am now, Faith. Or..."

"Or what?," she asked.

"Or," he said, wounded at the thought, "we're never going to get past this."

She nodded, tears now escaping her eyes. "You're right. We're never going to get past this." She took a deep breath. "Sam, maybe it's time for me to just finally move on."

Oh, wow. She'd really said it. And now, she couldn't believe she'd even thought it.

"Gracie, I will *never* be able to move on!"

As soon as he left that night, Faith had called home, and Gracie was the one who had answered the call. With tears streaming down her face and near hysteria in her voice, Faith had told Gracie everything there was to tell. They had picked apart the evening – from Sam's words at the banquet, to his comments about her, to the climactic blowup that had seemed to be the final nail in the coffin of their relationship. Gracie had gone from being strongly on Team Sam to being a casual observer to finally being on Team Faith. She was easily swayed, especially by her sister's tears.

"Oh, yes, you will," she said, echoing all that she had been saying for the past thirty minutes. "And you'll move on with someone way hotter, which wouldn't take much, frankly."

Faith stopped sobbing for a moment. "You think Sam is... ugly?," she asked, horrified.

"Well, he's certainly not the best looking of the bunch. Not even the best looking brother in his family, honestly."

"I think he's gorgeous."

Gracie sighed. "Well, he's *not*. I don't think you've ever seen Sam Huntington clearly."

Faith thought about this, about all that she probably still didn't know about Sam, about how she had been baffled by his behavior, what he really thought –

Gracie, sensing her sister's puzzlement, jumped on the opportunity. "I mean, really, Faith," she said. "You've been in love with him since... well, since before you were even old enough to tie your own shoes."

"Sam used to tie them for me at church," Faith sobbed mournfully.

"Oh, well. See? What did you know back then, when you were so young?"

Faith took a deep breath. "Well, not much. Just that he was kind and sweet and gentle. And that he loved Jesus, even then, even with as young as he himself was."

"That sounds great and all," Gracie said, "but what kind of future can you build on who he was then? And, I mean, how could a little kindness back then have any part in who you are now?"

Faith considered this. "You know," she said softly, "I thought the same thing, Gracie. And I told him so, told him that I didn't know if we'd even like each other as adults, you know? But he wanted to see me, kept at me to see him, and I did. And we got to know each other, apart from who we were all those years ago. And it was the biggest, most wonderful surprise to find that the very things I loved about him then, before I even knew what it meant to love someone... well, they're the very same things that make him who he is now. He's still kind and sweet and gentle. And he still loves Jesus. And I don't want to, Gracie, but I still love him."

Gracie remained silent for a long moment. Then, exasperated, as she herself began to cry all those miles away, "Then why the hee-haw did you send him away, Faith?! You're making *me* want him with the way you're talking about him!"

"Have you not been listening?!," Faith shouted at her. "He *hates* the people in my life, my career –"

"I don't think that's it at all. So, he's a little insecure around all your hoity toity friends, so what? Frankly, it would take a little getting used to for *any* boyfriend. Manfriend. Whatever."

"I thought you were on *my* side," she said.

"I'm not on anyone's side right now because you're both crazy," Gracie huffed. "Did something happen? Because what you're describing with Sam? Is just a little misunderstanding. Not a reason to end it all. Did something happen to make you blow everything out of proportion?"

"He told Dr. Jones that he killed --"

"Besides that, Faith. Before that."

Faith considered this for a moment. "Well, no, I don't think so."

"Oh, come on," Gracie said, "any more browbeating him for what he did all those years ago? Never calling? The rejection, rejection, rejection –"

"I've never been that melodramatic about that," Faith insisted.

"Please."

Well, perhaps she had been. "Okay, so maybe. But I haven't..."

Then, she thought back to the night in the guest room. And the rejection she felt. And the small, barely perceptible ways she had been freezing Sam out since then, slighting him so delicately that he...

... well, that he had picked up on it. Finally. Which only added to his exasperation that night.

"Oh, Faith, have you screwed this up?"

Faith frowned. "No. At least, I... I don't think I... " A deep breath. All that she had resolved earlier, washed away in his truck as she had yelled at him, said all that shouldn't have been said, felt all that she'd promised not to feel.

"Gracie... yes. I've screwed this up."

"Why? What happened?"

Faith sighed. "I went to his room in Florida, when we were there visiting."

"Yeah. So?"

"Gracie," Faith said. "I. Went. To. His. Room."

Gracie took a breath. "Oooooohhhhh."

"Yeah."

"Well," Gracie said softly. "I'm not even sure what to say about that. Seeing as how you and Craig never so much as... well, even thought about one another naked, right? Well, actually, I'm sure *he* thought about it at least a –"

"Nothing happened," Faith said.

"With Craig? Yeah, I figured."

"No, with Sam," Faith sighed. "And not for lack of trying on my part. He sent me back to my room. Told me he wanted to do things right. Flat out rejected me. Brought back all these memories of back then, and –"

"Okay, first of all, Faith? You're really dumb."

"Hey, that's –"

"Because," Gracie barreled on, "a man who tells you that he wants to do things right? Is not *rejecting* you, you twit. Let me guess? It took Sam a while to say that to you, right?"

"Yes. He had to think about it."

"Of course he did! Because he didn't *want* to send you away. But he did because he was doing the right thing. You know what I'd give for a guy who was that godly, that honorable?"

"Well, Sam's available," Faith muttered. A pause. "Gracie, I would totally *not* be okay if you went after Sam, and –"

"Not going to happen because I think he's ugly, remember?"

"Well, praise God for that."

"Yes, praise Him for many things. Mainly for Sam doing the right thing and for him putting up with you when you keep on lingering on what happened all those years ago. The man has apologized and made amends! When are you going to just let it go?"

Faith groaned. "It's so hard, Gracie. You don't know how it felt all those years to –"

"But that was *then*. And honestly, could you blame him? You two have been over it. And tonight? Was probably just Sam reacting to the ways you've been icing him out. Not that he was entirely right, but you've got to show him some grace. He's shown you *more* than enough lately."

"it was supposed to be easier, right?," Faith asked sadly. "He was supposed to do everything right, and –"

"I don't know where you're getting this, Faith," Gracie said. "Maybe because you idolized him when you were a little girl. But he's not perfect. He never was, and he never will be. And neither are you."

"I know that," Faith said.

"And," Gracie said, emphatically, "just because something's not perfect doesn't mean it can't be amazing."

This was it, wasn't it? What she already knew...

"I just don't even know if he... if he's serious," Faith said softly, wondering at all that she had messed up, still searching for an excuse. "If he's not just going to take off like he did. I mean... it's not like he wants to marry me or anything."

Gracie said nothing for a long, long moment.

"Gracie?"

Silence.

"Stephanie. Grace. Hayes. You *know* something!"

Gracie groaned. "Oh, man! I'm not saying *anything*, Faith! Nothing!"

And the thought of Sam, serious enough to want to be with her forever, despite all that she'd done to convince him otherwise, had her clutching her hand to her chest, horrified that she'd thrown it away.

Everything that she'd ever wanted. Gone. Because she couldn't handle having something amazing because she was so hung up on making everything perfect.

"You know something, don't you? Gracie, tell me what you know!"

Gracie spoke quickly. "Just go see Sam. Go tell him you're an idiot and that you want him. Do it now before you regret it!"

And with that, Faith hung up the phone and rushed out to her car.

Sam sat in his unfinished house, surrounded by loads and loads of candles.

Scott? Had done a spectacular job. Thirty minutes earlier, Sam had been impressed when he stepped in to find his brother's handiwork, surprisingly thankful that Scott still hadn't made his quick getaway.

"Oh!," he had whispered when Sam came in, turning to run and hide.

"It's okay," Sam breathed out. "She's... not coming. No need to rush off."

Scott stopped and studied his brother for a second. "She's not coming?"

"No," Sam breathed. "Change of plans. But wow. This looks great. Thanks, man."

"Hey, no big deal," Scott shrugged, looking around as well. "So, we're rescheduling for another night... or what?"

Sam shook his head. "It's... over."

"What?"

Sam tossed his tuxedo jacket on the unfinished ground and started tugging at his tie. "I think her exact words were that it was just time to move on."

"After all these years?" Scott crossed his arms over his chest. "What did you do?"

Sam frowned. "Why is this my fault?"

"Well," Scott began, "last time I checked, she was in love with you. Has been since she was a little girl. Clearly, you must have done something to mess this up."

"Nope," Sam tried for a laugh that fell short. "Just being me."

"What happened at the fancy party?"

"Ahh, well," Sam said, getting the tie off at last and running it between his fingers. "I met loads of people. Important people, with very important jobs, and very important letters in front of *and* behind their names. Which, you know, was intimidating enough *without* Faith being so cold to me, like she's been since we got back from Florida."

Scott looked confused. "Why do you think she's been like that?"

Sam shrugged. "I don't know. Probably the same old thoughts running through her head, about how stupid I was eight years ago when I never called or wrote or made any attempt to start a real relationship with a sixteen year old girl."

A pause. "She's still hung up on that?"

"I didn't think so, but... it would appear there are still some hard feelings."

"I'm sorry," Scott frowned. "For what it's worth, I think she's making a mistake."

"Well, thanks for that."

"Maybe Faith... well, maybe she's just scared to really give her all." Scott watched him for a long moment. "Are you sure that was it?"

"Well," Sam sighed, going back to how tonight had gone exceptionally wrong... mainly because of him. "I told some important donor that I killed people while I was a Marine."

Scott blinked at him. "Well, good grief, Sam."

And Sam looked up at him. "That's the second time I've said that tonight after not admitting it to anyone for.... years, Scott. That's got to be a sign that I'm finally getting past the past. Or that I'm just more screwed up than I thought."

Scott bit his lip for a second, clearly thinking about what to say to help. "Yeah, I got nothing, brother."

Sam, miraculously, managed a smile at this.

"Apart from whatever you're still going through with the truth of that and what it must have done to you... well, that just wasn't polite dinner conversation," Scott said.

"No kidding," Sam agreed.

After a long moment, Scott spoke up. "Are you okay?"

"Yeah," Sam nodded. "Are you ashamed of me now? Like Faith?"

"I could never be ashamed of you," Scott said. "And I doubt that Faith is either. Hey, Sam?"

And Sam looked up at him. "Yeah?"

"Don't throw it all away because of one bad night, okay?"

Sam considered this for a moment, unable to speak past the lump in his throat.

Scott seemed to sense this. "Do you... you want me to clean all this up?," he asked, looking around. "Go on back to the house, and I'll take care of this, so you don't have to –"

"That's okay," Sam said. "I'm going to hang out here for a while."

Scott nodded and left.

And thirty minutes later? Sam was still sitting there, the stupid ring box sitting next to him, mulling through all that had gone wrong, wondering where he would go from here.

Faith sped her way through the city, switching highways, roadways, lanes, and streets faster than was wise, making her way home to him. And she prayed, for wisdom to know what to say, for peace to accept what her actions had earned her, and for grace to forgive herself for hurting him.

But only after she told him she was sorry. Only after she made sure he was okay. Only after she tried everything in her power to won back what she'd lost.

She saw the low, warm lights from inside his house, so she bypassed Marie and Scott's driveway and sped forward to his. And as soon as the car was in park and her keys were out of the ignition, Faith found herself running in her heels, hurrying to the front door, where she didn't even bother knocking.

There he was. Sitting there on the floor, with candles all around him, looking up at her with surprise.

"Sam," she murmured, her eyes filling with tears again.

"Faith," he said, getting to his feet, even as she made her way into the room.

And there was no way to tell who made the first move because they moved together, reaching out for one another, touching, kissing, being... Sam and Faith, together like they'd been for so many years.

"I'm sorry," she murmured, just as he offered "I'm sorry" as well.

They stared at one another. "Are you okay?," she said through her tears. "What you saw, what you did in combat... are you okay?"

He nodded, his hand on her face. "Yeah. Yeah, I'm okay. I was wrong to say what I did --"

"I was wrong to back you into that corner," she said.

"You didn't," he murmured.

"Yes," she swore. "I did. I was wrong, Sam..."

And they watched one another for a long moment, acknowledging all the wrongs between them.

"It's been a tough week," he said. "For both of us."

"There will be tough weeks," she said softly.

"But they'll be worth it," he answered. "I love you."

"And I love you, Sam," she said. "I've tried my entire life to make everything perfect. And everything will *never* be perfect. And I'm going to be childish and wrong and all the things you probably hate about me --"

"I don't hate anything about you," he said. "And I shouldn't have said what I said tonight, but I kept on, knowing that it wasn't right, just trying to be someone --"

"You *are* someone," she said. "Just like you are. Post-Afghanistan, post-lake house, post everything we've been through. You're Sam Huntington." She held his face in her hands. "And I swear, Sam, from this moment on, I'm going to believe the best about you. Every time."

"No pressure," he murmured, thinking about how wonderful this was. The expectation that he would be the kind of man that he wanted to be for her. For Christ.

She smiled at him. "You'll do the right thing, though. You always do."

His smile disappeared for a moment. "Do I? Can you trust me, even if I don't always do the right thing? Can you trust me enough to believe the best about me?"

She looked at him and meant every word. "I can. And I will. No more looking back." She swallowed back tears, her voice cracking. "And I'm not going to let you leave. Ever. Been there, done that, and I'll not ever let you leave again --"

And she couldn't get the words out because his lips were on hers. And she began to cry, happy tears, as he kissed her and held her close, until they broke away from one another, where he stared into her eyes, wiping away her tears with his thumbs as she continued to hold his shirt in her hands.

"You gave me hope, all those years," he said softly. "Knowing your heart, knowing who Christ is to you, called me to more when things were hopeless."

"Really?," she asked softly.

"And I'd love you for that alone," he said. "But now... it's so much more. Closer to Christ, every day, to His goodness, to His sovereignty, in this new season with you. And I want a life full of newer, richer seasons with you."

She nodded, kissing him again. "Me, too, Sam..."

He released her for a moment to pick up the ring box, then got down on one knee. "I planned a perfect proposal, but after tonight..."

"Not perfect," she whispered. "But still amazing."

And he smiled at her. "Will you marry me?," he asked.

"Sam," she cried, wiping away tears. "It's Grandma Trish's ring."

"Is it what you wanted?"

"Just exactly what I've always wanted," she said, no longer looking at the ring but staring down at him.

CHAPTER TEN

Faith Hayes was in love with Sam Huntington.

Well, that's not true anymore. Now, it's Faith Huntington is in love with Sam Huntington.

And I'm in love with her. And always will be.

I promised her this three months ago, as we said vows, and I've been coming home to her ever since. And I've been coming out of the nightmares, only to find her face inches from mine, pulling me away from the past towards a better future.

"Hey," she murmurs even now, as the images I want to leave behind disappear as she stares down at me, her hand on my face. "Sam... wake up, sweetheart..."

I focus on her eyes. Then on her hair, which falls in long waves towards my face. And then on her lips, one that she's chewing on as she watches me with concern.

"Hey," I manage, reaching up to touch her face. She closes her eyes for just a moment at my touch. "I woke you up."

"Already awake," she says softly. "I'll likely have to leave in a few hours for a delivery. First baby. The mother keeps calling me."

"And you can't get any sleep in the meantime because of me," I groan. "I'm sorry."

"I'm not," she murmurs, snuggling in next to me, her hand on my chest, her head on my shoulder. "Think you can sleep now?"

"Probably not," I answer.

"Then, let me ask you a question," she says, and I can hear the smile in her voice.

"Let me guess," I say, the nightmares departing as I pull her closer, fully aware of this game, reminding me even now of when she played it back by the lake house so many years ago. "My best memory from..." I look down at her with the question in my eyes.

"Our marriage," she says contentedly. "All three months of it."

"Too many," I declare, my mind going through the best moments, the happiest times...

"So naming one shouldn't be a challenge," she laughs.

"The wedding night," I say, my mind even now roaming over the details and –

"When you woke up yelling at 4am and caused such a ruckus that I fell out of bed?"

I groan. "I really wish that hadn't happened."

"I thought I had dislocated my shoulder," she says. "Which would have been fun to explain to everyone. Wild honeymoon and all."

"Ruined," I say. "Almost got in an ER visit your first night at Mrs. Samuel Huntington."

"Not ruined. It didn't have to be perfect to still be amazing," she murmurs.

That's our mantra. Not perfect but still amazing.

"And you," she whispers, raising up on that very same shoulder so as to look at me more closely, "were so tender and careful and so sweet after that. Amazing. So wonderful to me...you kissed it and made it all better."

I think about this, about how every physical desire has found its fulfillment in her, in this marriage. I think about the years and months of honoring her, of deferring this enjoyment, of telling her how wanted she was, of praying for patience and integrity until we could covenant together to be one...

She was worth waiting for, most definitely.

"And," I say, my heart uttering yet another thankful prayer as my hands are reaching up to bring her close so that I can kiss her again, "your injury totally got you out of carrying any heavy loads into the house when we moved in a week later."

"That it did," she grins. "Marie and I had so much fun watching you and Scott carry everything in while we sipped lemonade and supervised."

"Smart of Marie," I say, "getting herself pregnant yet again so soon after Hannah was born. She hasn't lifted anything heavy their entire marriage."

Faith smiles at this. "Maybe we'll be as lucky as they are, huh? Soon, I'm hoping."

"A baby with bald Thibideaux genes," I murmur, smiling.

"I can't wait," she says, lying back down, draping my arm around her as she laces her fingers through mine. "I really can't."

I can't either.

We've talked about what might happen. Faith might continue on with Elaine Charles, ideologies dissimilar as they are. Or she might do what I've thought was inevitable from the beginning – begin her own clinic, her own ministry.

Either way, I'm supportive, ready to be her plus one whenever she needs me, happy to do what would help her, knowing that she honestly believes the best about me, that she respects who I am, and that she's in this forever.

"Ready for the big test today?," she murmurs, kissing my hand.

"Yeah," I say. "Though I did well enough on the last one that I could flunk this one and still pass the class."

She smiles up at me. "But you won't."

I won't. I took a semester off, at Faith's suggestion, making sure in the interim that I was doing this for the right reasons and not just to prove a point or try to be someone I'm not. And I found that I wanted to go back, that the skills I was picking up were actually helpful with what I wanted to do – work with Scott, building up his business, our business, together.

When I told Faith I was going back, she declared herself my unofficial support group and gleefully researched the ins and outs of dyslexia, so much so that she herself is somewhat of an expert on the subject now. She helped me make modifications to the way I study and take tests, and the difference it's made has been enough to make school tolerable.

I told her just last week that she should have been there when I was in high school, suffering through my classes. And she told me that she *had* been there. I just didn't remember her, clearly.

She can say even this with a smile now, confident that we've finally moved beyond who we were, the lake house, and the insecurities that made things difficult not so long ago.

"What are you smiling about, Sam?," she says, looking at me with a smile of her own.

"Nothing," I say, smiling even as I move over her. "Just thinking of how great it is that you're here, I'm here, we have a few hours to kill…"

She wraps her arms around me and kisses me slowly. "We do, don't we?"

"And I was thinking –"

Her phone rings, interrupting the great idea I was having.

"Babies," she mutters, frowning at me. "They just have no respect for office hours. I'll probably need to head over there sooner than later."

"And this morning was going to be perfect," I say to her.

And she kisses me again and whispers, with adoration in her eyes, "Still amazing, Sam. So amazing."

ABOUT THE AUTHOR

Jenn Faulk is a full time mom and pastor's wife in Pasadena, Texas. She has a BA in English-Creative Writing from the University of Houston and an MA in Missiology from Southwestern Baptist Theological Seminary. She loves talking about Jesus, running marathons, listening to her daughters' stories, and serving alongside her husband in ministry. You can contact her through her blog www.jennfaulk.com

Made in the USA
Lexington, KY
25 September 2014